COURTING SCANDAL

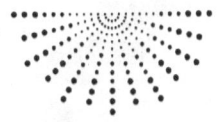

JAIMA FIXSEN

To Ivy, the dear friend who calls me Mom.

ESSENTIALS

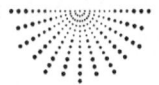

London, 1805

aura knew perfectly well she couldn't expect to be given what she wanted—it was up to her to take it. Just now she wanted money for her brother, more than she wanted a dress with long enough sleeves, meat for their table, or candles. Bad enough their mother must sew late into the night in these grim rented rooms. They were used to barely getting by, but watching her work with nothing but the light of the fire was painful. Thirty pounds Laura needed, an impossible sum that meant everything.

Thirty pounds would kit up Jack so he could go to sea with Dr. Drysdale on HMS Leander as surgeon's mate—a real apprenticeship with prospects, not like his job as an apothecary's assistant peddling laudanum and patent remedies. Yet here was Jack's letter drying on the windowsill saying he couldn't raise such a sum or leave his mother and his sister. Laura set down the bodice she was trimming and traced her finger over Jack's beautiful script. He wrote as stately as a minuet, no matter how cheap the paper, and his reasons were perfectly honorable. And foolish.

...express my gratitude for your kind offer...with the greatest reluctance I must decline...

Their best chance gone for lack of thirty pounds. Laura pressed her hand over her eyes and held back a bitter laugh. Dear Jack. He would never complain. His life was hard enough without being saddled with a mother and a sister. He must go with Dr. Drysdale. She'd make sure of it.

"I need some air," Laura said. Even if the air carried the smell of fetid streets. Glancing at her mother, she folded up the letter. "I might as well carry this round." She slipped it in her pocket.

THE LETTER DIDN'T COME UP AGAIN until they sat down for a hasty meal of bread and beans.

"Thank you for delivering my letter," Jack said, mopping the edge of his bowl with a piece of bread.

Laura shrugged. "Figured I might as well save the postage."

Jack accepted this with a grunt. They were accustomed to making do with every imaginable economy: thrice-brewed tea or straight hot water, darned socks and worsted caps, rationing out coal and sharing a single orange.

Laura set down her spoon. "I still think you should go. We could sell the earrings," she said. They were the last of the jewelry, tucked away in a faded velvet bag. Maman said it looked absurd, wearing pearls in her ears with a mended dress of printed cotton.

"But what would you do while I was gone? The sewing won't keep you," Jack said.

Laura shifted in her chair. "Maman, perhaps you could ask our uncle—"

2

"She will do no such thing," Jack interrupted. "And neither will you."

Laura bit her lip. Nine years ago, when they'd washed onto England's shores scared, starved and grieving, they'd gone to the duke. Laura didn't know what transpired, but she knew dukes didn't slave for shillings and wear second-hand clothes.

"Why not? Is he such a skinflint?" Laura turned to her mother, who shrugged.

"Let it be, darling. Jack's right. Your uncle made his intentions clear and I don't like to make my sister's life more difficult."

"We're his family—"

"Wife's family," Jack corrected. "That's different."

Laura snorted, but beneath the table her fingers clutched her skirts. Jack's letter was in the Thames, not with Dr. Drysdale, and she'd gone to Mayfair this afternoon, not the park. It took all her courage presenting her shabby self at her uncle's front door, but it hadn't mattered. Her uncle, the Duke of Saltash, was 'not at home.'

"You could go. I've a plan to look after us, Jack," Laura said, her eyes on the scratched table. Saltash wouldn't help and Maman wouldn't ask, but she had one last idea. She hadn't doubted herself this afternoon, but now her stomach threatened mutiny.

"What is it this time?" he asked. Over the years she'd thought out a dozen brilliant ways she could keep them hosed and shod, but none of them were practical enough for Jack. "I forbid you to turn highwayman." His smile faded. "Even if we had a pistol, I doubt we could buy the shot."

Maman smiled, reaching to wrap one of Laura's errant curls around her finger. "You and your ideas. How you would have shone! Do you remember France?"

"A little," Laura admitted, gratefully escaping into the past.

Soft carpets, parquet floors, slippers of satin with embroidered toes, a velvet-eared pony. And her favorite, a small theatre in their English-style gardens done in shell-pink and gold. All ash now, scattered in the wind. Her last memory of their home was of it burning.

"You would have made all the gentlemen laugh and fall immediately in love with you," her mother said.

"And now I charm the grocer. Much more to the purpose, I think." Laura forced a smile. Jack would never leave, not so long as he thought they needed him. She would get the thirty pounds. And a career, something that paid better than stitching...tonight.

They cleared away the dishes and Jack retired to his room to brood and study from borrowed books. Her mother sat down to the pile of sewing. Two of the costumes still needed alteration and they were due within an hour at the theatre.

"Let me manage it." Laura plucked an old-fashioned lace stomacher from her mother's hands. Maman insisted they were fortunate just to be alive, but days like today Laura didn't agree with her. Maman wasn't meant to be so exhausted, suffering from chapped hands and pricked fingers. In France, when she held a needle, it was for embroidery. "You rest. I can carry them over and finish there," Laura said as she folded up the sewing. Her scheme wouldn't work if she had Maman for company.

"It's not too heavy?" Maman asked. These days she looked like a stiff wind would blow her out the door. She hadn't noticed Laura taking in the burgundy silk bodice and lowering it an inch.

"Of course not." There was enough gauze in the bundle to lighten the stiff taffetas and heavy brocades. "I'll make sure to ask Mr. Rollins for next week's costumes." Whether or not he'd send them after her plan unfolded tonight...

"Are you unhappy?" Maman asked. "When you smile there's always a frown still in your forehead."

"I'm fine. Don't worry," Laura said, to herself as much as to her mother. "Go to sleep, Maman."

Her mother hid a dainty yawn behind her fingertips. "Very well. Good night, Laure." When Maman said her name, the French pronunciation always came out.

Slipping her feet into pattens, holding her bundle close, Laure Seraphine Edouard Lecroy-Duplessis, now simply Laura Edwards, whisked down the stairs and into the street.

PETER SHARP, who kept the back door of the theatre, was waiting for her. "Running a little late, aren't we? Twice now Her Mightiness has sent down asking for her dress," he said.

Laura shifted the bundle to her hip and laid her free hand on Peter's arm. "I need you to help me."

"I already fobbed off Her Mightiness," he said, flashing his gap-toothed, jack-o-lantern smile.

Laura pushed away her qualms. It was too late. She'd already altered the costume. "Good of you, Peter, but I'm afraid I'm asking for much more."

"You in trouble?" he asked, lowering his head and dropping his voice. The muscles in his forearm jumped beneath her fingers.

"Not exactly. I need a better job." She explained the predicament in a rushed, staccato whisper. "I want Her Mightiness's." It wasn't fair to ask, but she couldn't manage without him. It was no small thing, plotting to dethrone the theatre's reigning actress, Mrs. Sylvia Long.

"You? An actress?" Peter scratched the back of his grizzled head. "That's no kind of a job for a girl like yourself. Not so easy as it looks, either."

"Peter. I can do it. You know I can."

"You say the lines to me well enough, but—"

Well enough? Night after night she had him in stitches, earning chuckles from the stagehands and quelling glares from the curtain pullers. Last week Peter's sniggers had brought down an acid complaint from Mrs. Long and a threat to speak to Mr. Rollins, the manager.

"It's different on stage. What will you do when they cuss at you and hurl fruit?"

"Throw it back if I catch it. Throw a kiss if I don't." For years she'd watched from backstage corners and cheap seats in the pit, deciding how to improve a glance or a gesture, how to fix the pitch and cadence of the words. She was eighteen, and her legs and her bosom would never be any better. Unlike Her Mightiness, Laura had a backside for breeches parts. She needed this chance.

"And there's another thing," Peter said, still trying to dissuade her. "What about them lizards that prowl the green room? That's no place for you. I'm not letting you turn harlot."

"I won't. That's not always necessary. Think of Lucy Green."

Peter grunted. "Lady Eversdale? Don't count on that. She got lucky. Knew she had to choose eventually but managed to pick the right one, one that would marry her. I've kept my door twenty years and that's only happened once."

"Yes, but even before, when they called her the White Hart—"

"That worked because she played the foil to yon temptress, Mrs. Long, who's got neither whiteness or a heart, so's I can tell."

"I'll be the new White Hart then," Laura said.

"You know I love you," Peter said. "But you're no Lucy Green."

She didn't have the inches, or the alabaster skin. But she could act, even if it was only in front of Peter and the stage-hands. Before the pikes and the blood and the fires, she'd spent her days in a menagerie of actors and writers—the best from the Comédie-Française. Her father, the Comte, had loved nothing better than staging one production after another in his private theatre to audiences of family and houseguests. The obliging directors always found parts for him and his pet of a daughter. For her fifth birthday Laura had a costume with jeweled slip-pers and fairy wings and a speech of forty lines. They would have praised her no matter how badly she'd done, but afterward, when her fingers were still tingling and her face flushed, Laura overheard the lead actress, still in a Marie Antoinette wig and with her face done up with patches, whisper to her counterpart, "A shame perhaps, that the little girl is born what she is. A natural talent."

The actor, busy ungluing his false mustache, gave a grunt. "She'll be like her father. Stage everything she likes in her own theatre and play games with us. We aren't toys, Berthe."

The leading lady pouted, coy as a cat. "No? But I like to play."

It was then the actor saw Laura's eyes in the mirror. Hastily shushing his companion, he brought her back to her father. "A talent and appreciation to rival your own, my lord. You must watch her or I think she'll hide herself in one of our wagons and run away to Paris!"

Her father laughed and brushed a careless knuckle over Laura's chin, already talking about the next play, the next part. There were not many, and the last stage he climbed was a scaffold.

"I'll be better," Laura insisted to Peter. She'd have to be. "Besides, I'd rather queen it in the green room than fetch and carry for Her Mightiness and mutilate my fingers with her everlasting sewing! Please, Peter. I won't tell a soul you've helped me."

"Not a chance," he said, moving away from her like she'd confessed to a disease. "She'll have your head. And Mr. Rollins will—"

"Not if I bring down the house," Laura said. "I will, Peter. You know I can. Please."

After a bit more pleading he gave in, but kept up a steady mumble of foreboding as he showed her where Mr. Rollins hung his keys.

"Wait here," Laura whispered when he hesitated outside the dressing room door.

"Nope, I'm all in," he said. "You'd better shine, my girl, because it's both our jobs if you don't."

"What kept you?" Sylvia Long snapped as Laura and Peter sidled into her dressing room.

"I lost a button," Laura lied, advancing behind her. Mrs. Long sniffed, her attention on the application of a second layer of rouge.

"You'll have to help me into it. I won't have it smearing my face. What are *you* doing here?" she asked, fixing her eye on Peter through the mirror.

"I'm just the muscle," Peter said. Before Sylvia Long could speak, Laura threw the gown over her head, muffling the shrill scream. A manicured hand lashed out, scoring Laura's arm, but a second later, Peter had the claws pinned behind her back.

"Quiet down and we won't harm you. You just aren't going on stage tonight is all," he said. She struggled to wrestle free, yowling through the crumpled petticoats until Peter clapped a hand over her mouth.

"Everything all right?"

Laura spun round before the inquiring stagehand could throw open the door. She widened it a crack, speaking in a low voice. "I got the waist measurement wrong. Won't take me a minute to let it out, but you know..." All the staff were familiar with Mrs. Long's tantrums. The stagehand nodded and vanished down the corridor, glad he wasn't to blame. Laura locked the door.

"Can she breathe?" Laura asked, alarmed by the bite marks on Peter's finger and the arm he had hooked around Mrs. Long's neck. Her heels drummed on the floor. She wrested a hand free, raking her nails across Peter's face, but a cuff, a curse, and a look from him quickly drained the fight from her.

"She can breathe," he said, binding a handkerchief over Mrs. Long's mouth. "Just." With surprising efficiency, he fastened her hands and feet with stockings. Peter could look quite terrifying when he wanted to, Laura realized, noting the pallor of Mrs. Long's face and her dilated eyes. That scar, the missing teeth...

"Do you think we hurt her?" Laura whispered as they bundled her into an armoire and locked the door.

"Her pride, yes. And if Mr. Rollins doesn't kill you, you'll have to watch your back the rest of your days. She'll be fine. It's you and I who are bleeding." He inspected his wounded finger, motioning with his head to the scratches on Laura's arms. They were bright enough she'd have to powder over them.

"Old cat," Peter said. Something thumped in the cupboard. "Quiet, you, or I'll have you carted away." His eyes crinkled at Laura. "Expect I've lost my job, and I'll look a right mess tomorrow"—he probed his left cheek—"but I did enjoy that. You better get dressed."

The bell rang, warning that there were only five minutes till curtain. Breathless, cursing her clumsy fingers, Laura struggled with the fastenings of the gown, taking a few tentative steps in the heavy silk. Turning to the mirror, she plucked up a stick of charcoal and stretched up the curve of her brows. The burgundy of the gown didn't flatter her, but balanced with rouge on her lips and rice-powdered skin, the effect was tolerable. Besides, move and speak right and no one would notice the dress. She'd never bared so much décolletage, but the altered costume seemed to frame it all rather nicely.

Someone pounded on the door. "Hurry up, Sylvia!" Mr. Rollins said.

"Almost ready," Laura said, her mouth full of pins as she speared a wig of gold ringlets over her own hair. She moved, dipped, took an exploratory jump, but the piece stayed in place. There was a flurry of bashing against the armoire that Peter silenced with another thump.

"Well?" Laura turned back to Peter, grinning as she curtsied, stretching out her arms.

"You're the very devil," he said. "Go. Start a riot."

Heart pounding, she slipped into the dark corridor, hastening past the backstage moths who didn't see past the wig and the gown. Only when Laura stood in the wings, her toes just outside the glow of the stage, did she meet the prompter's eyes and realize he'd noticed the switch. She asked for silence with a single finger pressed to her rouged lips.

He answered with a hint of a shrug. *On your head be it.*

At least her furtive glance showed the Duke of Saltash's box was empty. She could face that hurdle later. The music swelled, racing to the finish, still barely discernible above the rumbling audience. Some buffoons in the pit were calling for Mrs. Long. Well, they were in for a surprise. Laura crossed herself once, silently begging for help from every possible source: the ghost of her father, the Virgin, the lucky ribbon tied round her thigh.

The music stilled. Laura fixed a saucy smile on her face, cocked her hip, and swept onto the stage. Staring myopically into the lights, she pulled in the gasps, the brilliance, the finery of it all, making it part of her own skin. Her lips slid back from her teeth and the words leapt from her throat, curveting into the boxes, prancing off the ceiling.

Surprise gave her a second's advantage. She would not waste it. By the end of the prologue, she would steal their hearts.

2
INCONSEQUENTIALS

London, 1813
Eight years later

*F*amily. They were nothing but trouble. If he weren't inordinately fond of his half-sister, Jasper would never abandon London at this time of year, not if she were birthing a litter of children instead of merely one—he hoped. Apparently the odds were less promising when women dropped more than one. Everyone seemed optimistic: Sophy, his half-sister; Tom, her husband; and Tom's plump rattle of a mother. Even the numerous physicians Jasper consulted said, to the best of their knowledge and without examining the lady in question, it seemed there was no reason for alarm. Henrietta, his other sister, already the mother of two terrifying sons, told him he was taking leave of his senses—she doubted Sophy would enjoy the experience, but the birth would proceed exactly as it ought.

"Is it wrong of me, though, to wish she might have a girl?" Henrietta asked.

"I don't have opinions about the sex," Jasper informed her. "Do you think—"

"Stop worrying. You're worse than Mama," Henrietta retorted. "Just go. And give Sophy a kiss from me."

Henrietta, though invited to Chippenstone, had smugly informed him she was required to stay home as she was also in an interesting condition. It made one feel quite overwhelmed.

"You won't stay to see the boys?" she asked, seeing he was ready to leave.

"I'd rather not," he said. The younger one was cutting teeth. On his brother, judging from the yowling penetrating the drawing room walls. "I'm going to the theatre tonight."

Henrietta pouted, but only half-heartedly. "Then you go to Suffolk tomorrow? Promise me you'll tell me anything that passes between Sophy and Mama."

"I wouldn't get my hopes up," Jasper said. "The Mater might forget temporarily in the fuss of the birth, but it won't take her long to remember why she forbade the marriage." Sophy, always a game little thing, had eloped.

"Oh, go away. I can't stand you when you're gloomy." Henrietta paused mid-dismissal and eyed him narrowly. "Are you sure you're all right? Everything seems to nettle you lately."

"I can't think what you mean," Jasper said, bending to plant a swift kiss on her cheek. "Give my regards to that husband of yours. And tell him it's positively indecent you're breeding again. I've a mind to put a bolt on your door."

"My dear," Henrietta said, her cheeks betraying her with the slightest blush, "I'm afraid this time, you would have had to lock his."

Jasper bowed and fled.

———

At half past six Laura knew she had plenty of time to reach the theatre. She'd be in trouble though, if she delayed any longer. Peter and Mr. Rollins didn't like her venturing out after daylight hours. It made getting about much more complicated.

"Everything's in the basket," Laura told Alice, the girl doubling as her maid and understudy. "If you take the longer way down St Martin's Lane, I'll catch up with you at Mr. Rollins' house." Laura didn't like putting the theatre manager to all this trouble, but the last few months she'd been forced to conceal her whereabouts. None of her neighbors must connect Miss Edwards, a spinster of straightened circumstances, with the actress Gemma Holyrood. She didn't fear them, of course, just who they might tell.

With Alice on her way, Laura packed away her brother's letters. Tomorrow or the next day, when Jack came home they could weep together and remember Maman. For now, it was best to put those feelings aside and forget herself in her work.

Shedding her morose mood with her day dress and apron, Laura retrieved her disguise from the box under the bed. It took only a moment to lace up the breeches and pull on a shirt and leather vest. She slung a ragged coat over her shoulders and stuffed her hair into a worn-out hat. Pulling the brim low, she ran down the stairs on light feet, glad at last to be released into the street.

Enjoying her man's stride, she made short work of the distance to Mr. Rollins' house where Peter waited just inside the servant's door and Alice in a room upstairs. With Alice's help, she effected the second change—pinning up her curls, garbing herself with the usual delicate white muslin dress. Her grimy man's neckerchief was exchanged for Gemma Holyrood's gold chain and simple cross, her face powdered, her neck and wrists dressed with rose scent. Quite the production, and all to keep away a man who responded to her stage presence a little too much.

"Ready, you think?" Laura asked, turning around in front of Alice.

"Lovely as usual, Gemma," Mr. Rollins put in, sticking his head round the door. "Are you ready to go?"

Picking up her shawl and fan, Laura followed Mr. Rollins outside to the carriage waiting to take them to the theatre and waved good night to Mrs. Rollins and her three daughters still at home. Peter and Alice climbed up with the driver and they set out rumbling through labyrinthine streets. They made fitful progress with innumerable stops and starts, wrestling through the clogging press of carriages, ramshackle hackneys, and crowds on foot.

"I hate all this extra bother for you," Laura said, looking past the serrated rooftops to the purpling sky.

"I don't," Mr. Rollins said. "Your guilt over it has kept you from asking for a larger share of the receipts. We've had a very profitable quarter."

Laura smiled. It was true enough. She knew what she was worth and liked to be well paid, but Rollins was her friend. His help, in her current difficulty, was worth more than she could say.

"Do you think he'll come tonight?" Rollins asked.

"Probably, just so he can glare," Laura said. "Don't worry about me—I've got iron nerves." She knew how to make it look that way at least. Acting skills were useful off stage and on.

"I know you do," Rollins said. "Here we are. You ready?"

He helped her down from the carriage, displaying her for the early arrivals come to fill the pit. With lifted chin but a warm smile, Laura cut through the crowd, acknowledging the flattering clamor with a raised hand and a nod. Maman's court training had proven useful after all.

Inside, Laura stepped into the waiting arms of the stage-hands, ready to bustle her to the dressing room. Rollins was summoned to manage the chaos accompanying an intermission performance of an acrobatic trio and departed for the box office. "Break a leg, my dear," he called to Laura over his shoulder.

It was a relief to slip into the relative quiet of her dressing room and see nothing but flowers. Last week she'd unwrapped a package and found a dead starling, its neck twisted and wings broken. "I think we pulled that off rather well," Laura said to Alice as they got her into her third costume of the evening—an elaborate sacque gown of blue brocade and a pale blonde wig. Worries left her as Alice powdered her shoulders and décolletage. Laura smiled. Tonight's role was one of her favorites, but the best part of them all was Gemma Holyrood. Threats and glares were nothing. She'd survived broken hearts, bad reviews and oily admirers. There was a play to put on tonight. She was ready.

———

AFTER VISITING HIS SISTER, Jasper returned to his rooms in St. James where he read the newspaper and then draped it over his face and took a nap. He woke, changed his clothes, spoiling only three neckcloths before getting the knot right. When his friends arrived to accompany him to the theatre he was arrayed in his full glory, but frowning and rereading a letter from Sophy.

"Pardon? Yes, I'm ready," he said, stuffing the sheets of paper under a Vincennes vase. He groped inside it for his quizzing glass and found instead a crumpled letter from a scandal-seeking widow. This he tossed to the fire. His second fishing trip for the glass proving successful, he draped the ribbon round his neck and slid the glass inside his waistcoat pocket. He sighed inwardly, noting his friend André Protheroe was again wearing a new coat and skintight pantaloons.

"Haven't given up yet?" Jasper asked.

"No," André said cheerfully. "She's still the most enchanting thing I've ever seen, and if I succeed you'll owe me two hundred pounds."

There was no disputing the actress Gemma Holyrood's considerable charms, but after nearly a year Jasper felt their wager over her had gone stale, sunk now to the back pages of the betting book at White's. "Wait until she's long enough in the tooth, then she might take you," he said and yawned. Seven years Miss Holyrood had ruled the London comic stage. In all that time rumor supplied her with only a single lover and even that one was debatable. The fellow, identifiable only by his height and swarthy complexion, had appeared with her a handful of times over the years. No one knew who he was, but he was the only man besides the theatre manager with whom she'd ever been seen. Although each sighting sparked feverish speculation, Miss Holyrood's mystery man never spoiled her persona. She always dressed in white, her only ornament a chaste gold cross.

They'd all tried to win her, of course, without any success. She'd flirt and laugh and send witty replies to his flowery notes, but she'd never let any of them see her outside the green room. Jasper had given up hopes of cutting out Protheroe and taking his money months ago, but that didn't stop him from trundling down to the theatre at nearly every chance. She was something of a habit with him and he did like looking at her.

Jasper followed André into a hackney carriage, seating himself by another friend, George DeClerc, known to his intimates as Boz.

"She'll never take you, Protheroe," Boz said. "Not when she's keeping the Duke of Saltash at bay."

"That old stick? Is he courting her?" Jasper frowned. The man was mean to dogs and a brute to horses—you never bought either from him.

"Well, he's been hovering almost since coming to town," Boz said.

"Yes, but he's delusional if he thinks he's flirting with those scowls. He looks more likely to kill than kiss her," Jasper said. The man was like a vulture, but despite his obsession with Miss Holyrood, he hadn't discarded his current mistress.

"She doesn't take fright, though," Protheroe said, a little downcast. "And she doesn't slight him." More than once they'd seen her bow to the duke's box and blow kisses. "He's a duke. She'll take him no matter what he looks like."

"Not unless he drops his current ladybird. She's got too much self-respect not to insist on that. I'm more worried about being cut out by the Mystery Man," Jasper said.

"That masked fellow? Hasn't been seen in over a year," Boz said.

"But he's been cropping up for a long time. The Morning Chronicle said yesterday they'd learned his identity," Jasper told Protheroe. "It's Chisholm."

"No! Is he that tall?"

"Jasper, you're a worse gossip than my sister," Protheroe said.

"I'll show you the article," Jasper protested. "It could very well be. I presume it isn't you since you haven't claimed my two hundred pounds."

"Alas, no," André said. "But I don't agree that he's her lover. He could be merely a confidante. A friend."

"Believe it if it makes you feel better," Boz said.

"Thank you, I will," said Andre.

Boz snorted. "For all we know, he's her pimp."

"You would think so," Andre retorted, turning icy.

"Enough! Just let me enjoy the play," Jasper interrupted. This one was more subversive than usual, but he always enjoyed the plays of Elizabeth Inchbald. With Miss Holyrood in the principal role of Maria it was delicious. He'd already seen it twice.

"What is it again?" Protheroe asked.

Jasper sighed. *"Wives as They Were and Maids as They Are,"* he said.

Boz grunted. "Mouthful isn't it? We'd be better off leaving all women be."

André laughed. "And so we shall. Except for Miss Holyrood."

"Good luck to you," Boz said sourly.

THE AIR WAS dense with smells of sweat, perfume, and the heat of innumerable candles. It was usually more fun to prowl in the pit, but tonight Jasper was happy to climb to the theatre's boxes, which displayed their inhabitants like oysters yielding pearls. Up here there was at least the illusion of cooler air, and he wouldn't have to worry about pickpockets.

Across the theatre sat Miss Lowell and her sister—both fast, but not nimble enough to catch him. Further up were his country neighbors, the Misses Matcham. Despite a two-inch difference in height they were equally boring. Jasper saw a good number of the jeweled hags from his mother's coven and a sad lot of roués, already salivating over the bosoms and arms out for viewing. Telling himself he wasn't shameless enough to belong to that fraternity, Jasper turned his eyes to the stage, tamping down his eagerness. Miss Holyrood, though unattainable, was worth every glance.

She parted the curtain with her slippered foot, giving a glimpse of her lovely ankle before stepping onto the stage. She curtsied, bestowed a few kisses in general directions, then spoke:

"Good ladies, kind gentlemen, welcome to our play,
Forswear bad fruit and sneers and yawns,

If ye allow, we'll please anon,

With tales of love and gallantry."

Jasper raised his glass to his eye. Beautiful features, but sometimes he thought he was caught more by the happiness in her eyes and the buoyancy of spirit he inferred from her light movements. No wonder the manager always sent her out to plead indulgence in the prologue. A script was hardly necessary for those expressive eyes and fingers. Jasper knew he wasn't the only one captivated by her teasing smile and gently rolling hips as she sauntered across the boards. Miss Holyrood finished and bowed to generous applause. Protheroe, the silly fool, leaned on the edge of the box, his eye fixed to his glass—mirroring his own pose, Jasper realized. He straightened his back and tucked away the glass, imagining the wink she gave was for him, instead of the audience at large. His breath hitched as she lifted one arm, the loose sleeve falling back to reveal a dimpled elbow. He'd read an ode to that dimple last winter, proving he wasn't the only admirer of that delicious bit of flesh. She also dimpled when she smiled. Jasper was quite sure that if he ever got a glimpse he'd find another pair of tempting dents right above her round little bottom.

It was a good play, the exits and entrances both farcical and fast, the story jammed full of peril, humor, and sly wit. Jasper liked her in this role almost as much as he liked her playing Lydia Languish, though he thought the costume for that one suited her better. Melting and mellow by the final curtain and giving wholehearted applause, Jasper didn't resist when Boz suggested they try to cram their way into the green room. It was good sport, after all, edging through the crowded corridors, bribing the blunt-faced doorkeeper for a few inches of space on her dressing room floor.

Inside they were packed close enough he could smell both his neighbors and see nothing but gentlemen's heads. Past experience told him Miss Holyrood spoke from behind a screen as her maid lifted away her heavy costume. The lucky fellows who were closer would catch a glimpse of soft arms and bare shoulders. Beside him a hopeful Protheroe rose up onto his toes. Jasper, who hadn't come to admire the enamel-like properties of some fellow's pomade, knew there were better ways and jammed his knee into the leg in front of him. The man half-stumbled and as he righted himself, Jasper slid into his place. He could see her now, chestnut curls swept high on her head, smooth shoulders visible above the scrolled edge of the screen. Her skin was warm, slightly golden, her cheeks bright, flushed from the heat of the stage and her own success.

"A triumph, Miss Holyrood," he said, holding out the bouquet he'd purchased on his way down from the box, noticing now it was violets, done up with paper lace and dove grey ribbon. Pretty enough but paltry next to the foliage spilling over the dressing table. The silent maid—it was months now since the elderly French one had been replaced by a new girl—took them from his hand as she circled the room depositing her armful of posies onto an empty chair. Miss Holyrood emerged from the screen clad in a thin silk dressing gown with Japanese flowers and a wide blue sash. It was thin enough that he could see the lace-edged shape of her underclothes beneath. His mouth went dry.

"Gentlemen, you overwhelm me," she said, moving to the table. Jasper, who was quick, beat the maid to the brush.

"Thank you, Mr. Rushford," Miss Holyrood said, accepting it from his hand.

"Will you trust me to take out the pins?" he asked, knowing he was asking in vain.

"Alice always does my hair," Miss Holyrood said, seating herself on the stool. "I can't be sure, Mr. Rushford, that you have a sufficiently delicate touch." She buried her face in the flowers as another man pushed forward, offering a folded letter.

"Lord Willbank, you shouldn't," she said, making it disappear into the folds of her robe. "You too, Sir John?" But she paused before taking the next one, meeting the gaze of the Duke of Saltash. "Your Grace. I daren't accept such honor." Her voice was low, but determined.

Saltash held it out a moment more before sliding it back into his pocket. His grimace chilled the room, but only for a moment. Miss Holyrood had turned back to the mirror and was calling out questions. "Do you gentlemen approve the play?" she asked. "I fear Miss Maria is a regular hoyden. What would you do if all women were so independent-minded? I'm not sure you'd care for it."

Saltash quelled the chorus of denials. "No gentleman would care to have his female connections behaving in such a manner. Your Miss Maria, I think, learned her lesson by the end."

"I am sorry you disapprove, Your Grace. What sort of character do you fancy? Ophelia? Mrs. Siddons in *The Grecian Daughter*? Some do favor tragedy, but I'm afraid I have little talent for it." Letting the duke fall from her attention, she reached into an offered box of sweets. "Mr. Shortcross! You've learned my weakness! I really shouldn't," she said, popping one into her mouth and licking sugar from her fingers. Jasper shifted, suddenly uncomfortable in this crowd of men watching her eat. It felt distasteful and he didn't like the currents swirling around Saltash. She might be quick and clever, but she was no match for a duke. Baiting him was reckless.

She ate a second sweet, chattering as her maid combed out her hair, until interrupted by a noise, some commotion nearer the door. "Gemma!"

Miss Holyrood was still.

"Gemma!" the man called again. White faced, she rose in

time to see a tall man plowing into the room with assurance and wiry strength. Her fingers leapt to her mouth.

He was tall, dressed in black, his face hidden by a half-mask. Beneath it the hair was deep brown, a shade darker than her own. Jasper felt an elbow in his kidney, heard Protheroe rasp in his ear. "The Mystery Man!"

"So I gathered," Jasper said, wincing.

Miss Holyrood looked stunned, but there was no mistaking the delight dawning in her face. "Jack! I never thought to see you today!"

"Love sped my journey." He swept to her side and captured her hands. Jasper would have snickered, if not for the blush creeping into her cheeks. She was happy—more than happy to see this man.

Ignoring the muttering behind him, Jasper catalogued the man's eyes, the shape of his chin, but found nothing familiar. He didn't know him. But he must be someone, waltzing in and claiming her like this in front of Saltash and twenty other hangers-on. Bold maneuvers, but she didn't resent them. Jasper realized with a pained twist of his stomach that she loved this man. He'd seen his sisters tinted with that sublime pink wash too often to mistake the significance. On them it made him uncomfortable, not envious. He sidled towards the door.

"What's the mask for?" whispered Protheroe beside him. "Who could be that pretentious?"

It was a little much, Jasper agreed, but Miss Holyrood seemed to find it attractive. The fellow had no trouble carrying it off.

Miss Holyrood came to herself, recalling the others in the room. "Forgive me," she said, smiling at them like she did at the curtain before making her bows. "An old friend. What can one do? And you have been so kind to me." Hearing the dismissal, her astonished admirers began to move out the door. Jasper lingered till the end, failing to catch Miss Holyrood's whispered conversation with the unnamed gentleman, but meeting her unguarded eyes when she glanced at the door. They brushed over him and fell on Saltash, still looming like a gargoyle in the corner. "Excuse me, gentlemen," she said and curtsied, leading the man she loved through the opposite door.

"Good night, Fair Cruelty," Jasper said, bowing to her retreating form. Whether it was his words or Saltash's disgruntled snort, Jasper couldn't say, but she glanced back one more time, her mouth curling into an impudent smile. Though it was too late, Jasper blew a kiss, then took himself outside to the company of his friends and the cool of the dark. Miss Holyrood's lover must be one devil of a fellow—at least Jasper hoped so, for her sake.

3

PLAYACTING

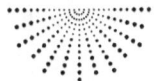

*L*aura leaned against the door until she was sure no one would follow her. "Jack, I thought my heart had stopped!" she exclaimed. "I didn't expect you till tomorrow at the earliest!"

"That's only part of my good news," her brother said, gathering her into a fierce hug. "I missed you."

"Me too." She squeezed hard. Some things just couldn't be expressed in letters. It was a miracle every time he returned, hearty and whole. She pressed her cheek against his shoulder, stifling a laugh. "What possessed you to come in like that? I can only imagine what the papers will say tomorrow."

His coat was new and he smelled of soap. "Don't give it a thought," he said. "How are you?"

"Happy you're home." She gave him another squeeze. He looked different—older, his face tanned. He chucked aside the mask, throwing it on the prop table. "What's this?" she asked, tracing her finger over a white line running alongside his right eye.

"Splinter. Damn close, but nothing that couldn't be stitched right."

She made a face. "Don't tell me you did it yourself."

"I won't. You look well," he said turning her round.

"Why, thank you," she said, curtseying as if she were on stage.

His nose twitched. "Yes, well, I've news."

"News?"

He nodded and she felt uneasy at the firm set of his lips.

"Jack..." she began.

"Listen. I've done it. I'm all but fixed, with a house and everything."

"You're leaving the navy?" It was what they'd always planned, but things were different now they were only two. "I—"

Jack saw her hesitation, rushed over it. "You needn't work anymore. My friend Bagshot wants me to come set up in Suffolk— his wife's about to deliver and the local physician's set to retire. I've enough saved to buy the practice and surgery in Bury St Edmonds. As for a house, Bagshot said he'd loan me the rest. Normally I wouldn't accept, but Laura...I can't leave you alone like this. Not anymore." His eyes flicked once more to the green room door.

"Jack."

"It was different when Maman was alive," he went on. "But a maid isn't the same—"

"Alice and Peter take very good care of me," Laura said, her voice warning him to stop.

He gave her a look. "You're telling me no one harasses you?"

"Not more than I like," she said stolidly.

"Or makes things unpleasant?"

She shook her head.

"Even our uncle?" he asked delicately. "I was surprised to see him here."

"Empty threats," she said.

"Maybe. But if you were me...watching them look at you like that..."

The old argument. Again. "I'd be proud," Laura said. "Can't you be?"

"I am," Jack insisted. "It's just...none of them know about Laura Edwards."

"Peter does. Mr. Rollins."

"I meant them." He jerked his head in the direction of the closed door. "If you left London, you could be yourself all the time. Be something closer to what you were born to be."

She loved Jack. Without his letters, she couldn't have borne their mother's loss. And this promise of a settled, prosperous life had always been what the three of them had wished for, worked for. Jack blamed himself for the separations, though she'd forced them on him—his first voyage, his training in Edinburgh, another two years with the navy. And each time they met, he'd promised her it wouldn't be for much longer, that soon he'd be taking care of her and Maman. He was so earnest about it and loved her so much. How could she tell him she didn't want to go?

"You could have a real life. Marry. Have children," Jack said.

"You know I gave up that idea a long time ago." It was one of the more interesting ironies of her life, but outside the theatre she lived as quietly and cloistered as a nun. "It's impossible," she said. Even if Laura Edwards attracted a marriageable man, what was she to do—never tell him? The strain of it would poison her. And if she did tell the truth, no respectable man would wish to marry her, not if he was sane.

"I'm going to see him—them—Bagshot and his wife," Jack explained. "They told me to bring along my sister. I said she would come."

The words hit Laura like a punch. "You didn't," she said. "The play's set to run for another week!"

"I've been gone more than a year," Jack retorted. "What will the Bagshots think if I leave you behind? Aren't you glad to see me?"

"I am," Laura protested. It would have been nicer if he hadn't made such a scene in her dressing room, but—"There's my work, you see."

"You don't need it anymore. I can easily look after us. And I couldn't have done it without you."

"That's why you came in the way you did?" she demanded, her voice sliding out of control.

"Stories need a good ending. This one's yours. Gemma Holyrood retires with her lover and lives happily ever after. No one will ever know any different."

Laura steadied herself with a long breath. Never mind she'd thought the speculation over Jack's identity hilarious or even occasionally useful. Just because he was her older brother he was not allowed to—to manage her. "What if I don't like your script? Well enough for Gemma if it were true, but what about Laura Edwards?" Her voice turned sing-song, sarcastic. "Laura Edwards the dutiful, if not-so-young-anymore lady vanishes from London forever and keeps house for her brother. After this that's what I'd do?" Too late, she stopped her tongue. Jack couldn't have looked worse if she'd slapped him.

"I thought you wanted us to be together," he said stiffly.

"I do," she said, repentant. "But I've—I've come to love this," she said, gesturing at the tools of her art: hair plumes and cosmetics, elaborate costumes shrouded in muslin to keep off the dust. Shoes and boots and breeches, old-fashioned tricorne hats. Laura Edwards might have done for her once, but she liked being Gemma Holyrood. So much more interesting than the woman who'd lost her mother and lived in quiet style in a shabby district of London. She could act for at least another five years before a younger girl replaced her.

"You've made so many sacrifices for me," Jack began.

"Maybe it wasn't a sacrifice," she muttered, massaging her forehead so she wouldn't have to look at him. "Maybe I wanted this all along." It was true, though Jack had never seen it. Even when she was only a seamstress she never wanted to work anywhere but the theatre. She could imagine her father here. He'd have loved seeing her speeches, discovering the workings of the mechanical sets...

Jack turned away, walking to the shelf of shoes, nudging a crooked one back into line. "You can't stay here forever," he said. "And after that scene in your dressing room—"

"I know." She was lucky. Many girls never made it half this far. It couldn't last. Five years ago Rollins had replaced Sylvia Long, no longer Her Mightiness. Sylvia made her living blackmailing old lovers now. Her memoirs would be published next year and apparently it cost at least twenty pounds to keep a man's name out of them. Rollins had a new scandal-maker to play opposite Laura, a pert and pretty harlot named Sarah who'd become a good friend—but Laura's acting career was like walking a tightrope with everyone waiting for her to fall. She'd sold herself as the angel and chances were they wouldn't forgive her if she ever played whore.

Jack switched to French, their language for secrets, for things that mattered, perhaps the deepest, truest thing about them. The words were laced with pain. "Laure, would you just try? You owe me that much. All along, I believed—"

French made her cry and think of Maman. Laura answered in English. "I did too. I just didn't expect it this soon."

"It's been eight years." He sighed. "Maybe it isn't your dream anymore, but it's always been mine."

She knew life was hard for him. Leaving her and Maman

again and again, the last time knowing Maman's health was failing. Time at sea could be ruthless and bitter, never mind the danger. Jack had got fevers...that new scar...and stitched together broken men as their lifeblood dripped through his fingers. And all the time he'd felt guilty for leaving her.

Jack slid his hand into his pocket. "You really meant it, didn't you, when you told me you didn't mind. I thought you were just being brave."

God forgive her. She couldn't hurt him so. Laura swallowed, licked her lips. "I'll come. As soon as the show's over." She had to try. Maybe she could work less, perform only during the Season and join Jack for the rest of the year. Being with him didn't mean she had to give up everything.

Jack swallowed. "Laura, I spoke to Mr. Rollins tonight."

She fought the urge to clench her hands. He was excited about his prospects. She could undo whatever he'd done.

"You can come with me tomorrow if you wish."

She drew a deep breath. He was offering it as a choice, so she could compromise too. "I see." She didn't like it, but it was the reason one had an understudy. Alice wasn't terrible and she'd be over the moon at this chance.

Yes, she owed it to Jack to at least go to Suffolk and weigh her options. Less time on stage wouldn't be all bad. If she took fewer roles a year it would help Sarah, who'd like having first pick of the parts. "I suppose it's been a while since I took a holiday," she said evenly. "I expect if I asked, Mr. Rollins would give me a few weeks' leave."

FEARING he might lose her for good, Rollins offered a month. "Is this just a holiday? Or does your brother know of your trouble with Saltash?" he asked.

Laura glanced to the door of Rollins' office, making sure it was shut. She shivered in spite of herself. "I can't let him know." If he did, Jack would end her career at once. She wasn't going to allow Jack or a demented old man bully her away from the stage. "Two weeks is all I need. All I want," Laura assured him. "You know I couldn't keep myself away any longer."

"Two weeks then," Rollins said, scrawling out the notice he'd have printed for the playbills. "Let me know if anything changes."

Suppressing a sigh, Laura buttoned herself into her Miss Edwards cape, avoiding her reflection in the window. Without the bright white she used for Gemma's off-stage appearances, she looked drab as a mouse. She set the bonnet squarely on her head—it was such a staid thing there was no point even trying to put it at a more fetching angle. Halfway to the door Laura stopped, remembering one last thing. She reached under her collar for the clasp of Gemma Holyrood's gold chain. Unclipped, the necklace slid into a pool of gold in the palm of her hand: precious, more than just metal, it was the symbol of who she was. "Keep this for me." She slapped it onto Mr. Rollins' desk.

"Of course," he said, sweeping it into his hands without looking up. He knew she'd be undone if he looked at her with solemn eyes.

"Will you explain to the others?" Laura asked. She'd rather let Mr. Rollins break the news to Dan, the lead actor, and Sarah and Alice. Not saying good bye gave her good reason to come back; besides, Laura didn't think she could keep a smile on her face when Mr. Rollins told Alice the news. She was pleased Alice would have a chance, but this show was having a spectacular run and it was hard handing it off. "Just tell them I'm on a short holiday."

"No one needs to know more than that," he said.

Mr. Rollins escorted her out of the office where Jack was waiting. "You take good care of her, Mr. Edwards."

"I will," Jack said, oblivious. She'd never told him that two years ago Rollins had insured her for a thousand pounds. She didn't keep secrets, exactly, but she knew it pained Jack a little that she was such a success. Even Maman, who'd chaperoned Laura's dressing room and seldom missed a performance had never boasted about her daughter the actress.

"See you in two weeks," Laura said, waving good bye to Mr. Rollins and Peter. It was a pledge.

4

A WANDERING BREEZE

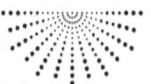

*J*asper was good at avoiding discomfort, especially the self-inflicted kind. Nevertheless, he put off his departure the next morning so he could walk round to Covent Garden first. It was a whim he couldn't justify but harmless—though he had no real reason to go, he also had no reason to resist.

Besides, he liked London's vast inventory of people, pleasures, and amusements. The market here, for instance, where you could easily spend an entire morning watching people whistling, walking, and bargaining: tired mothers with heavy baskets of shopping and children clinging to their skirts, nimble crossing sweepers and stall keepers with stout shoulders and wide aprons. Afternoons you could drink yourself stupid at Watier's Club (a poor idea) or a seedy tavern (generally worse) or at any one of a dozen gradients in between. Evenings were for flirting, cards, scrutinizing people at the theatre, and a glittering parade of dinner parties. Once you tired of that you raced to Brighton for more of the same—it wasn't a bad place, Brighton, and when it palled there were the Shires and Newmarket. As a matter of fact, Jasper couldn't think of any truly disagreeable place, except home, and he certainly wasn't going there. Sophy had tactfully invited him to stay at Chippenstone. And though London was the most agreeable place of all—generally, he qualified, stepping over something indeterminate and odiferous—it wasn't a bad thing to exchange the summer stench and heat for the quieter pleasures of the country.

After all, things never got too quiet with Sophy around. Even if she was turning soft-eyed and weepy and quite unable to ride, she had a knack like no one else for making him smile. He should bring her a present. He stopped to admire a posy of pinks, moving away before the flower seller got too hopeful. Pretty blooms, but they'd wilt in this heat before he ever got within hailing distance of Chippenstone.

He bought an orange instead, dropping the peels as he walked, eating the segments one by one. It was tasty and sweeter smelling than the milling crowd, but oranges were untidy fruit. Even after wiping with his handkerchief his fingers were sticky, forcing him to leave off his gloves. Circling round a wheelbarrow of fish and the jaw-cracking cries of the vendor behind it, Jasper turned the corner and strolled up to the theatre where red ink bulletins slashed across the notices for the current play.

"Hmm," he said to no one in particular. Miss Holyrood would not be appearing in this evening's performance. Seemed she and her lover were having a happy reunion indeed.

"They say she's sick," said a smirking flower seller crouched next to her baskets, resting her back against the wall.

"Pity," Jasper said. "Do they think she'll recover quickly?"

"Lawks, I don't know!" chortled the woman. "But they say with diseases of the heart—"

"I'll take that one," Jasper pointed out a flower. Removing the fading bloom from his buttonhole, he dropped it to the ground and replaced it with the carnation he'd chosen.

"Very nice, sir, if you'll forgive my saying so," the woman said.

Jasper dropped a coin into her outstretched hand and moved away, retracing his steps. So Gemma Holyrood was apparently indisposed... He'd half expected something like this, but instead of the satisfaction of proving himself right, he felt disappointed.

Mild the feeling may have been, but it dogged him all the way home and most of the way to Suffolk.

WHEN JASPER ROLLED his curricle to a neat stop in front of Sophy's house late that afternoon he was pleased with his time. It was only quarter past five, a new record for him.

"Jasper!" It was Sophy, wide and ungainly, lurching much too quickly out the door.

He snapped his watch shut and dived from the curricle. "Madness, my girl!" he scolded, catching her arms. "What in heaven's name are you doing on your feet?" She looked like a porpoise scarcely able to stand, clumsy now instead of moving with her usual lightning rapidity. Her birdlike wrists were thick, her fingers hot and swollen. Inside his thorax, Jasper felt something wrench.

"You've been suffering," he said. "Why haven't you told me?" She was too little, too young for this.

She laughed. "I'm so glad you've come," she said—apparently all he could expect by way of reply. Marriage seemed to have made his little sister immune to criticism. Overall Jasper didn't mind, just wished that she'd still heed *his*.

"I like what you've done with the gardens," he said. Though maybe it wasn't the profusion of flowers in the beds, but the tempting benches she'd tucked away beneath the trees. She'd always had the ability to brighten a place. "Henrietta sends her warmest love," he informed her. "And your nephews a wet raspberry."

She grinned. "Laurence or Will?"

"Whichever is the older one I think," he said.

She squeezed his hand. "I do miss her," she admitted. "But perhaps it isn't entirely unfortunate they couldn't come. I shouldn't have thought this house would ever feel full, but Laurie is something of a presence, isn't he?"

"Yes, like the nine-headed hydra," Jasper said. He frowned, reassessing her size. It still wasn't quite...believable. "Maybe you should be lying down. In quiet."

"I'd never have taken you for such a fusspot!" Sophy wrinkled her nose. "Come inside."

He let her steer him into the house, keeping a firm hold of her arm. She smiled, amused by his caution, and gave him a tolerant pat. The servant helped him out of his caped driving coat and carried it away with his whip, hat, and gloves. Jasper took a quick glance in the mirror. Tolerable, if he could just fix that unwanted crumple in his cravat...

Sophy moved to his shoulder. "If you want to help you could drive me to Cordell tomorrow morning. I'd like to see Lady Fairchild. Tom is willing to bring me, of course, but I thought it might be easier the first time if—"

He'd rather take a pummeling at the boxing salon than take her to his parents' home, but Jasper spun around to face her. "You haven't seen them yet?"

She shook her head. "We've been writing. I get letters every week, but—well, you know how it is. She writes fairly affectionately, so I think she's forgiven me, but she hasn't tried to see me...I think she supposes that would be admitting she was wrong about Tom and you know—"

All this roundabout was making Jasper's head hurt. "She is wrong," he said. "So is our father. You aren't to blame for any of this." Lord, hadn't they put her through enough already? He was easy tempered, but listening to her excuses for them made his heart pound and his arms tense.

"I was willing to lose them for Tom," Sophy said quietly. "But if I don't have to...she was always good to me, Jasper, as good as she knew how."

That wasn't saying much. "And Father?"

"I'm not as fussy about apologies as you are," she said. "If he's willing, I'll meet him part way. Really, if I expected them to grovel—"

"I would," he put in.

"Then I would end up never speaking to either of them again and that would be a pity. They are my family, Jasper, the only parents I have."

"I think Sally is wonderful," he said, reminding her of her mother-in-law.

"She is. You might not understand, but it means—it means a great deal to me that Lord and Lady Fairchild love me, in their way."

No matter what he said, she still thought of herself as the friendless bastard delivered eight years ago to their door. "You deserve better," he said.

"If I was choosy with my affections I'd be as lonely as you are. Who is there to love if you only take those who've made no mistakes?" It stung, though she said it half-teasing. "I'm sorry," she said, her eyes contrite.

"No," Jasper said. "I forbid you to be. If you are forgiving and apologetic and stand this close, I'll singe your wings. So they are both still at Cordell then?"

Sophy nodded.

"I'm surprised one hasn't killed the other and dropped the body into the lake," Jasper said. He looked about him, but there was no Sally, no Tom appearing on the wide stairs. Sophy had cornered him alone. This was important to her.

"I want to see Lady Fairchild and I'm tired of this ridiculous waiting. I have something I wish to ask her," Sophy said. There was no dissuading her, not when she had that set to her chin, so he relented with a smile. She always did insist on going her own way.

"Very well. I'll take you wherever you wish to go so long as Tom approves, even into the terrifying maw of my mother's drawing room. I shall suffer afflictions—blighting glances, a lecture—but I can endure any trial for your sake. How is Tom taking things by the way?"

"If he can stand it, so can you," she said.

The impending birth or the in-laws? Maybe she meant both. Jasper held her at arm's length, studying her. The ungainly bulge looked comical on her, but her eyes were bright and unshadowed. Tom took good care of her, which pleased Jasper, but he didn't know that she should be permitted to climb stairs. Before she reached the first one, he took her arm.

"I know how to make use of the bannister," she said, her hand sliding along the gleaming marble. He made a noncommittal noise, watching her slippered feet. Her dress was too long and she climbed slowly, spending her breath.

"I can't ever seem to get enough air," she admitted, pushing against her belly.

Jasper stopped. "Is that a corner? What have you got in there—a bureau?" As he watched a lump slid from one side of her belly to the other.

"A foot." She winced. "Maybe an elbow."

"No horns?"

She grinned. "Time will tell."

The pause had given her back her breath and they climbed

the rest of the way. Jasper lingered at the top, pretending to pick a piece of lint from his sleeve.

"I don't know if Tom and Lady Fairchild will ever be friends," Sophy began.

Jasper snorted. "I shouldn't think so." Folly to wish for it. His mother and Tom Bagshot were as likely a pair as Napoleon and the Tsar of Russia.

"Jasper." It was her own familiar smile she used, but her eyes were sad. "Are you angry on my behalf or your own?"

"I think it's actually my nature," he said, evading her with a glib answer. "I'm a beastly fellow, always have been."

She could forgive if she chose—he couldn't very well stop her—but he didn't have to like it or trust his parents. He wasn't convinced they deserved to be forgiven after forbidding Sophy's marriage and casting her off. The way he saw it they'd earned every one of their regrets. He'd grown accustomed to the heat of the vengeful little fire he'd nourished so long on the coals of their pangs. It wasn't well done of him, but he wasn't like Sophy, gifted with a kind heart. He was like his parents: vindictive, selfish, and proud. Sophy might share Lord Fairchild's unruly copper-colored hair, but she took after her mother.

Jasper hadn't reached nine when his governess, Miss Prescott, disappeared, but he'd never forgotten her. You outgrew boyish adoration—thank God—but you didn't forget caring and sympathy and the person who kissed you when you ripped up your knees. Impossible, unless you were a much worse fellow than he.

"Tom about?" Jasper asked, more than ready for a new subject. "Or did you feed him to the lions?"

"He's waiting for you. In the library."

Jasper made a face. "I was hoping you'd feed me."

"I will," she said. "If only to fatten you for the lions. Come on."

Sophy brought him to his brother-in-law in the library where she introduced him to a pile of sandwiches, which he promptly reduced to smears and crumbs. Between bites Jasper enquired after Tom's business, confirmed he had no objection to Sophy visiting Cordell Hall tomorrow and (after Sophy left) warned Tom again that if any harm ever came to his sister he'd beat the tar out of him.

"You're welcome to try," Tom said, smiling as he set aside his brandy. Tom was good with his fists and had a punishing right Jasper wouldn't mind seeing demonstrated on someone besides himself.

"You couldn't stop this madness?" Jasper asked. "My parents will only hurt her again. And insult you."

Tom shrugged. "She wants this. Whatever happens, she's got a home to come to and arms to cry in. She misses them more the closer we come to the birth."

That hurt him, Jasper saw. "I've heard the condition makes females even more irrational," he said. "This must be a symptom. Henrietta says she weeps over novels. Sophy will get over this. Really, I think one meeting will cure her of the notion. It only took a few meetings to convince me I'd happily trade your mother for mine. How is she by the way?"

Tom laughed. "Top of the trees and you know it." Sally Bagshot had never been happier with her son married and her first grandchild on the way. "Expect she's sitting with Sophy, making sure she rests."

"Someone has to. Should she really be using the stairs?" Jasper asked.

"If you can stop her... My mother wanted to give you time with your sister. She said she'd see you at dinner."

"When's that?" Jasper's eyes dropped to the empty plate. Travel always made him ravenous.

"Eight."

Jasper raised his eyebrows. It was a late hour for the unfashionable Bagshots.

"You aren't our only company. Means I have to dress for dinner," Tom said, his frown telling Jasper what he thought of that. "Friend of mine, John Edwards. Jack. He's a physician. I want someone on hand I trust."

Jasper nodded approvingly.

"He's just back from overseas so I told him to bring his sister. They've been a long time apart. I'm hoping he'll take up the practice after Jamieson retires. We'll need a new doctor in the district. He's a good sort, so don't play any airs with him."

"Would I ever?"

Tom laughed, a rough bark Jasper couldn't resist answering with a smile.

Tom waved him away. "I've work to do and I expect it will take you half a day to change."

"My dear fellow, there's plenty of time." Jasper consulted his watch. "There's a good two hours. I can manage, if I sacrifice my shirt points."

Jasper traipsed upstairs to his usual room where his bags and valet waited. He might jest with Tom about his fastidiousness (and Tom's lack of it), but he was perfectly capable of achieving a respectable transformation in three quarters of an hour, slightly less if it was truly urgent. Tom might be able to slap himself together in under ten minutes, but that was lamentable not praiseworthy. Sophy's husband had his good points, though—he wasn't as unfazed about the impending birth as he pretended and had invited a physician friend to stay. A neat solution and Jasper liked him the more for it.

Jasper dressed with care in his best linen. Sophy and Tom wouldn't care a fig about the arctic peaks of his shirt points or the sublime cut of his coat, but Tom's mother would notice and recognize the compliment. With time still before dinner, Jasper sauntered downstairs hoping to find Mrs. Bagshot. He'd appreciated the chance to greet Sophy alone, but was looking forward to greeting the elderly lady. Jasper was fond of her grey-haired, cushiony person; she was blessed with sweetness, shrewdness, and good sense. She wasn't in the drawing room, or the Egyptian salon with its crocodile-legged furniture and bright, overly gilded walls—an absurd fantasy, like a setting straight from the stage.

Jasper picked up a newspaper and made himself at home stretching out his legs and crossing them on the sofa. Nothing interesting in the society items—just the usual snippets about wives misbehaving and an update on a stale divorce. To make up for the dearth of scandal the editor had put in a piece about Thomas Ward, the boy supposedly born of an incestuous affair between Princess Sophia and her brother the Duke of Cumberland: a decade-old controversy and not worth stirring up in Jasper's opinion. At this point who cared if the boy was fathered by Cumberland or General Garth? Jasper lowered the paper and considered the copy of *The Castle of Otranto* on the nearby table, but decided to leave it alone. He'd read most of *The Mysterious Mother* and one gothic novel by Walpole was surely enough. His ears pricked at an interruption, prompting a smile of relief. The door clicked open and someone entered with a quick, light tread.

"They should paint you after you've had the baby, lounging here like Cleopatra," he said without turning around.

Silence. Jasper turned the page and glanced over his shoulder, wondering why Sophy wasn't laughing—and found it wasn't her. Of course not. Her footsteps didn't sound that softly, not anymore. "I beg your pardon," Jasper said as he set aside the paper and vaulted to his feet. "I heard someone come in and assumed it was my sister." He gave an elegant bow, but it didn't appear to mollify the lady. She stared at him in a fixed way like she'd been cornered by something truly horrifying.

It was true that a well-mannered fellow would have risen for any female, sister or not, but in the country at what he'd thought was essentially a family party...well, Dr. Edwards' sister was either a stickler or painfully unused to society. "I'm Jasper Rushford," he said, hoping to convince her he wouldn't pounce.

She nodded, but didn't offer her name or come any closer.

"You must be Miss Edwards," he said, unwilling to play the correct game and run away, waiting for a formal introduction at dinner. He liked coming to Sophy's house where rules were unknown or ignored. Escaping the tiresome code was one of his chief pleasures here, not that he'd ever admit it.

"You think Mrs. Bagshot as Cleopatra?" she asked, finally thawing enough to speak.

"The younger one," Jasper explained. "But I'd kill to see the elder in the role."

She cracked an involuntary smile. "Goodness no. It's a much better part for you."

Perhaps not a stickler after all? She had a charming smile. "Does that mean I have your permission to resume my attitude of decadent recline?"

She glanced swiftly at the open door. "Yes. But I recommend exchanging the newspaper for a better prop."

"Excellent notion. I'd exchange this newspaper for almost anything—nothing but drivel and tepid scandal today. Perhaps you could massage my feet and peel grapes for me."

"I'm afraid I haven't the right costume," she said, stiffening.

True enough. There were better things than that dark blue stuff to set off those chestnut curls. The clothes looked...wrong for her, though they were perfectly appropriate for her station. Maybe females of the middle class always looked like that.

"Have we met before?" Jasper asked, tilting his head, hoping it would improve his study of her. There was something in the shape of her face, the angle of her chin...

"We haven't yet," she said, schooling her face to blankness so swiftly it made him blink. "Excuse me." She moved for the door.

"Fine, fine," Jasper said, annoyed he'd lost her. "I'll wait until you're presented at dinner." He would wink at her if there were grapes with dessert. With a smile he sprawled back on the sofa, reaching out a languid hand for the newspaper. His attention wouldn't fasten onto the tight rows of print though, or even the cartoons and advertisements. He was thinking about Miss Edwards and the strange way she'd left him and what it was about her that seemed so oddly familiar.

5
ILL WINDS THAT BLOW NO GOOD

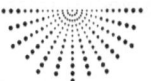

*L*aura marched down the hallway and rapped on her brother's door.

"Come—"

Before he could finish she barged into his chamber. "I have to get out of here."

"What's happened?" Jack set down his watch chain and the fob he was struggling to latch onto it.

"Your friend's brother-in-law. Did you know he's a regular at the theatre?" Let Jack unravel the rest.

He sat down, thumping against the high mattress. "Did he recognize you?"

"He asked me if we'd met before."

Jack winced.

"He was reading the paper," Laura continued. "What if some mention of Gemma Holyrood jogs his memory? I'm going back to London."

"You can't. We just arrived."

"Then you'll have to tell your friend who I really am." What a disaster that would be.

"I don't think Tom would mind..." Jack began.

"And his brother-in-law? His wife?" They weren't the same kind of people as Tom and his mother. Anyone could see that.

"I'm more worried about the village," Jack said.

Of course. His future patients. They wouldn't want their wives and daughters attended by the brother of an actress. "Then I have to go. We'll invent something."

"What? A dying relative? Tom thinks we haven't any. And neither of us has got any letters."

Laura leaned against the dressing table and folded her arms. "It'll be odd I grant you, but what of it? I'm not needed here. It's you they want."

"They're trying to be kind to me. They know I've just come back. They don't want to steal me away from you."

"Tell them we've quarreled." It was fairly close to the truth. "Tell them I'm an unmanageable harpy with the devil's own temper and—"

"Laura. Tom knows you mean everything to me."

She glared. "Then what do you suggest?"

"Well, he hasn't actually recognized you..."

"Yet," she qualified.

"Maybe he won't," Jack said. "You are, or at least you tell me so, quite a wonderful actress. Act." He smiled tentatively. "You won't necessarily be giving up your career, you know, staying in the country."

"I just don't like the part," she grumbled.

"It's my sister you'll be playing, not a mouse," he retorted.

"Yes, but she can't resemble Gemma Holyrood." Anything could give her away—a smile, a glance, a laugh. The only characteristics left for Laura Edwards were the old, the dour, the awkward, and the plain. She also had plenty of scope to play dull-witted and stupid. She never should have teased Mr. Rushford about Cleopatra. "I'll have to be—to be—" She couldn't say it.

46

"He won't be around that long. A few weeks—"

"That long?"

Jack leaned away, shrugging shiftily. "Babies come when they come. Tom wanted me here in plenty of time. Bit anxious about it, in fact," he said.

"I'm not doing it for that long. A couple of days. Just until I invent a reason to get out of here." She pushed away from the dressing table and strode toward the door.

"Just don't—don't overdo it," Jack said.

She pinned him a full five seconds with her glance, then released one of their mother's sounds, a Gallic noise erupting from her throat that was the very essence of frustration. "Bah! You think I'm so stupid?"

Jack knew better than to answer and let her bang out the door.

Outside in the hall Laura collected herself, relaxing clenched shoulders and tight fists. She didn't like any of this, but she knew better than to expect the world to order itself to please her. Jack was right. She may as well treat this as a challenge, a test of her skill. Pursing her lips, she turned for her own room. It was too late for major alterations, but there was still much that could be done with the subtle use of cosmetics. She wished she'd worn a wig instead of her own hair, even if it meant days of sweat and prickles.

He's already seen you blonde, she reminded herself.

LAURA CAME DOWN to dinner in the full panoply of her trade, her complexion dulled, shadows brushed into her cheeks and beneath her eyes. Unnecessary tactics, she discovered, for her opponent didn't step onto the field. Aside from a formal introduction of perhaps a dozen words, Mr. Rushford didn't spare her a glance and devoted himself to Mr. Bagshot's mother.

"See? You worried for nothing," Jack whispered as he took Laura's arm and escorted her to the table.

She knew it was childish to fume behind a false smile as she helped herself to duck and roasted vegetables, but the man had been her devoted admirer for months. He'd promised her kisses with his eyes, reached after her trailing gauze (her Titania costume was scandalous but wonderful), stood in his box and applauded. There'd been witty notes delivered with flowers, tributes to her elbows and ankles—all the symptoms of passion, destroyed by a coarser face and plainer frock. It was terribly lowering.

She was just a prop—noticeable only when gilded with the romance of the theatre. How naive to think *she'd* become something different, when it was only lights and a stage. Laura took a spoonful of cauliflower, waving away the cow's tongue. The footman offered the plate to Jack who helped himself to a thick slice and ladled on a heavy coat of sauce. Masking her distaste, Laura prodded her food until it was clear of the gilt and painted flowers edging her plate. It had been a lifetime since she'd seen a table so laden with silver and flowers, but she ate automatically, not bothering to reach for the salt. This character had no tastebuds and only took timid sips of wine.

"You must be so happy to have your brother restored to you," Mrs. Bagshot said from the end of the table, recalling Laura to the conversation.

"Oh yes," she said, longing to simper or make a scene. She could play vulgar and at least that would be interesting. But it wasn't her role. She was anonymous, dull as a dictionary. "Thank you for inviting me here." Her spine was rigid, her fork precise as a scalpel.

"You must consider yourself at home," urged Tom Bagshot's young wife. "Have you seen the town?"

Laura shook her head. *You are porridge. Disinteresting.* She kept her face still, her eyes blank. "I'm sure it's lovely."

"It's a pretty place. And we've our eyes on a house for you, close by, but near enough to the surgery in Bury St Edmonds. It's a charming house, though it needs a feminine hand. Do you garden?"

"I'm afraid not, Mrs. Bagshot." Gardening was probably an acceptable pastime for this persona, but Laura knew nothing about the subject. She'd have to think up a suitable fossilizing hobby—history or cutting paper silhouettes.

"Please call me Sophy." Tom's wife smiled at Laura, still undeterred. "It gets so confusing otherwise. Perhaps Tom and your brother will take you by the place tomorrow. Or you could look in on the village."

"If it's no trouble." Laura felt bad for her, trying so hard to coax smiles from her conversationally handicapped guest, but it couldn't be helped. She smiled, a facial contraction without any warmth. "That would be nice."

It was easy after that to slip into silence. Jack and Tom were lost in shared memories of their time at sea when Tom had been impressed onto the crew of the Leander. His stint in the navy had been shorter than Jack's, but they had grown close in the year they sailed together. Mr. Rushford, looking far too comfortable for a man in such impossible shirt points, volleyed witticisms at Mrs. Bagshot and his sister while Laura dissected her vegetables. Even after the meal when Sophy excused herself from the drawing room to rest upstairs and Tom summoned Jack meaningfully to his study, Mr. Rushford devoted himself to the elderly woman, winding her knitting, which covered his breeches and coat sleeves with fluff. Laura sat at a small table on the other side of the room all but forgotten, trying to convince herself this was due to her convincing performance and not Rushford's shallow snobbery. She wasn't a pathetic creature dependent on adoration and praise. She'd just...become used to it. She reached for a nearby deck of cards and started laying out a half-hearted game of patience.

Past sixty and gently fading, Mrs. Bagshot had the fragile, translucent glow of a fine tea saucer. Despite the clever way she set down her knitting at intervals, Laura noticed an occasional tremor in her fingers. Tom and Sophy hadn't seemed to notice, but Mr. Rushford, for all his smiles, watched keenly. Why else was he always ready with a quip at the right time, so she could put down the needles and clasp her hands?

Laura moved a card, studying them.

"I'm knitting for the parish now," Mrs. Bagshot told him.

"Yes, I expect Sophy's infant has enough jackets for every day of the year," he said.

"There's plenty," she said. "But they grow quickly and who knows? There might be more of them."

"Infants? Yes, I suppose so."

She turned the knitting, counted off the row, but fumbled the first new stitch. Before her mouth could pucker, before the shaking grew more than a twitch, Mr. Rushford had her hands in his.

"You're a marvel," he said, with a smile and a squeeze.

"You're a rogue," she answered. "But a charming one."

He acknowledged the compliment with a nod, releasing her hands. "Let me get you a footstool," he said and rose to fetch one from across the room.

"No, I think I'll put it away now, so you can stop waiting on me."

"And deny me my greatest pleasure? You wouldn't." He was skilled, acting a farce but making the feeling sincere. He liked Mrs. Bagshot, Laura realized, and wanted her to smile and laugh.

Mrs. Bagshot rewarded him with both. "I'm quite comfortable and Miss Edwards—"

"Don't worry about me, ma'am," Laura interrupted. Dull mouse she might be, but she was not allowing Mrs. Bagshot to force Rushford to notice her. She was not an object of pity to be targeted with intentional kindness.

"You are so quiet there. May we join you in a game?" Mrs. Bagshot asked.

"I think I'm tired," Laura said, hastily scooping up the cards and destroying the nonsense plays she'd made to cover her scrutiny of them. She slid the cards together, tapping the sides even. "From the journey. I've no head for it tonight."

"Oh, we can count penny points and—"

"Truly, Mrs. Bagshot. I've no wish to play. Is it—am I allowed to walk in the garden? I'll sleep better after a turn outside."

"Of course you may! Remember, you are quite at home." Mrs. Bagshot hastened to tell her where she might like to walk, where to find a comfortable seat, where the flowers were at their best, and which of the long windows were always left unlocked. Laura, making for the door, nodded without catching the details.

"Are you sure you don't want company?" Mrs. Bagshot finished.

"Oh, no. I shan't be long." Laura slipped from the room and down an impressive gallery to a larger formal drawing room with a collection of bronzes and seascapes. The windows stretched from the floor to the ceiling, giving a view of the terrace. The latch gave with a well-oiled snick and Laura escaped into the cool of the evening.

Her persona didn't help, but even without it this place oppressed her. She didn't belong, yet it brought back uncomfortable memories, faded sketches of another life. She remembered the smell of gardens in the evening, the eye-pleasing symmetry of neatly clipped hedges, the loosening of muscles one felt gazing out at a stretch of green lawn. Quiet trees, aged stone, gravel paths that glistened as the sun dipped out of sight: she had known all these. But it wasn't memories of gardens or chateau that pricked her eyes and made her nostrils flare. It was her grandmother, stately in red-heeled shoes and a towering wig with a miniature ship tossed in its waves. Her eldest brother, handsome in his military uniform. Her father, the lines of a hundred thousand carefree smiles embellishing his mouth and eyes. And her mother, hosting salons, maintaining a large and glorious correspondence *avec les Pensées*. As a child Laura didn't understand this as more than the pleasures of thick stationery, lavender ink, and scented sealing wax. Now she knew better. Her mother, an intellectual beauty who'd never so much as laced her own gown, had learned to cook underfed chickens and bargain at the market for fruit and eggs. She'd toiled as a seamstress and played maid to Laura for years, keeping a wary eye on her only daughter, helping her manipulate the crowd from the stage and behind the dressing screen in the green room.

Remember, Laure, the way to flirt is to flit in and away. To tease, but to surrender nothing. A dandelion puff tossed on the wind.

That lesson came after her first run as Lydia Languish, with the heady rush of success burning under her skin. Then, during a failed revival of She Stoops to Conquer:

That one's a danger, Laure. You must be careful with him. Let other girls wreck themselves on him...

The second time Laura did the play, when her Kate Hardcastle was the toast of London, she got careless with her heart. Young Lord Harvey caught it and slipped it into his pocket. Her mother said nothing, just quietly handed Laura a written list reminding her what she might lose if she accepted Harvey's offer of carte blanche. The next day Laura sent Peter the doorman with a tactfully worded refusal, bearing no hint of the heart wringing it had taken her to pen each word.

"You did right," her mother said afterward. "He's handsome as ever a man was, but he never tips the doorman. If Peter doesn't like a man it's best keep to him at arm's length. With a fan in your hand, too. Harvey would love you my darling, but not for long."

They'd cried and laughed together over the gossip in the papers, danced with joy at some reviews and hurled others into the fire. Maman always fussed over Laura's costumes, even after she was too weak to go to the theatre. From her bed she inspected every tuck and every seam, making sure it was shaped just so.

She never admitted missing her life in France where she'd had a house and gardens like these. If she were here she could have told Laura what to do with the troublesome Mr. Rushford. Laura sighed, tearing a leaf from the hedge and rolling it in her fingers, letting the green juice soak into her skin. It was sticky with a bitter scent.

6

INVESTIGATING

*W*hen he left Mrs. Bagshot Jasper was reasonably certain Miss Edwards was still outside. Twice he'd looked round at the sound of someone passing in the corridor, but the first time he saw a footman, the second a housemaid. Miss Edwards did step quietly though. He might have missed her, so he strolled out to the terrace to investigate. It was dark now but there was a half moon, enough light to venture beyond the perimeter of the house. He watched the shadows but nothing moved. There was no breeze.

No reason why she shouldn't sit out as long as she pleased—Bagshot's gardens were extensive and safe from prowlers. Still Jasper found himself descending the wide steps to the paths that quartered the lawns, his steps on the gravel beating a pulse that was too loud, too quick for the night. He slowed down and moved to the grass.

He knew his way even in the weak light round the box trees, beneath the elms. Her dark gown would hide her more effectively than it had in the drawing room or at the dinner table. Was she shy? He hadn't thought so, not when she mocked him in the Egyptian salon. He'd meant to quiz her about it at the dinner table, but she was so self-effacing that even when you looked straight on her edges seemed blurred. In the drawing room she'd chosen a seat in the shadows as far from him as she could get. He'd watched covertly, looking for an expression or a trick of movement to explain the sense he'd seen her before— maybe she spoke like one of the ladies he knew or had a similar way of dressing her hair. After a second glance, Jasper was certain that none of the ladies he knew styled their hair like that. The chestnut mass, gathered clumsily above her neck and ears, seemed duller than it had in the library, her eyes tired, her skin sallow. He didn't care for that dark gown or those long sleeves. If it was her way of talking that was familiar he couldn't say; she'd relinquished about a hundred words all evening.

He could ask her, but it was an awkward question, insulting. Besides, where could he have met her before? She lived the retired sort of life necessitated by constrained finances and the death of her mother. It would be a good thing for her, settling here with her brother.

Jasper finished the shortest circuit and glanced up at the house. She might have completed her walk and gone in ahead of him; it was growing late. He was ready for brandy, a book and a good doze—soon, after one more pass through the park. He'd take the longer path this time. She might have been tempted by the dainty bridges spanning the water and lingered there. Quickening his pace, Jasper set out again, passing the maze. He was no help to her if she'd ventured in there for he'd never mastered the trick of it, and his wretched sister refused to part with the secret.

He walked out of sight of the house past the cutting gardens, the stables, and the empty kennels. At the turn into the wilderness he saw her, but some instinct drew him back into the shadows. He knew from the way she stood, she'd come out here to be alone.

She moved after a time, walking slowly, a gently stepping piece of shadowed sky. At the path's crossing she paused again, glancing back where she had come, then looking ahead to the square little bridge that would conduct her past him and back to the house. Weary, she leaned against the rail, her head dropping, her study turning inward or perhaps to her clasped hands. Her neck was pale and thin in the dark, too slender to support that heavy twist of hair. Tempted to step forward, he halted as her pale hand dashed up to her cheek—brooding he could interrupt, but not tears.

Muffling his feet, he stepped back behind the kennels meaning to hide until she passed, but as he moved she turned her head, framing it in profile against the weak light of the moon. He stopped, arrested by the arabesque curves of lip and chin. He knew them, knew the short nose above and the straight brow, not quite as high as fashion decreed. As he blinked she finished turning, the features melting into shadow once more. Jasper moistened his lips, uncertain. It was some trick of the light, some fancy of his own brain. Lord knows he thought too much on Gemma Holyrood. She was not, could not be here. He waited but the moon didn't move and neither did she, refusing to oblige him with another glimpse. She just wilted against the low wall and Jasper couldn't say if it was fact or the contortions of his own mind that made him see the forlorn pose of Gemma Holyrood's Titania. She sighed, a tremor that ruffled the water and flew into the trees. Pulling herself upright, she set off for the house, the crunch of her footsteps fading in the distance.

Jasper waited until all was silent, frowning as he picked a loose bit of paint on the kennel door with his fingernail. Miss Edwards and Gemma Holyrood...surely not.

. . .

A CAUTIOUS HUNTER, Jasper dawdled in his room the next morning, trying to time his arrival in the breakfast parlor with Miss Edwards'—guesswork, since she'd been put on the other end of the house. He passed the time writing in his diary.

> *Driving time to Chippenstone: average sixteen miles per hour with two changes at Chelmsford and Braintree. Ostlers at the Red Lion confoundedly slow, but gained time in the last ten miles. Good road.*
>
> *On inspection, S appears a baffling size but well. Physician on premises. I'm to second her in a duel with the Mater today. Shall try to keep blood off the carpets.*
>
> *Interesting developments in wager with P re: seduction of actress G. H. (remember—stake raised to £200 in April). Either I'm mad or she's here, masquerading as a genteel spinster! The mind reels...*

The more Jasper thought on it, the more impossible it seemed. Sitting here with a pencil in his hand yesterday's suspicions were hardly credible. Gemma Holyrood? Here? Not bloody likely. A good look-over at the breakfast table should give him the truth.

> *If I'm wrong (and therefore mad or hopelessly infatuated) recovery will likely require drastic measures. Walking tour? Scotland?*

It had worked as a cure once before.

Pocketing his palm-sized notebook, Jasper made his way to the sunlit breakfast parlor. Some blessed soul had restrained the decorators here. It was done up in a soothing combination of white and pale sea green with dreamy watercolors on one wall and a view to the gardens on the other. Tom and Dr. Edwards were down already, seated at one end of the table and discussing Sophy's examination—not something Jasper cared to hear at any time, but particularly awful when contemplating breakfast.

Tom, seeing his face, colored and broke off. "Jack, will you wish to ride this morning?"

Dr. Edwards accepted and helped himself to more eggs. "Morning, Rushford," he said as Jasper took the seat opposite. Jasper was on his second piece of toast when Miss Edwards slipped in, added one or two morsels to her plate, and sequestered herself at the far end of the table. She ate with concentration, barely looking up. Jasper stared without staring, getting up and walking to the sideboard again, but all this gave him was a view of the top of her head.

"Laura, would you care to take a turn about the gardens?" her brother asked.

"Yes, please," she said, meek as a child of six. Her voice was rough as if from disuse. Jasper frowned. It wasn't easy to super-impose the features and flair of Gemma Holyrood on this one. He studied her fingers, trying to recall if yesterday they'd looked so red and chapped. Perhaps she'd soaked them overnight in lye and combed soot into her hair. She kept her chin tucked so close he couldn't get a glimpse of the line of her neck. Long sleeves again, so no hope of spying the elbows. The eyebrows were heavy, drawing together over the nose. Perhaps she'd darkened them. She'd recognize him, wouldn't she?

Don't flatter yourself. Gemma Holyrood always accepted his gifts and his admiration, but never with more than the same pleased smile she gave everyone else.

Beside him Tom slit open a letter. Jasper watched the message play across his face. "You are not pleased with the cream of your correspondence?" Miss Edwards didn't react to the quote from *She Stoops to Conquer*, one of Miss Holyrood's most acclaimed roles.

"Magistrate informs me he's taking very seriously the matter of my stolen poultry," Tom said, puzzled. "Didn't know I'd lost any."

"I think your mother may have mentioned it," Jasper reminded him delicately. "Her blue bantam."

"Yes. I'd forgotten."

Jasper helped himself to sugar, clinking his spoon against his cup.

Since Sophy was taking her breakfast upstairs these days, she arrived last, dressed for her visit. It was a pretty blue muslin gown with a matching pelisse, but she hesitated in the doorway, fussing over perfectly faultless gloves. Jasper understood immediately.

"Mater will approve." He took a last sip of coffee. Her chip straw bonnet with velvet ribbons was an especially nice touch, one his exhaustingly fastidious mother would appreciate.

"You look ready." Jasper rose from his seat.

"I am, but—"

"Confound your buts!" Jasper cast a covert eye to the far end of the breakfast table where Miss Edwards in demure silence pretended to eat her egg. If she recognized the line from Sheridan's play she didn't show it. Best save that puzzle for later, Jasper decided. He smiled at his sister. "Do you wish to go or not?"

Sophy settled her shoulders with a quick breath. "I do."

"Don't be too long, love." Tom laid down his letters and glanced over his shoulder to give her a reassuring smile. "You know I pine when you're away."

She laughed, telling Tom he'd survive for an hour or so, but her fingers lingered as they brushed across his shoulder. His hand came up, closed over hers and gave it a squeeze. She bent, whispered something in his ear, then left him to his letters. "Jasper? Is my chariot ready?"

It was. Jasper helped her inside then settled himself beside her. "Come here," he said, nudging Sophy closer. "Let me cut the wind." It wasn't a sharp breeze but her gown was thin. "There's a rug by your feet if you need it."

She gave him a look.

They rolled gently over the bridge and down the drive.

"May we go a little faster?" Sophy suggested. "Don't you want to amaze me with your fearless handling of the ribbons?"

"Certainly not."

At this pace it might take a half hour to cover the two miles of road between here and Cordell Hall, but he wasn't risking speed, not with this cargo. He'd never say it, but she was precious.

7
COMING HOME

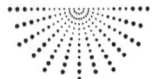

*C*ordell Hall was sufficiently large and sufficiently weathered—silently announcing itself as the home of persons of lineage and gentility. It had the right number of turrets and inconvenient architectural oddities and a luxurious number of windows, most with the original wavy glass.

Jasper assisted Sophy from the curricle, noting the nervous flexing of her fingers.

"I'm as scared as the first day I came," she admitted.

"But a little larger," Jasper said.

"True." She smoothed her gown ruefully. "Getting around isn't too difficult, but sometimes I forget and bump into things. And there's just no room to breathe." She smiled. "Not for much longer."

This time she didn't act like it was a concession to take hold of his arm.

The staff were well trained—much more dignified than the lot at Chippenstone—and the door opened wide with pleasing promptness. After that, dignity disappeared. Jenkins, the perfect butler, beamed and clasped Sophy's hands, chiding her for not sending word ahead of her arrival, while Sophy joked with Timothy the footman.

Partway collecting himself, Jenkins gave Timothy a stern look. "You. Hop along. Tell His Lordship and Her Ladyship that Miss Sophy's come home."

Timothy sped up the stairs, hallooing as he went. In seconds Sophy was surrounded by a housemaid who'd abandoned her duster and Mrs. Lawson, the housekeeper, who gathered in Sophy like an octopus until she practically disappeared.

"Our girl is back," Mrs. Lawson said. "Did you ever think to see the day?"

Jasper adjusted his neckcloth, put off by the fussing and wiping of eyes. He almost jumped when Jenkins whispered at his shoulder.

"It's good of you to bring her, sir." Jenkins smiled as he did when he used to jolly Jasper out of the mopes by inviting him into the pantry to polish silver and decant the wine.

"I drove her," Jasper said, fiddling with a button on his cuff. "It was nothing."

Accepting this statement with a skeptical lift of the brow, Jenkins joined Mrs. Lawson in hustling Sophy to the drawing room. They hadn't made it past the first bust of marble when they were stopped by a noise from the stair.

"Sophy!"

Jasper turned and froze at the sight of his mother rushing downstairs. Without thinking, Jasper moved to catch her. He was used to her colorless complexion, but didn't think he'd ever seen her as waxen as this. If she didn't break her neck tumbling to the checked marble floor, he might need to keep her fingers from Sophy's throat. She looked terrifying.

"I know it's too soon—the scandal—" Sophy stammered behind him. "But I missed you and—"

"My dear girl," Lady Fairchild said. Tears sprang from her

eyes as she swept past Jasper with the force of a summer squall. "Why didn't you send for me? I'd have come. A single word and I'll come." Her hands wafted over Sophy's cheeks like they were delicate sugar spun frost. "You ludicrous child," Lady Fairchild said, crushing and kissing her. Jasper wanted to look away, but he couldn't move.

"Well!" his mother said, disengaging at last. "I presume someone sent for your father?"

"I believe he's outside," Jenkins put in.

"Yes, and if you aren't thrilled to pieces by this new horse of his, Sophy, I think you'll break his heart all over again."

Jasper snorted, but no one paid him any mind. Lady Fairchild went on as if nothing happened. "Mrs. Lawson? We will have tea. Sophy, I expect we have only a short time before your father comes in and I want all your news first. Then you may speak with him of horses or whatever you please."

With an arm around Sophy's shoulder, she shepherded her into the drawing room. Jasper lingered in the hall, tracing his finger over the surface of the console table, polished so smooth it shone like still water. He didn't trust himself to speak. He should be happy. Dammit, he was.

"Will you join them, sir?" Jenkins asked, deferential at his elbow.

"No." Jasper produced a smile but more was beyond him. "I'll leave them be. If they ask I'm walking down to the lake." He wanted to curse. Or to weep.

———

SOPHY WAS TOO BEWILDERED to speak. She didn't think she would have managed the walking without Lady Fairchild directing her.

"Tell me, are you well?" Lady Fairchild asked, settling her on a sofa.

"I am. The doctor said all is progressing just as it should." Still amazed by the force and fervor of her stepmother's greeting, Sophy glanced at the space beside her. Lady Fairchild filled it instantly, keeping hold of Sophy's hand.

After the rupture, after months of silence when she used to ride out to look at Cordell from a distance, after careful and guarded letters this was sweet-scented balm—or else she was dreaming. Sophy sniffed, knowing she was lost if she gave into tears. Beside her Lady Fairchild blotted her own eyes.

"It's too late to lend you my handkerchief," Lady Fairchild muttered. "Shall I send for another?"

"No need." Sophy swiped at her eyes so her cuffs could catch the moisture. "It's so good to see you."

"Thank you for coming," Lady Fairchild said, resolutely folding away her handkerchief. "We've longed to see you. I think your father's worn a path through the fields between here and Chippenstone. He—I—we are both so sorry."

"We can put it behind us, surely," Sophy said. "Perhaps we already have." It surprised her the way Lady Fairchild spoke, linking herself to her husband. The best Sophy had ever seen between them was an armed truce and those tended not to last. Much could change in a year, but it would surprise her if her father's marriage ever changed that much. You got so accustomed to some things they became certainties. It was a question for another time. She'd come for other reasons. "I wanted to ask you something."

Lady Fairchild waited, expectant.

"I don't mean to be morbid," Sophy began, twisting in her seat a little. It wasn't easy to say. "And I have every expectation of..." Long life and health? That sounded like the yeomanry toasting her father in the local tavern. "I have no reason for alarm. But since I'm soon to be a—a mother I must think of every eventuality and it is possible I might be taken prematurely from my child."

The struggle to speak of it left her short of breath. Even now the loss of her own mother colored her thoughts, warning her to be cautious and prepared.

"You must miss her. Now, especially." Lady Fairchild took a breath. When she spoke the words tottered feebly, a newborn foal's first stumbling attempt to stand. "She was such a pretty thing with the most engaging smile. Like yours, you know. I'm sorry she isn't here for you."

Sophy's eyes filled with water, shutting out velvets and damasks, the paintings on the walls. Her hand winched tight around Lady Fairchild's fingers. "Will you come? I want you with me," she said, knowing she sounded desolate and small, but unable to put it any other way.

"Of course. If you knew how—it's been such pain, keeping away."

Sophy breathed again, steeling herself for the last, the highest hurdle. "Will you be my baby's godmother? If something were to happen to me, I know—I know you'd do your best for her."

"Are you certain?"

She'd thought of asking Henrietta, but ever since Lady Fairchild's first haughty and impulsive letter Sophy knew who she wanted it to be. Lady Fairchild was exacting, difficult, and seldom gave way, but she discharged all her duties with honor. She loved even when it warred against her instincts. She would do her best for this baby, just as she had for Sophy.

Sophy answered with a sharp nod, unable to speak. Lady Fairchild, too, failed to find words. It happened so quick, Sophy wasn't entirely sure about the swift kiss Lady Fairchild pressed onto her fingers. By the time she caught her eye, their joined hands were back in her lap.

"Her?" Lady Fairchild asked. "Isn't Mr. Bagshot to have a son? Well, I suppose I can be trusted to provide a silver rattle in either case."

SELLING SUFFOLK

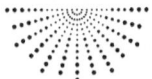

*J*ack must have observed how little she ate at breakfast. After Tom's wife and Mr. Rushford departed, he begged off the proposed morning ride. "If you've no objection, Tom, I'd like to take Laura for a walk down to the village. She could use some fresh air." To her, he added, "Bad night? You look tired."

"He's a terrible flatterer," Laura said, with a glance at Mr. Bagshot.

"Travel is fatiguing. Rough roads, strange beds. Admit you are human. Give yourself time to settle in," Bagshot said. "A walk sounds a fine idea. May I join you?"

The three of them set out moments later. Tom Bagshot, to give him credit, was very kind and plainly intent on keeping both Jack and her in Suffolk. "It's a nice corner of the world," he said, slowing down so they might take in the view. Admiring the green expanse before her, broken by a tall, white windmill, Laura wasn't quick enough. Jack spoke first. "Only a fool wouldn't be content here. You're a fortunate man, Tom."

They passed a cottage skirted by neat rows of cabbages and

onions. A man toiled over them, pulling out weeds with a long handled hoe. "Hallo Phipps!" Tom called. The man straightened.

"Mr. Bagshot, sir. Good day to you." Phipps smiled as he approached, brushing his sleeve over a sun-browned face. They exchanged a few words and Tom presented him to her and Jack. "I'm persuading Dr. Edwards to take over for Dr. Jamieson. We'll need a new doctor in these parts."

Phipps nodded and said he hoped they would stay. "And how's Miss Sophy—er, Mrs. Bagshot, I mean."

"Edwards?" Tom asked, turning to Jack.

"Well indeed. I don't think it will be long," Jack said.

Tom promised to bring Phipps' best wishes to Sophy and they set out again.

"Good people around here," Jack said.

"They are," Tom agreed. "Took me a while to realize it. We were outsiders, you see, until I married Sophy. But she's very well liked among the farmers and the villagers, and they've been kind enough to extend their goodwill to me. I didn't use to spend much time here." He grinned. "You and Miss Edwards won't have any trouble. They'll take to you right away. There's no little anxiety amongst them about Jamieson retiring. I want you here, but it was Sophy's idea to persuade you to stay. Come on, I'll introduce you to a few more."

After the next house, and a long discussion concerning the householder's dogs, Laura was beginning to feel superfluous. Jack, she could see, was already feeling at home here. She'd fit in too if she remained the self-effacing sister. That kind of person could disappear anywhere. But suppose she didn't want to?

"You see how nice it is? The place is ideal," Jack whispered when Tom disappeared into someone's garden to collect a rose clipping for Sophy. "Beautiful and you'll have friends close by. I can support you quite easily here and you won't have any troubles with Saltash. I know—" He forestalled her objection with upraised hands. "I know you said he isn't a problem. But he will be, Laura. I saw him watching you in the green room. As a doctor I felt inclined to warn him of the dangers of apoplexy."

"The world would be better off without him," Laura muttered.

"My thoughts exactly," Jack said. "So I kept the advice to myself. But there's no need for you to bait him. Not anymore. He's nothing to either of us."

"Shall we push on?" Tom reappeared with a potted clipping in his hands.

"Why don't you go on with Jack," Laura said. "I'm wearing new boots and my left foot doesn't like them. I think I should get back to the house before I break out in blisters. I can bring Sophy her rose."

"You know the way?" Jack asked.

"I have eyes," Laura said. "It's not difficult." In such flat country it would be a challenge to lose your way.

They agreed and Laura set off happy to be alone but also feeling guilty about it. Jack liked it here and she hadn't told him the truth about Saltash. Perhaps it would be best to accept Tom's offer. Jack would certainly think so, especially if he knew the whole of it, but she'd never let Saltash intimidate her before. She wasn't about to start now.

Despite what she'd said to Jack and Tom she wasn't in a hurry to get back to the house. Sophy and Mr. Rushford might have returned and it was best to avoid him as much as possible.

"This is the way to Mr. Bagshot's house?" she asked a young boy playing by the crossing, just to confirm.

"Yes, miss. And yonder's the way to Cordell."

She had time on her hands so she took the second way.

· · ·

HER LUCK WAS OUT—SHE hadn't gone far when she spotted Mr. Rushford beating his way through the field on one side of the road with savage swings of his walking stick. Rooted to the spot Laura could see no place to hide. The nearby hedges weren't tall enough to conceal her even if she was willing to risk a swipe of his stick. As she turned to dart away the movement caught his attention.

"Miss Edwards!" he said, surprised.

"What are you doing here?" she asked, provoked into rudeness.

"Avoiding my mother. She lives there." He pointed backward with his stick through fields and gardens to a faraway house. Even at this distance it was imposing.

"What about your sister?" Laura asked. He was supposed to be with her.

"She's inside. Weeping, no doubt, all over the Mater. It's just what she wanted. Suppose I should be happy for her." But he didn't lighten his scowl.

"I didn't realize this was the way to your house," Laura said.

He stepped forward, stopping her retreat. "How would you? No one said. Please don't run off. I'll lose the bad temper. I'm nearly always put out, you know, after conversations with my mother." He forced a smile.

Laura's throat went tight. "I'd give the world for five minutes' speech with mine."

"I'm sorry," he said, his voice softer. "She's dead?"

"Last winter," Laura said. She'd promised Jack Maman would live until spring, when he'd at least have a chance of coming home. It was stretching the truth, but they'd both wanted to believe it.

"You miss her," he said.

Laura didn't answer. He sighed. "I do seem to step wrong

whenever we come across each other. I doubt you'll believe me, but I'm not usually such a clod. If I promise to mend my ways may I bear you company?"

He looked repentant, if you ignored the glint in his eye, a token of malice or mischief. Laura didn't care for either. Best to avoid him. "I prefer to be alone."

"It's nearly afternoon. Rest your feet a little. Won't you come into the garden?" He gestured to the grounds behind him. "I should like my flowers to see you."

She sniffed in spite of herself. "Sheridan again? Haven't you any words of your own?"

"He puts it better," Rushford said. "Come walk with me."

Laura didn't move. "It's roses, you know, not flowers. And I'm supposed to carry this one home for your sister. You should go back to her. And speak to your mother," Laura added.

He made a face. "Must I?"

Laura nodded.

"My valor is certainly going," he began, quoting again. "It is sneaking off! I feel it oozing out as it were—" he paused, searching for the next words, so she helped him finish.

"Out the palms of your hands? Yes, I know that one too. You must be quite an admirer of Mr. Sheridan."

He glanced at her sideways. "And Mr. Goldsmith too. You?"

"I don't read plays," Laura lied. "But if I did I wouldn't trouble with those silly ones."

"Never? Are you sure?"

"Didn't you say you were going?"

He sighed. "Too cowardly. I can't help myself."

"Nor can I, I'm afraid. Good day, Mr. Rushford."

She stalked away before he could get a better look inside her bonnet.

"I'll see you at dinner," he called after her.

Not tonight, Laura told herself as she stepped over a rut in the road. She was inventing a headache.

———

SOPHY'S FATHER, William Rushford, Lord Fairchild, hastened across the grass. Any faster and he'd break into a run. His breath was quick, his heart bursting against the confines of his chest. All thoughts of his promising new yearling, the owls taking up residence in the old dovecote, the tall corn ripening in the south pasture were gone. Jogging around the corner of the house he barely noticed his son Jasper exiting the rose arbor and heading for the lake. William checked but didn't take the chase. Sophy was here; if his son wished to be present, he'd have stayed indoors. The cordial skirmish that would inevitably break out between them could wait. William rushed through the house but stopped outside the drawing room door to wipe away the nervous sweat seeping from his palms. He'd imagined this so many times it scarcely felt real.

"What have we here?" He pushed open the door. The instant before they looked up Sophy's bright head bent close to his wife's blonde one produced a disorienting wave of déjà vu. William wasn't sure if he'd walked into his drawing room or a memory. He crossed the room too startled to perform the formalities.

"You've grown," he said after a good look at his daughter. He'd seen her from a distance back in the spring, when he used to trail behind her horse out of sight. Pregnancy put an end to her exercise and she'd kept to her own gardens after that. He hadn't seen her up close or heard her speak in more than a year.

"A trifle," she said, glancing down at her swollen belly.

"It suits you," he said. "You look well." Her face, though a little fuller than he remembered, suffused with her familiar lightening blush. Her shoulders still looked too small and finely spun to keep her together. "Come, give me a kiss," he said, holding out his hands and presenting his cheek.

She complied, dutifully, still a little wide-eyed for his liking, wary as a child with a wolf-hound.

"How is your husband?" William asked. Bagshot wasn't here, but William assumed he must have consented to this visit. "He won't object if I should call on him?"

"I suppose that depends on what you have to say," Sophy said, her chin high as a flag pinned to a mast.

"My apologies, to start." William wished they were familiar enough for him to laugh regretfully and chuck his daughter under the chin. "I imagine those are a necessary foundation to any friendship between him and I. And I hope there will be. I've missed you too much."

It was *all* too much. His wife's eyelashes already clung in spiky points and a trembling heartbeat pulsed beneath the soft web of skin strung across his daughter's collarbones. They weren't accustomed to each other's unveiled emotions and their moment together had probably exhausted them. Georgiana, his wife, was drawn from worry and lack of sleep, and though it had been many years, he recalled something of the emotional storms that broke on expectant mothers. He must be tender with these two loves; he must not push them.

Inserting himself at Georgiana's side, though it meant they had to share a single cushion, he turned the subject, asking Sophy if the baby was likely to be as long-shanked as his father. Bagshot in his stocking feet was taller than anyone ought to be. He told her about his horses and only smiled, instead of breaking into a grin, when he learned she'd kept herself apprised of their progress in the racing newspapers.

"Have you bred Hirondelle?" he asked, because it seemed gentler to leave her be and inquire after her horse.

Sophy grimaced. "I'm not sure if I can inflict this state on any creature I care about."

"Horses make a great deal less fuss," William argued.

"Maybe, but this feels ghastly."

Georgiana jogged his elbow. William left it at that and asked Sophy about her garden instead. He could tease his wife about prudery later.

9

MALCONTENTS

*J*asper wasn't going to speak to his mother. His temper had cooled—mysterious Miss Edwards was an excellent diversion—but saying what he wanted to say to Lady Fairchild would ruin the day for Sophy. So he rambled about the gardens, checked his watch, and wished he'd asked Sophy how long she wanted to stay. Thinking about her didn't help, nor did the knowledge that she had more right to grudges than he. Before his scowl could set in again he quickened his pace.

The lake looked pleasing in the sunshine. Beyond that, past the welcome shadows of the woods in the tiny churchyard, the flowers he'd sown back in the spring were blooming. Jasper bent to twist off a few withered blossoms and scrape off a bit of moss creeping over the name on the headstone. Julius Francis Rushford, Beloved Son, it read above a pitiful span of years. His little brother.

The small mound was well-tended and the sight of the flowers growing over it soothed him as it always did. Fortified, he returned to the house and collected his sister, reminding her she'd promised to return home in good time. He was more polite than usual to his mother, blandly civil to his father, and didn't interrupt Sophy's contented silence on the drive home.

He brought her inside and left her in her husband's arms. Escaping Sophy's warbling treble—more squeak than speak— and the uncomfortable sight of her shedding tears all over Tom's waistcoat, he sought sanctuary again, feeling increasingly restless. He was glad Sophy was happy and yet...

A quarter of an hour pacing the terrace only made him more fractious, so Jasper gave up prowling and went inside. Tom's library was generally an interesting place. Most of the unread classics had been boxed away, making room for Tom's oddities on the shelves: weirdly-shaped rocks, fringed leather shoes brought back from the Americas, a bit of iron machinery, and a tarnished silver cup commemorating a boxing match. Stacks of half-finished newspapers littered the tables and a pile of correspondence was sorted in a wire organizer on the desk. Made Jasper tired just looking at it, but Tom enjoyed the workings of his business, inexplicable as it seemed. Jasper pulled down a book or two and inspected the lettering on the silver cup, but couldn't settle.

He strolled down the gallery, trying to interest himself in the pictures; he sought out Mrs. Bagshot, but learned she was again resting in her room. That worried him, her tiring so frequently. He wrote a letter to Henrietta, then tore it up because every word of it was odious and sat with his chin in his hand, staring out the window, almost sighing with relief when his attention was summoned by the click of the latch.

"Forgive me. I didn't mean to intrude on your privacy." Miss Edwards was already half out the door, a black boot heel and a swish of green muslin skirt.

Excellent. He hadn't expected this pleasure until dinner. He had a whole store of quotes to throw at her and see if she blushed. "You aren't intruding. Interruption was never so welcome. I've been brooding and that's not healthy." Jasper rose and started after her. "Allow me to walk you to—where is it you're going?"

"I'm...there's really no need."

Maybe not for her, but he had questions. She wasn't getting away this time. "Were you looking for a book? A pen? Writing paper?" he asked.

She shook her head.

"Would you care for a walk to the village then, or the church? There are some nice windows and it's the resting place of some painter I probably ought to remember."

"I couldn't impose." The words were politeness itself, but there was no mistaking the rebuff in her face. Fine. He didn't need to play nice. Jasper looked over the severely dressed hair, the roughened hands, the blunt fingernails trimmed right to the quick. She ducked her head, avoiding his gaze, but he could pinpoint each little deception: compressed mouth, lines etched over the cheeks, flattened, thickened brows. She was the right height. Smudges aside, she had almost the right coloring. There was the profile she'd guarded so carefully this afternoon. He could see it plainly now. That, she couldn't change. And she knew her Sheridan.

Jasper leaned back against the doorframe. "This subterfuge is quite unnecessary," he said in the placid voice his family was so wary of. It had been a trying day and he had kept quiet in front of Sophy, destroyed his acid letter to Henrietta. Nastiness couldn't be constrained indefinitely. He knew her secret and she'd given him no reason to be kind with it. "Miss Holyrood, it has been amusing, but let's not pretend we aren't old acquaintances. Your other face is much more charming."

She stiffened at his side, her eyes fixed on the damask-lined walls.

"Does your brother know?" he asked.

"Of course he does! Right from the beginning!" she said, stung into answering.

Jasper relaxed into a slow smile. "Does he approve?"

"That's no concern of yours," she snapped.

"Is Edwards your real name? I'd never have guessed." She was uncomfortable, tensing like she wanted to flee. He realized he didn't want her to. It might be diverting to goad her, but if he didn't pull back the game might end right here. A sad waste, that. He could manage this better and spin it out into something truly entertaining. There were numerous possibilities...besides, already his mood was considerably lighter. "Doesn't matter, I suppose. I'll call you that if you like. But I think this visit will be much more interesting if you soften Miss Edwards' attitudes a little."

Her glance heaped scorn on him. "How much money do you have riding on me?" she asked.

It took some effort, but he absorbed the jolt into a single cough. "I beg your pardon?"

"Your wager. In the betting book at White's. I heard you and your friends laid down quite a sum over me."

Never mind how she knew—there were ways to winkle out the goings-on in that haunt of gamblers and gossips. Perhaps she'd bribed a waiter? No matter. Jasper feared he was blushing. Thinking about it only increased the heat rising to his forehead.

"Well, none of us have had to pay up yet," he temporized.

"Nor like to," she smiled sweetly. "An entertaining band of rattles, certainly, but I'm afraid none of you meet my standards." She'd returned to her green-room manner with a vengeance.

"Pity." He sighed. "I can't say I ever expected to do more than swoon at your feet."

"Don't."

"How about after dinner?"

"Certainly not."

"If you insist." He smirked. "Well, could I get you to promise not to take Protheroe or DeClerc? If I can't win at least I won't lose."

She glanced down the hall but nothing moved. They were alone. "I'd never—" she began in a whisper, breaking off to study him. "Actually your friend Protheroe is rather dashing."

He'd always admired how delicately she used her claws. "He drinks too much," Jasper said. "And I would buy you prettier horses."

"Oh well then. Horses. Why didn't you say?"

Yes. He'd envisioned it all, her driving a dashing phaeton with match greys in the park. Fearing his face might slip into transparency, Jasper told himself he wasn't seriously hoping, just making a good attempt at it, playing along, following her cues.

She warned him off, unwilling to let hope run away with him. "No, darling. I'm afraid not. Are you forgetting Brother Jack?"

"Yes." There was that. How troublesome. Jasper studied her through narrowed eyes and chewed the inside of his lip. "Your mystery lover." It was gratifying, how the blood tainted her cheeks. "You write yourself some fascinating scripts."

"I improvised," she said. "I didn't expect—well, when the papers first got wind of him, it seemed wise to make the best use I could of it. Even if I'd offered the truth no one would believe it. There's nothing exciting about an actress and her brother."

"You certainly caused a flurry of speculation. Just think—I could lighten despair in so many hearts if I told the truth," Jasper said.

She tapped her lip with a cruelly abbreviated fingernail. "You won't," she said confidently. "You like secrets too much."

True. They were one of his favorite indulgences. He wouldn't give this one away, not if it could buy him something better. No need to play that card now, however. The game was just beginning. Better to wait. "Your retinue was devastated to hear you'd decamped from London."

"Were you? I thought the story was that I was ill."

"Yes, in the country recuperating. If they could see you now they'd—"

"Yes," she interrupted him. "I'm not quite in my best looks."

"Not at all I'm afraid. I think you should change."

The brows flew up, approximating their usual curve. "Why should I do that, pray?"

"Because," Jasper explained patiently, "I'm going to walk you to see the windows in the church. Dull stuff I know, but it's what one does in the country. I'd hate for my magnificence to put you to shame." He made a show of flicking invisible lint from his sleeve. "Besides I'm tired of looking at you with that stuff on your face."

Surprise, chagrin, irritation: they flew across her face like swallows in the sky.

"My sister won't like it if her guests are neglected," Jasper said to forestall her acid retort before more than the fumes could reach him. "And I've had as much of my family today as I can stand." It was the truth, slipping out without the usual varnish. "Please? I'll even make up some history about the windows."

She laughed. "Very well. But I'm carrying an umbrella."

To hit him with presumably. The weather was still fine, a proverbial summer's day without any cloud.

"Bring an umbrella. Bring a poker if you wish," Jasper said expansively. "Much better for denting my skull. But come?"

She nodded and promised to meet him downstairs.

Not bad, Jasper thought. And he wasn't done yet. He might be able to stretch this out for weeks.

10

GAMBLING

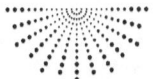

*I*t was folly to be pleased about discarding her disguise, but Laura couldn't suppress the satisfaction she felt as she sponged the worry lines from her face, restyled her hair and changed her gown. She was in an awkward predicament—but it was exciting.

It was far more pleasant to spar with Mr. Rushford now all was in the open, rather than skulking about with a sour face. She'd always considered his admiration of Gemma Holyrood a compliment, even if he'd only joined her train because it was the fashionable thing to do. There was a fussiness about him she'd never detected in his friends; it was no mean thing to be singled out by a man of such particular tastes though he played court to her in a casual manner. She'd thought him much like the others and underrated him—a mistake. He should be treated cautiously, but she couldn't seem to force herself to it.

You're pleased he knows. That you can be something of yourself again.

Laura fixed her mother's milky pearl drops onto her ears with a smile. She wasn't a green girl to be bullied about or seduced by smooth words and a handsome face. He was playing some game with her, but she was quick and knew her own rules. If she'd outplayed her uncle for this long she could manage Mr. Rushford.

What comes, comes.

She was good at improvising.

ONCE LAURA WAS SATISFIED with her appearance she returned downstairs. Mr. Rushford took her arm and brought her outside as carefully as if she were a piece of blown glass— and dull-witted besides. Freeing her arm, Laura explained she had eyes and could see (and step!) around uneven ground and gluey puddles without help. He was scrupulously polite, inquiring about her brother and her opinion of the countryside. It was unexpected—and wildly irritating.

"Have you always been devoted to the theatre?" she asked, trying to startle him back into the sly creature from before.

He smirked. "Heavens, no. Only since I found a talent that caught my attention."

She accepted the tribute with a nod. They talked of plays then, and if he was too free with his quotes from the stage, at least it showed he paid attention. He had opinions about every-thing: the staging, the props, the kisses her fellow actors pressed upon her.

"Do you like them?" he asked.

"What a question!" She turned away to cover her blush.

"Forgive me. I'm forgetting where we are. That's not a proper question for a young lady on an innocent country walk."

Someone needed to stick a pin in his acrobatic eyebrows. The way he used them was not innocent at all.

"What is that flower?" She pointed with her parasol—it was prettier, though less useful as a weapon than her umbrella.

"Do I look like Watt's Botanical?" he asked.

"No. Is that a book?"

"Yes, with two hundred color plates in it. The flower, if you must know, is meadow saffron."

"Oh." The blooms were purple, not golden, but before she could puzzle over it he spoke.

"Shall I be gallant, pluck you an armful, and swear that you put them to shame?"

"No," she said, suddenly wary. The exquisite politeness and theatre talk had relaxed her guard. She wasn't ready for—or wanting—romantic importuning.

"Good. They don't keep. They'll be wilted by the time we get to the church. I'd rather let them live."

He was teasing her, leading her on and then spinning her assumptions back at her—a good ploy and one she typically used without even thinking. Laura smiled. Perhaps she could learn a few things if she let someone else do the conjuring. Of course it wasn't wise, but the game pulled, irresistibly. It reminded her of long ago when she crept up on her unsuspecting brother and startled him with a shout and a clap. Or the trick they'd dared each other to learn, swallowing the flame from a candle. She felt the same light tremor in her pulse every time before stepping on stage; prudence and fear never held her back.

"I agree." She summoned an absent expression and patted his arm. "Leave these beauties be. Interference only destroys them."

"An admirable philosophy," Mr. Rushford said, leading her through the trees. Ahead, a stone wall appeared between the stout trunks supporting a tangle of brambles. "Do you extend it to other creatures?"

Was he talking about her again? Laura frowned into the rustling canopy of branches, sunlight veining the quivering leaves. Her ears opened to a hundred busy sounds. "Your birds here couldn't live in a desert. They ought to stay where they can thrive."

"My sister has a very pretty canary."

"Yes, and it lives in a cage and eats from her fingers," Laura said. She'd seen the bird chirping in the morning room.

"No hawk will kill its song."

"Pretty creatures tend to do well for themselves." Laura smiled. "Look at you." If one of them was a canary it was surely he. She was a jackdaw, a bold scavenger and not ashamed of any of it.

Mr. Rushford bowed. "A double compliment." He unlatched the iron gate in the wall, wincing as the hinges shrieked. "Efficient, this method of summoning the curate," he murmured. They had not ventured far into the churchyard, their feet skimming through the long grass, before the man appeared, stooped and garbed in the black of his calling. He bowed low to her and Mr. Rushford and returned his attention to her for a second scrutiny when informed she might settle in the neighborhood.

"Mr. Rushford will convince you of our district's charms," he said, still wheezing slightly from his swift walk to join them.

"The decision rests with my brother," Laura explained. Rushford again used that skeptical twitch of his brow. She ignored him and looked across the weathered gravestones to the uncompromising bulk of the church walls, the admonitory finger of the spire. It was exactly what a village church should be. "But I'm pleased with everything I see." Jack would settle them here and she would meet with the village women and dress the church with flowers. He'd encourage her to busy herself with the parish school while he snuffed out friendships with the local gentlemen and turned up marriage prospects for her like truffles.

"My people are Catholic," Laura said, fighting reflexively.

"Then you will belong to St. Jude's. It's a little farther, but not too out of the way," the curate said, not unduly perturbed by this news. She'd sunk in his estimation, but not irredeemably.

"Scots?" Mr. Rushford hazarded behind her.

"French." It came out crisply. There were all sorts of people in England with lingering French trappings—Huguenots, for example—who'd been around a long time. Then there were émigrés like herself, increasingly unpopular, stained by war and recent troubles. Neither gentleman asked what kind of French she was. Just as well.

"May I see inside?" Laura asked. "Mr. Rushford promised me some fascinating history."

"Did he?" The curate looked alarmed and glanced wide-eyed at Mr. Rushford.

"I was thinking of the troubles," Rushford said without blinking. "And the story about the monks' treasure."

"I don't think—" the bewildered curate protested.

"Leave it to me," Mr. Rushford said with a smile, sweeping her through the arched door. It was cool as a cave inside but illuminated with grand, kaleidoscope windows. The history he gave of ravages and relics lost and rediscovered was fabrication from the first word to the last, but as good a tale as any dramatist could conceive. Long before they quit the church, thanked the curate, and returned to the house, Laura recognized him. He too was a performer, perhaps as skilled a one as she.

11
HAZARDS

*S*ophy watched Tom—dear Tom—pace across the drawing room.

"What am I supposed to say to them?" he asked.

Not what he wanted to, she was certain of that. Tom hadn't forgiven Lord and Lady Fairchild. Yet.

"You could talk about your education," Sophy suggested. He'd hated his years at school and ended career there by tying up his chief tormentor, cutting off his hair, and running away. But it was a respectable institution and her father would appreciate learning he'd gone there. They needn't disclose the entire story.

"Should I mention I'm the one that gave Lord Harvey that kink in his nose?"

Sophy tilted her head, inquiring, but he didn't offer more. "I'm sure he deserved it."

"Yes. He fancied himself kissing my girl." Tom threw himself onto the sofa before she could finish her aggrieved gasp. He wrapped an arm around her shoulders, crossed his ankles, and thumped up the cushions. "She wasn't really my girl, Soph. A friend. Had her eye on a farmer."

"Good," Sophy finished darkly.

"But you see the point? You are my girl, my very own. I'm to overlook what he's done to you?"

Sophy twisted, trying to ease the pain in her hips. These days she thought she was in danger of coming apart. "He didn't stop our marriage."

"He would have if you hadn't been such a fool and come chasing after me." Tom intercepted her look and broke into a smile. "I'm glad you did, Sophy." His arm tightened around her. "I'm glad you did."

She waited as he traced a finger over the back of her hand. It wouldn't be easy but after her visit to Cordell yesterday she was sure their call today would go well. Almost sure.

"I know it hurt you. And I know it was hard to lose them because of me," Tom said.

"Choosing you wasn't hard. I've never regretted it."

"But you've missed them."

She wove her fingers into the spaces between his, tracing the callouses and the white scars. He still liked sparring with his fists, but only for sport—unless he and Jasper ever did lose it on each other. Tom had promised not to damage her brother's face.

"You're the only one I don't want to live without," she said.

"But you'd like to have them, too."

He knew—she'd told him—that didn't mean she loved him less. "If I can. I think it's possible. She wept on me, Tom."

"I know. And apologized."

Sophy'd never expected that. She wasn't entirely sure the Lord and Lady Fairchild she'd met yesterday weren't changelings or products of her hopeful imagination. Maybe they'd both got a hard knock on the head, most likely from butting against each other; if so, she wasn't going to complain about it. "Maybe you can talk about the baby," she suggested.

"Think it's safe?" he asked. "Lady Fairchild's letters fret

almost as much as I do." He muttered something more under his breath.

"Hmm?" Sophy asked.

"I said she's worse than the mate who crewed the Leander. Sure, she'd like us all jumping to the tune of her whistle. I won't do it, Soph." He didn't say it aloud, but she knew he didn't want to see her doing it either. She sighed. First Jasper, now Tom. She supposed there was a difference between forgiveness and appeasement, but she just wanted to be on good terms again. You could try, but you couldn't truly leave your family. Their quirks came with you in blood and brain, speech and skin.

She heard footsteps in the corridor. "Is it them?" she asked, trying to arrange herself more conventionally in her seat, but Tom kept his arm in its place around her shoulders.

"Not like this," Sophy hissed. "It's indecorous!" To welcome them curled up in Tom's lap on the sofa...

He glanced down at her belly. "I'm reasonably sure they understand how you got this way."

Choking down a laugh, she tried again to move away, but soon gave up. If he needed a firm hold on her to keep him in the room, so be it.

Lady Fairchild halted for a moment in the doorway, but didn't say anything, perhaps reading the truth in Tom's jutted chin and Sophy's conciliatory smile.

"How are you feeling today?" she asked as she stripped off her gloves.

Sophy replied that she was doing well, while Tom and her father sized each other up like wary cats.

"Bagshot. Thank you for receiving me," Lord Fairchild said.

"Sophy insisted."

At least Tom accompanied the words with a smile.

Lady Fairchild crossed the floor, picked up Sophy's outstretched hands and kissed her cheek.

"Forgive me for not getting up," Sophy said, motioning Lady Fairchild to the nearest seat. She sank into it without compromising her exquisite posture. Lord Fairchild positioned himself behind her, a hand on her shoulder. Lady Fairchild didn't flinch, but the sight of them touching still unnerved Sophy.

"I've been meaning—we've been meaning," Lord Fairchild corrected at a glance from his wife, "to express our apologies. Bagshot, I should have heard you out." He coughed. "You seem a good husband to Sophy."

Something quivered over Tom's skin. Sophy increased the pressure of her hand.

"You'd have trusted me more if you liked my lineage I suppose," he said evenly.

"Perhaps. But I'm learning. I had little opportunity to discern your qualities before the wedding."

"You could have if you'd wanted the chance."

"Yes, well, it was a mistake to dismiss you out of hand. Especially after I learned you were her choice." He looked hard at Sophy. "I'm pleased she made it."

Tom hesitated, then gave in. "As it happens so am I." He smiled, a real one this time. "Come on. You might as well sit down. Sophy? Shall I ring for tea?

"Yes," she said, glad for the excuse to busy themselves over cups and spoons and sugar. It would help except that she must have sweat through her gown by now. It was impossible to pour without moving your arms.

"I could use something stronger myself." Tom rose and crossed to the sideboard. "And you, sir?"

Lord Fairchild paused before reaching the chair, giving Tom a slight bow. "A brandy would be most welcome."

They both tossed them back rather quickly—a small thing, but something Sophy hoped might bring them closer to mutual understanding. They understood each other's discomfort at least.

THE VISIT WASN'T a resounding success, but it was a step forward Sophy decided, helping herself to another slice of pineapple for dessert that evening. Tom's father had built the succession houses and planted the fruits. She'd grown appallingly fond of them. Down the table Tom laughed with his mother, his tension gone. His fork spun in the air, stabbing again into his slice of cake. It must be good because even Miss Edwards ate with relish.

She seemed comfortable now and it did wonders for her. Sophy couldn't believe how pretty Miss Edwards was, now she'd relaxed. Faces always did look better with smiles on them and Miss Edwards wore plenty this evening. Jasper was telling her about the London theatre—she said she'd never been and he did have a way of bringing it to life with his critiques. Yes, Miss Edwards, listening with bright eyes, was in much better spirits, but the doctor...

"You don't care for it?" Sophy asked, with a glance at Dr. Edwards' untouched cake.

"A little too rich," he said.

"I often think so. Maybe some fruit?" Sophy suggested and earned a wan smile in response. "I'm pleased your sister is happy with us. It isn't easy being thrust into a houseful of strangers. I'm afraid I haven't seen much of her myself yet, but—"

"She seems on excellent terms with your brother," Dr. Edwards put in.

"Ye-ess," Sophy said. There was no way to pretend Dr. Edwards was at all pleased with this. She leaned closer and lowered her voice. "He's a rattle I know, but perfectly harmless. And she seems much happier than before, now he's put her at ease."

"I'll be sure to thank him for taking an interest."

Sophy glanced down the table. All was sparkling, not just the silver. She caught her brother's eye as Miss Edwards let out an effortless laugh, beautiful as an aria from a singer. Sophy bit her lip, then let it go before her frown was seen. Next to Tom she trusted Jasper best, but even when you knew the way to his heart he could be devious. She couldn't discern if there was more in his face than warmth from the candles. Perhaps the situation bore watching.

SOPHY FOUND she had little time for it though, with Dr. Edwards always measuring her ankles and feeling her pulse. She and Tom's mother had to finish fitting up things for the baby—she was supposed to direct things from her chair, but it was faster changing the nursery curtains herself than waiting for the footman.

Unfortunately this explanation failed to satisfy Dr. Edwards or Tom. They ordered her to rest and Tom enforced the command by supervising from the bedside chair. More tedious still was the fact she was expected to lie down each subsequent afternoon.

Her father and Lady Fairchild visited again and though Sophy wasn't used to calling Lady Fairchild Georgiana in her thoughts, she managed it most of the time when speaking. She couldn't see any warmth developing between her father and stepmother and Tom, but for her sake they were getting used to sitting in the same room. Sophy told herself to be patient. More would come with time.

"How does Miss Edwards pass her days?" Sophy asked Tom, recalling her resolution one afternoon. Really, to be expected to sleep on a day like today. It was too hot to be confined indoors, even with Tom waving a fan at her.

"Drives out with Jasper I think." Tom lowered the fan to turn a page of his book.

Sophy considered that. "Oh, don't bother." She snatched the fan and snapped it shut. "Doesn't do any good. Can't we walk outside?"

"In an hour," Tom said, unrelenting.

"Do they drive every day?" she asked.

"Most of 'em. But it's not your concern," Tom warned. "Let him take care of himself."

"I was thinking of Miss Edwards," Sophy said, indignant.

"She can handle him. And if not, there's Jack."

That was what worried her.

"You're very friendly with Miss Edwards," Sophy said, finally cornering Jasper on the walk back from the stables.

He stopped whistling. "Why not? Capital girl!"

"What if she falls in love with you?"

Jasper hooted, laughing so hard he had to brace his hands on his knees. Recovering, he poked her in the cheek. "If I could do that! Just think of all the fellows who'd call me out. If I didn't end up with bullets in my liver and spleen, I'd fill my whole appointment book with duels before I got done." He wiped a watering eye.

"Jasper." Sophy planted her hands where her hips used to be.

"Stop scowling. What a goose you are! I promise, there's no need to worry about Miss Edwards and me, but it is adorable of you to come give me a lecture."

He kissed her and was gone. Restricted to a waddle, Sophy knew there was no catching him. Maybe he was immune to Miss Edwards, but there had been all those widows: dashing Mrs. Forsythe, Lady Foote-Harding, and more recently that predatory Dowager Countess. Jasper might be entangled with her still, which would make Miss Edwards safe, though it was hardly fair. Jasper shouldn't flirt with her like this.

Next morning Sophy made a point of sitting down with Miss Edwards. "I've been so remiss in my attentions to you," Sophy said, pouring out tea.

"Not at all. You mustn't trouble about me," Miss Edwards said. "Heavens, I didn't come here to impose. Just to keep my brother company, and it's very good of you to have me. You're busy with your parents and your soon-to-be-born baby. I'm afraid I'm not much good with them myself. Well, I've never really had the chance to try."

"I haven't either," Sophy said. And though they drank two pots of tea and somehow laid waste to a plate of lemon biscuits, they talked only of Sophy's unborn child, imputing all sorts of characteristics to the creature punching acrobatically in her belly. Each time she remembered, Sophy tried to turn the conversation to Jasper, but by the time Tom summoned her for her afternoon nap, she hadn't succeeded. Miss Edwards was either blithely unaware or very, very clever.

"Should we worry about this?" Sophy asked two mornings later as she and Tom waved off Jasper and Miss Edwards, embarking on another jaunt to the town. Jasper always found some reason to absent himself before Lord and Lady Fairchild arrived. Sophy never warned him they were coming, so he must have a real sense for it.

"No," Tom said. "And I don't think we should tomorrow either."

Sophy frowned. She supposed he was right. Miss Edwards

was a convenient excuse for Jasper to avoid their parents. Of course, she was also pretty and pleasant company now she'd let him draw her out. But why on earth would Jasper think so many gentlemen were willing to fight over her?

12

CARE-FOR-NOTHINGS

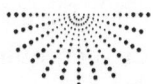

*I*t was a mere ten miles or so to Bury St Edmonds and Jasper was used to covering the distance in well under an hour. Though it was thrilling to drive at speed round corners and make Miss Edwards clutch his arm and squeal, he was in no hurry today. No point in returning before he could be certain his parents were gone. Yesterday he'd come back too early and had to kick his heels in the stables for an hour.

"To avoid your parents is childish," Miss Edwards told him. She'd picked up on the pattern of their outings.

"I love unsolicited advice. Have you anymore?" Jasper asked.

"I think we're less likely to overturn at this pace. Normally you drive like the devil's at your heels."

"She is—you know her as Lady Fairchild."

"Is that why you're taking your time today?" Miss Edwards asked, shaking a curl out of her face.

"Maybe I'm savoring the company," he said.

"You should. I won't be around for long," she said.

"Nonsense. Haven't I helped you choose wallpapers for your new house?"

"You've made plenty of suggestions, certainly. No. Jack will settle here, but my home is in London."

"Then I'll see you there."

"You might. But you won't have me all to yourself," she warned with a smile.

"Well, that's a crying shame. We get along so famously." He said it in jest, but it was true. They never had trouble finding things to laugh about and traded quips all the way into town past St. Andrew's Street.

She sighed, her eyes fixed on the famous Abbey Tower. "What tales will you invent for me today?"

"None if we get saddled with the caretaker again," Jasper said, making a face. Two days ago they'd gone through St. Mary's with the old man. "That was worse than being at school."

"I found it very enlightening," Miss Edwards said.

"Yes, well, I don't expect anyone tried to beat your history into you."

"Are you trying to make me pity you? I assure you I'm quite incapable of it."

She might be at that, depending when her people had come from France. "How long have you lived in London?" he asked.

She started at his abrupt question, a transgression of their unspoken rules—serious probing wasn't allowed, only silly impertinences. "Since I was quite small," she said, evading nicely.

That didn't tell him much.

"We came from France."

Ah. She smiled still, but he must be careful. He didn't know her exact age, but it didn't take an arithmetic champion to know she'd have been small during the Terror.

"It was a long time ago," she said.

"Your brother was never tempted to return to France?"

Some, he knew, made peace with Napoleon and repaired or even grew their fortunes.

"There's nothing to bring us back," she said.

Jasper licked his lips. He really shouldn't have broached the subject. He turned down a side street, threading the curricle through a jostling throng of carts, pedestrians, and street vendors. The lane, edged by narrow shops with swinging signs and open shutters, wove drunkenly up the hill. Before the Abbey Gardens came in sight, her hand clutched his arm.

He shot one eye at her but kept his attention on the road.

"He's seen us," she sighed. "You'll have to pull up."

Jasper brought his horses to a stop. Before he could ask who she meant, he saw the answer to his question trot toward them on one of Bagshot's chestnut hacks. If ever he'd seen a thundercloud, here was one brooding on the face of Good Brother Jack.

"Will he be pleased to see us do you think?" Jasper asked, hoping vainly.

"Not especially," she whispered. "You'd best be careful."

Seemed she had no qualms about feeding him to the wolves. "Dr. Edwards." Jasper nodded and tipped his hat.

Edwards ignored him. "Laura I thought you were staying home with your new book?"

"I put it away. Couldn't make myself finish. How was your meeting with Dr. Jamieson?"

At breakfast Edwards had mentioned plans to ride into town so Jamieson could introduce him to more patients and show him over the surgery.

"Are your offices down there?" Jasper twisted his neck to peer down the cross street.

"Yes."

"Let's go see them," he suggested. "I'm sure Miss Edwards would love a look."

Edwards' lips shrank together. "There's a patient recovering. I've just cut out an infected toenail."

Jasper's mouth twitched in a rubbery grimace. He could never do such a thing, not for any amount of money.

"Then you're free to come with us to tour the Abbey Gardens," Laura said. "Isn't it good of Mr. Rushford to take me?"

Edwards' grumble said what he thought of that, but he didn't hesitate to join and rode beside them the rest of the way up Angel Hill.

"He really dislikes me," Jasper whispered to her, aggrieved. "And I've been a perfect gentleman."

"I may have mentioned to him your first evening here that you were a frequent guest in my dressing room."

Jasper fought the impulse to draw rein. "Does he know I know?" he asked coolly.

"No, I haven't told him. But you can see he doesn't care much for our friendship."

"You are an impudent thing," Jasper murmured to her under his breath, keeping a wary eye on Jack Edwards. The man rode indifferently, but his hands looked alarmingly capable. *Toenails!* Jasper thought and shuddered. "I prefer a whole skin and your dear brother looks very capable of thwarting my desire."

"Are you afraid?" Miss Edwards asked with a coquettish tilt of the head.

"I don't like making scenes," he said.

"And I thought you an exceeding fine actor," she said.

He'd laugh if he weren't the one caught out in trouble. This would take careful stepping.

They did just that, pittering down the gravel paths of the Abbey Gardens, admiring the church and views of the river

Lark. "And this way you've a fine prospect of the town." Jasper pointed and held back a yawn.

"Lovely," Miss Edwards said. She started down the path, but as Jasper moved to follow her the doctor laid a hand on his arm.

"A word, sir," he said.

Here it comes. Jasper decided not to make too fine a point of it. "You're concerned about my attentions to your sister. Here? Or in London?" he asked.

Dr. Edwards took a moment to recover. "Both. She's not a plaything and you're a flirt."

"So is she," Jasper said. "A cracking good one. I assure you if it ever becomes necessary for you to run me through or give me a good drubbing, you'll be given every opportunity. In the meantime, let her take care of herself. She prefers it that way." Jasper prodded a lump of dirt with the point of his walking stick while Dr. Edwards pulled his jaw out of the folds of his necktie. "Better now?" He shouldn't needle the man, but Edwards made it so easy.

"I did not abandon my sister to pursue my career. And I take a great interest—"

"Of course you do," Jasper said. "I expect she'd have delivered you to the ship herself bound and gagged if you hadn't agreed to go." He was guessing, but was sure enough of his sudden insight to wager on being right.

Edwards' face sagged, confirming Jasper's theory. Poor fellow. Living amongst forceful women could wear the life out of you. Jasper laid a reassuring hand on Edwards' arm. "There were times I thought Sophy's antics would tie my guts in knots." Times too when he'd fully expected a broken nose, especially after she'd become acquainted with Tom. It hadn't happened, yet. Good thing too—spoiling the faultless profile he'd inherited from his mother would be a pity. "Sisters are tricky. I won't forget she's yours."

Edwards grunted, but took a long study of Jasper none-theless, weighing his words for sincerity and measuring him to the last quarter inch. His search was so protracted Jasper wondered if he knew about the rash he took every time he ate strawberries or that he'd once broken his left wrist. He sniffed and scanned the horizon, trying to act like it didn't trouble him. "Aren't you coming?" Miss Edwards called, swinging her furled parasol by the handle.

"Directly," her brother answered. "I'll take you at your word," he muttered at Jasper, the words slipped edgeways from the corner of his mouth.

"What's keeping you?" Laura puzzled, though the smirk hiding behind her wide eyes said she had a very good guess.

"We're just becoming more perfectly acquainted," Dr. Edwards said. "I think Rushford and I understand each other now, don't we?"

Laura glanced between them, her eyes narrowed with suspicion.

"Perfectly," Jasper said with a nod. "Shall we go on? I believe there's a fine prospect of the abbey from the north end of the churchyard."

Fine or not they'd be able to see the church from there and he was reasonably sure he was actually leading them in a northerly direction. If he wasn't, Dr. Edwards didn't give him away.

———

SOMETHING HAD PASSED BACK THERE between them. Though Laura had guesses aplenty, her curiosity to know exactly what had brought about this sudden truce between Rushford and her brother was almost painful. The way they were going on now you'd have thought they'd been cronies for years. Rushford had no interest in the new surgical techniques on which Jack discoursed with such enthusiasm, but he listened with such polite attention Jack couldn't tell. Her brother did tend to lose himself in his work. It was one of the unfortunate things she couldn't help but love about him.

Laura spun the handle of her parasol and watched the movement in her pygmy shadow puddled in the grass beside her. It wouldn't be such a bad thing to stay in Suffolk with Jack. Bury St Edmonds was a pretty town and Jack ought to have someone, a patient ear for when he rambled on about sutures and hands to massage the guilt from his shoulders the times that he failed. There was no one to fill the role but she.

Of course someday Jack would marry, someday soon she hoped. He was thirty but in no hurry. It was selfish of her to cling to London and the theatre when he needed her and wrong to hurt his chances. She shouldn't have told that curate they were French and Catholic. She'd been thinking of herself, forgetting she and Jack were inextricably connected now they'd come here together. It might have been better if she'd held her ground and refused to come. Though she had tried.

And Rushford—Jasper, his sister called him—well, she might tease and say she'd forget him back in London, but it wouldn't be so easy. She'd fallen into the habit of playing to him, seeing how long she could hold his gaze, watching for that quick upturn in the left corner of his mouth. She liked him throwing her lines and casting her secretive glances and knew with a sharp plunge these would be hard to give up.

Somehow, without noticing, she'd got attached to him.

Chewing her lip, Laura reviewed the past two weeks to find

when her heart had first softened. Maybe it was the lines of Sheridan or how sweet he was to Tom's mother or the sight of him, honed and polished, when he was dressed for dinner. It could have been the sly way he teased her or maybe it was the shock of sighting him that first evening sprawled indolently on Sophy's couch. Her mistakes had come gradually, inch by inch. Now she found herself in deep water, far away from shore.

She mustn't panic. The thing to do was slow the breathing and steady the heart, then work until your feet touched bottom. She'd done it before, reclaiming her heart from Lord Harvey and the unsuspecting actor Dan Bowen. Laura's mouth twisted into a frown. She should have paid closer attention—she knew better than to make this kind of foolish mistake. It might be wise to quit Suffolk now and take herself back to London. Rushford would have to stay here at least until the birth, and she could use the time to detach herself. Yes, she'd miss him at first and London wouldn't be the same if he stopped jostling his way into her dressing room. But even if he did it wouldn't be so intimate as this. She needn't allow the same closeness she did here. It would sting but a clean wound was better than a lingering infection. For now, she must say and do nothing—then she could pick up these memories later, smile, and turn them round in her fingers before returning them to their velvet box. Clever women knew to only wear jewels that suited them: ones they could afford.

"Do you sketch?" Rushford asked, surprisingly near her shoulder. She turned, raising a hand to shade her face from the sun. She wouldn't look becoming squinting up at him as if he was too brilliant to behold, but he nearly was, set against this backdrop of mammoth church and limitless sky, the sun performing alchemy with his fair hair.

"Jack does a little," she said. His letters were always decorated with drawings in the margins: ships, specimens, himself sprawled in a hammock with his toes burrowing out the holes in his stockings.

"A very little," Jack laughed. "Nothing fit to be seen. I wouldn't attempt the kind of detail required by all this masonry." Everywhere the eye touched were angles and arches, pediments and capitals.

"If it's too much to draw, pity the stonecutters," Laura said. "How long did this take to build?"

Rushford shrugged. "No idea. We could inquire if you like."

Laura shook her head. "No, I've seen enough."

He offered to show them the butter market, but Jack shook his head. "Best save it for another day. I should be getting back," he said deciding for all of them despite his single pronoun. "Besides, it's getting hot."

It was warm, but Laura didn't think the temperature to blame for her desire to return to Chippenstone—the pleasure she felt in Rushford's company was suddenly gone. She couldn't even blame Jack. Laura sighed. She probably wasn't meant to be respectable. She enjoyed her vices, such as they were, far too much.

Her attention inward, Laura left the conversation on the journey home to Rushford and Jack. With her brother riding beside the curricle, they covered the level countryside at a decent pace. Lulled by their voices Laura drooped in the sun, loose strands of hair stuck to her forehead, her fingers swollen inside her gloves.

"We'll stop for lemonade at the White Hart," Jasper murmured.

They bounced into a rut she was sure he could have avoided, throwing her against him. She gave him a look and the corner of his mouth hitched up the merest fraction, but he kept his eyes on the road. It was a bad sign, how much she enjoyed the feel of him.

The road dipped through a stream that was baked to a slender trickle, then twined through a stand of trees on the other side. Emerging into the open country Laura sighted a smudge of dust in the distant road that marred the finish of the cobalt sky. She tightened her grip on the carriage rail as Rushford slowed his horses.

"No one rides like that on this road," he said, eyes fixed on that far away smear. "Not without a reason. Careful," he said, as Jack drew in beside them.

"Fast, isn't he?" Jack said, stroking the neck of his sidling horse.

"I think it's my father," Rushford said. Laura could just make out a blue-coated rider and a giant, surging black horse.

"It is." Jasper flicked the reins. The unexpected lurch threw Laura backwards.

"Slow down!" she said. "Are you trying to throw me off?"

"Haven't lost a passenger yet," he said as he steered his plunging horses down the road.

"I didn't realize that made you invincible," Laura said through clenched teeth. "How foolish of me." If he heard he made no sign. Lord Fairchild was almost upon them, his horse lathered and blowing hard, a second animal saddled and running behind him. Working in frightening symmetry, Jasper and his father dragged their horses to a stop, ending practically on each other's toes. "Seen Edwards?" Lord Fairchild asked.

Jasper jerked his head over his shoulder. "He's with us."

"Here," Jack said, pulling up behind them. He glanced at Lord Fairchild. "Is it time?"

Fairchild nodded. "Yes. But my wife and Tom's mother—they said it didn't seem right."

"Her pains are coming quickly?"

"Quick enough we're all in a panic. But she's so small and her burden is..."

"Yes, I spoke to Tom of it. I'd best hurry."

"Ride Philippides." Lord Fairchild motioned to the horse on the lead. I'll take you cross country."

"Mine are still fresh," Rushford interjected. "If you take Miss Edwards I can take the doctor up in the curricle."

Fairchild shook his head. "Going through the fields is faster than the roads."

"Yes, but—"

"Laura doesn't ride," Jack said.

"Come along Edwards," Fairchild said, settling the matter and ignoring Jasper's troubled glance at his mount's heaving sides. Jack dismounted and climbed the spokes of the curricle wheel to get a leg up on the new horse. He was scarcely in the saddle when Fairchild unclipped the lead and motioned him to follow. "This way."

Next to her, Rushford cursed under his breath. Laura looked up at him.

"Forgive me," he said, collecting himself. Already they were back in motion. "We'd best make our way as swiftly as we can."

"Haste won't help if it kills my brother," Laura said as she watched the riders' breakneck pace through the tall barley, unable to rinse the sharpness from her voice. Jack was a decent horseman, but racing like this across fields and over fences was ludicrous.

"Jack will be fine. That horse hasn't thrown anyone yet."

"This could be the day," she said. It was already a grand one for things going wrong. Her wrist ached from her grip on the rail. "What about your father?" she asked. Jasper hadn't liked them racing off, she was sure.

"My father always decides for himself," Jasper said. "I tried to change his mind."

One wheel bounced over a rut in the road, but Jasper didn't slacken their speed. He was silent and sweat beaded on his lip as they rattled down the road. Laura clung to her seat cursing cathedrals, curricles, this poor road, and her brother's lack of one, praying no one's neck ended up broken and that her brother reached his patient in time.

13

SQUEAKER

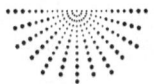

*W*illiam found Tom in the library, his white knuckles welded around an untouched brandy.

"You're wet, Fairchild," Tom said, looking up.

"Put my head in the horse trough," William explained. "Edwards is with Sophy?"

"Yes. Thank you for fetching him."

"Things came on unexpectedly," William said. Unlucky, but he didn't say that. He still felt unsteady even after soaking his head. Floundering into an empty chair, he braced his fingers together, trying to still the trembling in his knees.

A door slammed sending someone scampering down the corridor. Tom spun in his seat and sloshed his brandy, but the runner went past, unchecked. "Merciful God," he said, kneading his fingers into his forehead. There was a groan—not Tom's this time—quickly suppressed. Tom started from his chair, flying from the room.

Seconds later he was back. "Mother says I'm to get drunk if I can't take it." He stared at the brandy staining the arm of his chair. "Why didn't she speak earlier?"

He meant Sophy, William guessed. "It's new to her. How would she know? She doesn't complain."

"I know. That night she dragged herself to my doorstep her shoulder was out of joint—" Tom shuddered.

William nodded. "She used to hide the bruises she got, afraid I'd know she'd been thrown and not let her ride."

Tom closed his eyes and let his head fall against the back of his chair. "If your wife hadn't noticed, who knows when Sophy would have given in and said something."

"Georgiana's hard to deceive."

Tom made a motion approximating a smile but without any life in it. "Never seen Sophy take a scolding like that. Meek as a lamb." He didn't end it like one, but there was a question in it. William shrugged.

"Sophy grants Georgiana special privileges I wouldn't dare. I expect you'll have a word or two for her yourself, sometime when she's back on her feet and the babe's asleep."

Tom blinked twice. "No. Heavens, there'll be better things to say." For a moment he seemed afraid to speak. "But I tell you one thing—if we're ever in this mad fix again I'm not letting her send the doctor beyond the grounds, not for any reason!"

William said nothing. Instinct told him it was better to let Bagshot to try boring a hole in the wall with his eyes. "You won't drink?" he finally ventured.

"Sophy doesn't get that release," Bagshot spat. He stopped, tilting his head after some sound. "Lord, what are they doing?"

William shrugged. "You're confident in Edwards."

"With my life." Tom made a face, slumped into his chair, and covered his face with his hands. "But it's not mine. It's Sophy's."

William studied his hands. He could tell Bagshot that all would be well, but the words were counterfeit—he couldn't be certain. Chances were good, but they'd all been alarmed by the suddenness and force of her pains. Worse now by the focused silence blanketing the house. He could make no promise; no command of his would set all aright. But he ought to say something, so he lifted the first likely thing from the jumble in his mind.

"Once she got sick. Must have been a mere eleven or twelve. She never told the nursemaid. Ended up throwing up on my library carpet. Never felt like such an ogre. I think she'd have rather died than asked to be excused. Meant to get through the interview with me by sheer force of will. Doesn't like making a fuss. Never has."

Bagshot grunted, bitterly conceding the truth. "Doesn't like to ask, doesn't want to put anyone out...times like this it's awful to live with."

William huffed. "Sophy's only asked me for one thing. Except for this I can't remember her asking for so much as a glove or a stocking," he said.

"Well?" Tom asked, prodding him out of silence.

It was shaming, but it had to be said. William smiled ruefully at his son-in-law, at his lanky legs flung anyhow over the carpet, his coarse, sandy hair wrecked by nervous fingers. "She asked me for you," he said. This daughter of his, who until now had never dared to ask for love from her family, knew Tom Bagshot had a store of it. It knit his bones together and spilled out his anxious fingertips. Of course she'd wanted him. William swallowed, hoping the motion would quell the ache in his throat. "If you knew how I wish I had let her."

It would have been easier after that to let his eyes drift to the window or a distant wall. Tom stared at him hard, dislike chiseled in the set of his jaw. William kept himself still and let the sharp eyes delve him. Finally Tom spoke.

"I suppose the only true fool is the one who fails to realize his mistake." He tapped his fingers on the arm of his chair.

"Does it help?" he asked. "Putting your head in the horse trough?"

William pushed back his damp hair. "Clarity? Not especially. This mistake I recognized long ago. But I find the shock of cold water does lessen anxiety. I doused myself twice waiting for the birth of my son Jasper."

Tom glanced at the door, his thumb fretting against his second finger. "I don't want to be out of hearing distance."

"Bagshot, you—"

"Call me Tom," he interrupted.

"Tom." William smiled. "You can easily send for a bucket."

———

JASPER RETURNED and found the rules were changed. Sophy, Dr. Edwards, and his ferocious attendants, Lady Fairchild and Mrs Bagshot, were now the only ones allowed to make noise in the house. Miss Edwards disappeared without him realizing it and Jasper crept from room to room unable to settle. Finding himself in the dusty chamber which passed as the gunroom, Jasper cleaned the piece he'd given Tom last Christmas. It didn't look like he'd fired a single shot. He breathed on the window, then unlatched it and wandered into the Egyptian salon to rearrange the newspapers. The servants had disappeared, save for the ones rushing to and fro with hot water and towels. He didn't dare ask if it generally took this long. After the rush to get Edwards, Jasper had half expected to arrive to the sound of a baby's cry. Instead the hours ticked by, wasting the night and creeping towards dawn.

Jasper stopped in the library to share a plate of untouched sandwiches—neither his father or Tom were eating. Tom glared at him every time he swallowed, so Jasper pocketed a sandwich and returned to his wandering. Once he passed Dr. Edwards in the hall, his shirtsleeves rolled to his elbows, but he fended away Jasper's questions with upraised hands. One clutched a sinister looking pair of pincers.

"Don't say a word," Dr. Edwards commanded. "Nothing to Tom."

Then it wasn't quiet. Unearthly groans swelled into the corridor. Then he heard Sophy gasping, damning so vehemently the paper must be curling off the walls. Tom, stripped of his coat and chewing through his bottom lip, flew down the hall and hovered in front of the door, reaching for the handle then pulling back like it was a glowing coal.

"I can't stand it," he said and flung open the door. Another curse, not from Sophy this time, cut the air and the door slammed shut.

Jasper glanced at the library where his father hesitated on the threshold. "Was that Mama?"

"Wasn't Edwards." His father didn't look good. Wet hair clung to his forehead and stuck up in points from the back of his head. The shoulders of his coat were soaked through and drips of water spotted his dust-stained trousers.

"Your horse?" Jasper asked.

"Foundered half a mile from here. Edwards rode on and I ran on foot the rest of the way. I didn't matter by that point. We'd passed all the gates and hedges."

"You took a toss on the last one?" Jasper recognized the signs: stiff limbs, a suppressed wince with every turn of the head.

His father confessed with a half-smile. "Not so much a toss as a fall. Ajax's paces were off but he cleared it. Stumbled on the landing. Even then he took the brunt of it. I got clear before he fell. He was a gallant one. A gentleman."

"Is he all right?" Jasper asked, thinking he couldn't have heard his father right. He was too calm to have lost the horse—

Jasper had seen him weep over stillborn foals. Ajax was the prize of his stables, the work of his life.

"Had to shoot him. You'll please not mention this to your mother." More footsteps. Lord Fairchild passed a hand over his forehead. He looked white and puddly as a blancmange.

Jasper wanted to ask if it was usual for physicians to require barbarous claws, but fearing the answer he kept silent. Another gasp struck them like a lash. It was unbearable. Jasper turned to the door, giving up. Three paces down the hall he stopped, arrested by a furious mewling that ratcheted within seconds to a gale-force scream. Alive, thank God.

Jasper brought his fist to his mouth, exhaling hard. When he was composed enough to look up, his father was huddled against the closed doorway.

"Sophy?" Jasper asked.

"Can't hear anything over the babe," his father muttered.

They fretted for some minutes. "Just open the bloody door," Jasper said and shoved it wide. His eyes fell first on Edwards bent over a basin washing blood from his hands.

"All's well," he said with a haggard smile. Lady Fairchild worked at his shoulder rolling up a mass of soiled linen and moving briskly despite the tired lines in her face. She straightened, driving away renegade wisps of hair with the back of her wrist.

"A girl," she mouthed with a smile and shrug.

The parents were oblivious. Sophy was sweaty and damp, too tired to flutter a finger or breathe a word. Yet when Mrs. Bagshot finished swaddling the little squaller, Sophy's arms somehow shaped themselves into a cradle. Mrs. Bagshot settled the babe into them as lightly as if she were nothing but a bundle of swansdown. Tom knelt, wet-cheeked, at the bedside and broke off his incoherent stream of love words to look. Jasper stopped breathing. They all did, waiting for Tom to speak.

———

HE DIDN'T, just laid his head against Sophy's arm, quiet and complete, resting there as Edwards and his satellites circled and brought order back to the world. Gently the doctor coaxed them from the room, even Tom and his infant burden. Lady Fairchild stayed behind, obedient to the doctor's unspoken command. Sophy Bagshot was well and would be well, but he needed quiet and a steady hand to hold the candle so he could sew the little mother back together.

14
INDEPENDENCE

*A*fter the initial flood of relief ebbed, Laura wondered if it might be best for her to say farewell to the Bagshots and Chippenstone. She wasn't exactly necessary. Jack was busy tending his two patients and writing up an account of his successful forceps delivery, justifiably proud. Sophy had Tom's mother and Lady Fairchild who were both eager to tend her. It would be good, Laura thought, to remove herself from Jasper.

Except he'd done it first. The morning after the birth he disappeared. Just as well, Laura told herself, since Sophy, for absurd and inexplicable reasons, pressed her to stay.

Laura wrote Mr. Rollins to ask him for the extra two weeks he had offered before. It would take that long, she figured, to pick out the right words to explain to Jack. In the meantime she found ways to make herself useful: fetching books, bringing up trays, opening windows, helping the new mother walk up and down the corridor and, five days later, pace out the terrace. Sophy complained about Jack's strictures but accepted them all, knowing she'd have the entire house on her head if she dared vary an iota from her doctor's prescription. The little girl was christened Viola Frances Persephone, but Jasper, who reappeared for the ceremony, made a face at her given name and refused to use it.

"Ugh! Far too pretentious a handle for a little bug like her. Ollie is better. I'll call her that."

Laura listened with pricked ears, telling herself she was glad when all Sophy's pleas couldn't convince him to stay.

"I'll pop in to see you and Ollie in a day or two," he said.

"Viola," Sophy corrected.

"Ollie. Don't mind her. She'll catch on," Jasper said, bending to kiss the baby's soft head.

He was right. Even Sophy gave up on Viola after three more days, cooing the nickname as she kissed each walnut fist and gazed at stubby eyelashes. Ollie, indifferent to names of any sort, forgot the ugly trauma of her birth and waxed fat and happy.

It was a sort of dream, this life of turning pillows and melting over tiny fingers plump as pudding. Laura brewed possets, laughed with Sophy as they bathed Ollie, and watched mother and child sleep tucked away in the confines of Sophy's chamber, now a land of milk and honey. Jasper, whom she'd unconsciously begun to think of again as Mr. Rushford, stayed away.

"He really isn't interested in babies," Sophy sighed. "Maybe when Ollie is ready to learn to ride."

"He'll be back," Tom said without looking up from his letter. "He took his portmanteau but left his trunks."

Laura picked up Sophy's cup and refilled it with tea.

"Jack's gone to the village?" Sophy asked.

Laura shook her head. "Bury St Edmonds again." To meet with the solicitor about the house.

"I hope you make a great many changes," Sophy said. "The longer the workmen have it, the longer I can make you stay."

Laura knew Sophy truly liked having her about, but she wasn't needed. She'd done some good—she'd taken it upon herself to chasten the elder Mrs. Bagshot's maid, because Tom's mother really shouldn't suffer under such tight lacing and was far too good-hearted to complain. But that was attended to, Sophy was walking, Ollie feeding and sleeping. Lady Fairchild came by almost every day.

It was time to go back to her own life before London felt even farther away. There'd been a pleasing flurry of speculation when she'd first disappeared, but if she didn't return soon she'd be forgotten. She had to tell Jack.

Laura spent the afternoon predicting his objections and planning out her speeches—in vain. Rushford returned that evening and it proved impossible to avoid him and corner Jack. Her brother, ignorant of her own desire to steer clear of Rushford, was determined to prevent a tête-à-tête between them and unwittingly spoiled every opportunity for conversation. Laura slept poorly and rose early, planning to catch Jack alone. Instead, she was first to the breakfast table—with an unexpected letter waiting beside her plate.

It wasn't from Mr. Rollins. The single word, Saltash, franked the top corner. Laura's name and direction were in the same repressive handwriting, too blunt to belong to a secretary. She broke the seal, no longer hungry.

Miss Edwards,

You've ignored me this last year, persisting in your unseemly profession despite my pronounced opposition. I'm not sure what you meant by that ridiculous masquerade with your brother, but my informants tell me he plans to settle in Suffolk. If establishing him was indeed your ambition, and not making a vulgar spectacle, at last you have succeeded.

I can see no reason for you to flout my commands and return to the stage. Believe me, rumors of incest won't help your career or his. My daughter, Eugenie, will be presented this forthcoming Season and I expect both you and your brother to keep out of London. If you are not sufficiently wise to take my advice I warn you that continued opposition will bring unpleasant consequences. I have friends in Suffolk and no qualms about making it as uncomfortable for you as you have made London for me.

Saltash

Laura refolded the letter and laid it beside her plate. With trembling calm she sipped her tea and consumed every dusty morsel of toast, then escaped to the garden, keeping a sedate pace until she was clear of the house. At last she broke into a run, her feet slapping on the gravel. Unused to running, her breath soon whistled in uneven gasps and a cramp clutched at her side. Spit congealed in her throat and choked her. She spat in the gravel and wiped the hair from her forehead. Bolting for the woods, she veered from the path, following the stream that fed Bagshot's square moat into the wilder places where trees grew in tangled confusion and mushrooms and tufts of grass broke through the mat of dead leaves.

She'd fretted all through her first season acting, wondering what he'd do once he finally attended a play and saw her. He came once that spring, but the bolt from above never came. He hadn't recognized her.

She hated Saltash for that, for his letters with their thick ink strokes and lavish spacing of words. She hated staring up from the stage into the jowls of his box, where he sat with his thinning hair and his great gold watch. She hated his elegant Mayfair mansion and his castle up north, though she'd never seen it. The husband of her mother's older sister could have made things easier for them. He hadn't.

When her mother died and Laura was tasked with burying her alone, she faltered. The loss she'd expected, but not the bludgeoning grief. She marked the passing with a notice in the Gazette.

Marguerite Leonie Edouard Lecroy-Duplessis, Comtesse D'Aiguines, of France and lately of London, died in her home on January 5, 1812.

Laura didn't know if any of her mother's former friends would see it, but she wanted a record, some way the world could know it had lost a courageous lady. Nine days later she had a visit from Saltash.

"I was sorry to read about your mother," he said, filling up the door. Laura left her hand on the latch to bar his way.

"Thank you, Your Grace. Please excuse me." Before she could shut it he caught the edge of the door.

"May I come in?"

It had the form of a question, at least. Laura gave way and brought him into the little parlor looking over the street. She sat on the ottoman, releasing her clenched fists. She wanted to vomit—just days ago she'd found the letters he'd sent her mother. It seemed Maman had asked, once or twice, for help and sometimes asked after the duchess, her sister. Saltash's letters were all the same. The duchess wasn't well enough to write. He didn't feel obliged to send her children to school, offer them a home, or buy her son a commission in the army. One thing he offered year after year; to a family struggling to buy coal it was an insult. Laura burned with it.

"I'm surprised you knew where to find us," she said.

"The newspaper office told me." His fingers played against

the arm of his chair as he inventoried the room. Small house, small rooms, small windows...little sketches on the walls. He took note of the books from Hookham's library stacked on the fireplace and the shawl—Laura's last gift to her mother, hardly worn—draped across the round table.

"Is your brother home?"

"He last wrote from Gibraltar. He's in the navy."

Saltash nodded, pleased. "He's been keeping you? Good. But you'll need a new home. Can't live on your own now."

"Jack doesn't keep me. Or my mother," Laura said, before he could go any further. Her pulse beat in her ears like a troop of parading soldiers. "I kept him the first few years and paid his tuition at Edinburgh. He's a physician now, did you know?"

"You supported him? You couldn't—"

Laura smiled. It was revenge—of a sort. "You could have but did not so I took care of them the best way I knew how. Don't you recognize me?" she asked, for bafflement still clouded him. The words didn't sound like hers, they came so fast and brittle and sharp. It felt like falling—once begun, you couldn't stop. "You've seen me at least once each of the past six years. My aunt was with you last time. I remember she applauded." Laura remembered too, how ill the duchess looked, clapping genteelly, her bird-claw hands too thin for her gloves. She waited, containing her furious breathing and the urge to hurl something, watching the puzzle play across his face.

Drawing herself up, she continued. "All London knows me. I'm Gemma Holyrood."

For a minute he didn't speak. "But...the breeches...the rumors..."

"You took no interest in us, Your Grace. You forfeited the right to say anything. I thank you for your condolences on behalf of my mother and wish you good day." Laura rose from her chair, her rigid back ordering him to leave.

He stayed in place, still sputtering. "Gemma Holyrood? You cannot continue. What of our family's reputation? Your aunt, your cousin Eugenie?"

"Believe me, I have as little desire for our names to be connected as you do." Her skin crawled just having him in her rooms, and she couldn't trust herself not to scream the insults she longed to pour into his unfeeling ears. Ignoring the tremor in her fingers she reached for the bell. Peter, who'd likely been hovering just behind the closed door, answered before her fingers released the handle. "His Grace is leaving. Will you escort him from the house?"

"You will leave the stage," Saltash said, rising.

"Forgive me for disappointing you, but I will not. Peter?"

A glance at Peter's tough face and calloused fists had the desired effect. Saltash went, trailing thunderheads. Alone at last, Laura slammed her fist against her leg and broke into tears. It didn't help. Maman was gone. Crying, raging, even punishing her uncle wouldn't change that, and one moment of vengeful vindication was hardly worth revealing her secret.

A week later her landlord sold the house to the Duke of Saltash. It took Peter and a kind crew of stagehands all night, but they moved her to new lodgings before Saltash threw her out. They kept her new address amongst themselves. Undeterred, Saltash went to Mr. Rollins demanding he dismiss her. Laura answered with a sharp letter, asking Saltash how it would look if she went to the papers and revealed their relationship and his treatment of her family. She'd just finished a sold-out run of Twelfth Night and been congratulated by the Regent. Saltash didn't bother Rollins again, but he took to scowling at her from his box, sneering when the rest of the theatre broke into applause, and talking during her speeches.

Laura's nerves were tempered and did not break. He could not stop her, not with puny weapons like these. She bowed to him, blew him kisses, smirked, and gave him a fine view of her breeches, infuriating him more. His face grew thin and gaunt, his eyes as he watched her burned like coals, but he never missed a performance. When the scandal sheets hinted that Miss Holyrood had captured the Duke of Saltash's heart, she clipped it out and mailed it to him. He sent her back the dead starling.

After that she moved in disguise outside the theatre, her whereabouts a closely kept secret. A stalemate but Laura felt she had the upper hand.

Now in a stroke all was reversed. Saltash was right—no matter how she might laugh that Jack's mask was only a ploy, the gossips wouldn't relent, not with a story as bawdy as incest. It would destroy her career, but even worse it would wreck any chance of Jack's. They'd have to emigrate to America where he could doctor out of a cabin in Kentucky.

Quitting the stage would be hard enough, but to lose it all because of Saltash?—she'd rather move to Kentucky. Except that wouldn't be fair to Jack. Nothing must touch him, but she couldn't let Saltash win. Her mind spun, testing and discarding ideas. There had to be a way.

Her real name? That wouldn't change anything. Maybe if Jack married...but she had only days. Impossible to find her brother a wife in that short a time. Besides, even the best of brothers would balk at a solution as drastic as that. If only she hadn't played along and let the world think he was her lover. The gambit had afforded useful protection from time to time, but now it had spooned her right into the dish. Unless...

She could change the story. All she needed to do was give the audience somewhere else to look. You could make anything disappear if the action downstage was busy enough. Saltash could only threaten her with the speculation she'd created about Gemma Holyrood's unknown paramour—it was hers to control.

The world wanted to believe she had a lover? She could give them a better one. Someone elegant and disdainful, who played with society like he had it on a string.

It wouldn't be an easy game, but Rushford was the man for it. She would sweep into London and triumph on the stage and snap her fingers under the Duke of Saltash's nose.

15

MAD, BAD, AND DANGEROUS
TO KNOW

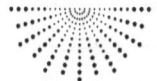

*S*he didn't intend to approach Rushford with sweaty hair and a rumpled dress, but he found her before she could return to the house.

"I've been looking for you," he said. "What's the matter?"

"Why do you care all of a sudden?" she asked, provoked by hurt she hadn't let herself acknowledge. He'd avoided her for days.

A bad start. She'd have to do better. Calming herself, Laura was putting together conciliatory words when he held up a folded paper between two fingers.

"You left this on the breakfast table. It's from the Duke of Saltash. How does he know who you really are?"

He was angry, she realized, finally understanding the mask-like tightness of his face, the colorless skin. "Does your brother know about him?" Rushford demanded.

Laura collapsed into disjointed laughter, wrapping her arms around her shoulders to keep herself together. It was too much. "You're jealous!"

"You owe me an explanation," he said, though he didn't say why. "What is Saltash to you exactly?"

She didn't like this face of his, stern, both judge and prosecutor. But she wanted him to help her—she couldn't succeed without him—so he needed the straight truth. "Saltash is my uncle. He doesn't like me onstage."

Rushford took a step back. Frowned. He didn't believe her. Well, she would read him the letter. As she reached for it he spoke.

"I should think he doesn't! Very high in the instep, Saltash." He still looked incredulous, but his voice was milder now. "I don't understand. If he's your uncle, why take to the stage in the first place?"

"I needed thirty pounds. He wouldn't give it to me."

Rushford barked—it wasn't quite a laugh. "I don't believe it."

"It's true. I was six when my father died and they burned our chateau. My oldest brother and grandmother also went to the guillotine, but mother and Jack and I hid."

She wouldn't speak of the months in a dark cellar, the nights they walked from one hiding place to another, the lies their protectors told to explain the bits of extra food smuggled to keep them alive. "Somehow she bribed our way out of France and we sailed to England with a cargo of Bordeaux wine. We arrived practically penniless."

"And Saltash did nothing?"

"He said we were welcome to use his box at the theatre." A kind invitation he renewed every year as they counted pennies and rationed food and coal. No wonder Maman had said nothing.

Jasper flinched. Laura plucked a leaf from the hedge and tore it into tiny pieces, scattering them over the grass and the skirts of her gown.

"So you took your revenge," he said studying her. "Though she be but little, she is fierce."

Laura dismissed his Shakespeare. "I prefer formidable."

"No. *Formidable*," Jasper said, giving it the French pronunciation. "You *are* wonderful, right enough."

Compliments were generally a good sign, but she wasn't sure she could trust his when they were coupled with that sardonic eye. "Saltash's daughter, my cousin, is coming out next Season. He wants me out of London. I don't believe I shall oblige him, but I'm in a bit of a fix. He knows about Jack and unless I quit London he's threatening to ruin things for him here."

"Letting slip that his sister is an actress?"

Laura shook her head. "No, Saltash threatens to reveal our secret incest. It doesn't matter that it's not true. Once they print it, it might as well be."

He laughed. "Play with fire and you'll get burned, Laura."

She sent him a look. "No one notices a pot burning in the midst of an explosion." If she failed and Saltash spread his incest story, she'd respond by revealing that he was her uncle. He could try and paint her black, but she'd make sure he didn't escape the spatters. Rumors of incest would ruin her and Jack, but if Saltash was squeamish about being connected to an actress, being known as the uncle of a debased one would give him a brain seizure. Victory, of a sort, but hard to enjoy after losing all she'd fought to achieve. You couldn't gloat over that in Kentucky. Much better if she outplayed Saltash and for that she needed Jasper.

"Explosions? Are you going to ignite one?" he asked.

"We are." Laura smiled. "How would you like to win that two hundred pounds?"

SHE COULDN'T BE SERIOUS. Jasper glanced back at the house, wondering if he ought to run. They were in full sight of the windows. Good God. She already looked like she'd been tumbled in the grass. He took another step back.

"I promised your brother," he began.

"Is that what happened? I suppose he made you promise not to take advantage of me."

Jasper didn't contradict her. She sighed. "Really, I could do without Jack's meddling. It needn't trouble you. What I'm proposing is really the other way round."

"Is it?" Jasper swallowed, trying to bring his voice out of the register of a boy soprano. "What are you proposing exactly?"

"Return with me to London. I'll be your new mistress."

She might as well have thrown a cup of scalding tea over him. Recovering, Jasper tried again. "Impossible. I told you, I promised your brother—"

"Why should he have any say? And why should you get to grow scruples at this hour?" She planted a finger on his chest. "What if I'd accepted you a month ago in London? Did you think of me as anyone's sister then?"

Jasper dropped his eyes to the damp grass.

"Well?" she pushed, relentless.

"The point is I do now," he said. Impossible to explain that London was entirely about the chase. He wouldn't have known what to do if he'd caught her. With the chances of winning her practically negligible it had seemed a safe enough game. She'd laugh if he told her his personal credo: no despoiling the innocent, no affairs, no mistresses. Anyone would laugh, but he remembered Fanny Prescott and what his father had done to her. And Sophy—it was none of her fault, but the world wasn't kindly disposed to bastards. He'd promised himself long ago not to make any.

"And that's supposed to finish it?" she demanded, incredulous. "One word carelessly thrown to my brother and it's over? Very well. I'll choose someone else. You may as well write your banker because you're going to have to pay up."

Protheroe? She wouldn't. "You mustn't—Miss Edwards—"

"No one will care about Jack—the man they think was my lover—once he's replaced by someone else," she explained. "They'll be wondering instead how the new one stole me. And with he and I flaunting our love so flamboyantly about town... well, there won't be any space in the newssheets for anything else."

It was true, every blithe word foretelling disaster. If Protheroe didn't leap at chance to acquire her she'd have her pick of at least a dozen more. Jasper braced his hands on his head, forgetting it would muddle his artfully disarranged hair. She peered up at him and stepped closer. "Perhaps you are willing to reconsider?"

Damn. He couldn't let her go to anyone else. But he wasn't going to break his word either. Nimble stepping, that's what this needed. Hopefully he wouldn't trip. "Seems I must." He couldn't see any other way he'd get a say in her behavior. Jasper squared his shoulders, hoping the motion would set the world in order again. No luck. She was still there, tapping her slippered toe on the gravel path.

"Good. Rollins—he's the theatre manager—needs me back in London."

It would be nice, since he wasn't allowed a real say, to at least have the luxury of a little time. Without it there was a good chance they'd both roast for this. He could afford it. No one ever faulted the man. When things went wrong she'd take the brunt of it. Yet he'd promised not to harm her and in his book, that also meant not letting her be hurt by anyone else. "When would you like to depart?" he asked.

"Tomorrow," she said. "I need to rehearse."

The question was, for which stage? "I can't leave before noon." It would be a miracle if he managed his preparations by then. He felt exhausted already.

"Do you always sleep so late?" She frowned.

"You'll find out I suppose," he snapped. *Not as practiced as she pretends*, Jasper thought, noting the quick convulsion of her throat. Just as well, but it didn't mean he had to be nice about it.

She glared and drew herself up. "I certainly will. I'll be ready tomorrow for twelve o'clock."

It was amazing that a person as disheveled as she could manage such an uppity flounce. Jasper watched her disappear into the house, frustrated that he knew no curse of sufficient potency to express his exasperation. He rubbed his forefinger along the bridge of his nose—it wouldn't look nearly so well once it was broken.

Better not wait. No hope for him if he didn't speak to Jack before she did.

"Edwards?"

"Rushford?" The doctor untangled himself from his chair and laid aside his notes as Jasper entered the drawing room.

"I'd like to speak to you, if I may." Jasper pitched his voice low so he wouldn't disturb Tom's mother who nodded away in the other chair, a tatty-looking novel splayed on her knees.

The two men tiptoed into the hall. "What is it?" Edwards asked.

Jasper glanced nervously at the stairs, half expecting Laura to make an entrance. "Can we speak in my room? It's more private there."

Edwards' look turned disdainful. He folded his arms. "I can't help you," he said. "Mercury isn't a cure."

"I haven't got pox!" Jasper hissed. Heavens, there were plenty of perfectly acceptable reasons for wanting a private word with someone, though telling a man his sister had propositioned you—and you'd accepted—wasn't one of them. There was just no good way to do this. Lord, how to even begin? Jasper only knew he was incapable of attempting it out here. "Just come. *Please*."

"All right," Edwards said as he followed at Jasper's elbow. "Usually though if someone wants a private word with me, it's pox. Are you quite sure you're well?"

"Perfectly sure." Face flaming, Jasper stalked at a carpet-devouring pace through the mile of corridor to his chamber, jabbing open the door, provoked into hitting something, even if it was only walnut wood. Did everyone think him such a frippery fellow?

"I like women you know," Edwards said, behind him.

"So do I!" Jasper said, spinning round, blushing so hotly he feared smoke would curl from his ears. Honestly if he didn't get this done soon, his head would explode—not exactly the fireworks Miss Edwards had in mind, but still newsworthy. Jasper drew a ragged breath and paced out the room.

"It's Saltash," he said. "He's threatened your sister and she refuses to capitulate. But she doesn't want to harm you, so she's decided to go back to London and she's making me be her mistress—I mean, she's making me make her my mistress. Damn it—"

"Slow down," Edwards said. "For your own sake you want to explain this better." He looked ready to chew rocks.

"It's not my fault!" Jasper spluttered. "She said if I wouldn't do it she'd take my friend Protheroe. Not only would he not understand the situation, he'd really tup her!"

A lightning strike of anger blazed on Jack's face. Jasper took a step back—there were cruder terms, but it hadn't been the best choice of words. "You have my promise already," Jasper said, raising placating hands. "And I swear again to you that I won't touch her. Saints alive, man, if I intended to would I be telling you this?"

"I don't know," Edwards said grimly. "Madness is a symptom of pox. It can come from inbreeding, too."

"For the last time I don't have pox! And we've never had strangeness in our family!" Not that kind at least.

"Indeed? This seems strange enough to me. You're telling me that, at my sister's request, you'll take her on as your mistress but not sleep with her?"

Jasper checked himself, his retort balanced on the edge of his tongue. It was a ludicrous scheme. "I can't think of any other way to make her mind me," Jasper said. "But by all means if you think she'll listen to you it will save me a world of trouble. I don't want a mistress, least of all your sister—but I do like women," he finished.

Edwards let out a breath through his teeth. It was an opening and Jasper took it. "She just needs another actor to play out her little drama. Can't be you because Saltash knows and he'll say it's incest and the gossip rags will gobble that up like ices on a summer day. Good luck doctoring the good people of Suffolk if that gets out. And better me than some other fellow. In public I'll play her game, but otherwise I'll put her in the charge of a very strict chaperone." He just had to find one. For both their sakes. After all, it was tempting. He'd never had a woman, but he'd fondled a few and was pretty certain Jack wouldn't like him trying that either.

"But how will it end?" Edwards asked.

"I don't know." Jasper threw up his hands. "How do these affairs end? The point is they always do. She'll face down Saltash, or not, and in all likelihood send me packing once she's done with me. So long as I make sure she comes to no real harm and no one besides us connects Gemma Holyrood to Laura Edwards, there's no difficulty and no scandal attached to you." He finished, half expecting to hear a thunderclap at such a blatant invitation to fate. So many things could go wrong. They'd all have to think on their feet. And another thing...now that he knew their real names—"Perhaps I should address you properly, Comte?"

Jack rolled his eyes. "I prefer doctor. I earned that title."

"As you wish," Jasper shrugged. "But just because you don't fancy yours doesn't mean I'm giving up mine." For now he was a paltry Honorable, but even when he became Lord Fairchild after his father, Jasper doubted he'd develop radical sympathies. Just as well Edwards disdained his title. Jasper was at enough disadvantage without being reminded that Edwards outranked him. "Does Tom know you're a count?"

"No. Please keep it that way," Jack said.

Lord, these two had a lot of secrets.

"I'd hoped she'd quit the stage. I wish she would, and not merely because of Saltash," Edwards said. "It would be easier."

Jasper looked at him. "I hope you're joking." It was a ludicrous plan likely to toss them all in the soup, but when you were losing a fight you used whatever weapons came to hand. "That man's actions were unforgivable. I would never ask her to submit to him." This wasn't a game. It was a duel and she'd asked him to stand second. He'd never held back when his friends' honor was at stake and he wouldn't now just because Miss Edwards was peculiar about the way she kept hers.

Edwards looked up, the tired lines on his face accentuated by the pale scar. "What do you want? My permission? I don't like it, Rushford."

Jasper didn't either but kept it to himself. "Your sister doesn't bother with niceties like permission overmuch. I'm telling you because you deserve to know the truth. I won't ruin her. I'll boil alive first."

It sounded suitably dramatic. Unfortunately Jasper suspected this might end that way too. He sighed. Two hundred pounds was not worth this amount of headache.

HURDLES

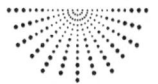

*S*he'd got her way, but Laura couldn't consider Rushford's agreement an unqualified success. The amount of arm-twisting required was mortifying. He was so reluctant you'd think she was crude and illiterate with sagging bosoms and rotting teeth. But it was done and he'd agreed. Now she needed to come up with a story for Jack.

She wandered the house looking for him without success, finally finding him the second time she looked into his chamber.

"What's the matter?" She stopped on the threshold, alarmed by the haggard look on his face.

"Why don't you tell me?" he said.

"I don't think you should take the house," Laura said. "I'm not ready for this, Jack. I need to go back to London. If you live in the rooms over the surgery, you won't need me to keep house for you—"

"I closed with the solicitor yesterday," Jack said. "The house is ours." He watched her, waiting for her to speak. She had nothing. "But you won't come." His eyes fell to his hands.

"I can't—"

"Won't," he cut in. "What are you trying to do, Laura? All along I believed you were acting for my sake—"

"I was!"

"You aren't now. Tell me, why are you going back to London?"

"I'm not finished there yet."

"Is that all?"

"Nearly."

He waited, but she kept her lips shut.

"Suppose I forbid it?" he said.

Again she didn't answer.

"You'd best go then." He turned away. Laura felt the floor slide beneath her.

"Jack—"

He shut his eyes. "Nothing you tell me will make this any better. Just once I wish you'd let me decide something. You didn't ask me about the stage—"

"You'd have said no. You wouldn't be a doctor now if I'd listened." His face and the set of his shoulders terrified her. He'd stopped walking away from her, but it felt like he'd already left the room.

"I'm grateful for my career. But what's the point of it if I can't do a brother's job and take care of you? I've lost you. Better if I'd kept working in that shop."

Laura cringed.

"Tell me the truth," Jack said.

"I'm not finished yet," Laura said. "It's a point of honor between me and Saltash."

He grunted. "That's all? Saltash doesn't matter. We do. Your name matters to me."

"Which one?" Laura demanded. "You'll do anything for Laura Edwards, but I'm not her, Jack. If I'm anyone at all I'm Gemma Holyrood. Don't take that away from me." She could fight Saltash, but it killed her to fight Jack. He wheeled away and braced his hands against the window, staring down at the front lawn.

"I don't care which name you use, Laura. It's you I care about. Unlike you I've learned that winning some battles will lose you the war. He's not worth it."

She was crying—something she hated, especially in front of Jack. Stammering, she bludgeoned the scalding drops from her cheeks. "You think I'm—why shouldn't I feel the same when you try and decide for me? You don't get to do that, Jack."

"I never have. Not like you've done for me."

"I haven't!" she spat back. "I decided to do what was best for both of us. What I wanted to do because you needed me to do it. I wasn't going to be a—a useless weight holding you back. And I wasn't going to be held back either. Not then and not now and certainly not by that bastard Saltash!"

"Stop hating him," Jack said. "It makes you unreasonable."

"I might if you weren't so forgiving," Laura snapped. "He did nothing for us, Jack, and now he thinks he can take away what we have."

He stiffened. "I don't know how it's escaped your notice, but I'm a grown man, Laura. Your older brother. It would be nice to be treated as such, even if only once. I'd take care of Saltash, but you won't let me."

Laura swallowed.

"When do you go?" Jack asked.

"Tomorrow. Mr. Rushford is taking me."

Jack raised his eyebrows at her, but she gave nothing more. "How kind of him," Jack said. "I trust he'll drive safely."

EYES BURNING AND LIPS COMPRESSED, Laura returned to her room to pack, hating herself. Telling Jack more was impossible—

he'd never permit it, and she wasn't going to let that stop her. Besides, Jack would learn the rest from the papers soon enough. She'd face it then. This way at least she'd avoid risking a scene in front of the Bagshots who still didn't know her for Gemma Holyrood. Better for her and Jack and Jasper too if they could keep that secret.

Besides she had no words for it. It wasn't a comfortable bargain, this arrangement with Jasper, even explaining it to herself. Every time she thought of him her brain skidded to a stop. But she needed a lover to wield against Saltash and Jasper Rushford was the likeliest candidate—and that was all, she told herself squashing the maggoty guilt stirring in her middle.

Very well, it wasn't all, and she should know better than to lie to herself. Nothing wrong with the truth. Since she was finally at the point in her career where she was trading on her virtue, why shouldn't she have the man of her choice? If she was going to have a lover it should be someone she liked. He was the one who'd pursued her, after all—no need to be embarrassed by her attachment to him, Except he'd dropped her and she'd been uprooting those warm feelings for nearly two weeks now. He'd been baffled by her proposal, almost annoyed and certainly not amorous. Shouldn't he be at least a little in love with her? Feelings, at least her own, didn't change that fast. At the very least he should be pleased to have her at last.

She'd surprised him, that was all. And perhaps it wasn't so unusual, beginning this way for this kind of arrangement. There was a fair bit of business to clear away first. Laura wished she and Rushford had got a chance to settle some particulars. Ignorance was very unsettling.

Frowning, Laura rerolled a pair of silk stockings and put them in a muslin bag to fit in her trunk. This would be easier to do if she'd some experience mistressing or some answers—like where she was going to live. And when he thought the mistressing would start...

Good heavens, she wasn't a girl to take fright at the thought. Rushford had all the appearance of a competent lover. Anyone would be who'd brought indulgence to such heights of perfection. That posed another worry—she wasn't as sophisticated as she let on. She mustn't be gauche or reveal her inexperience. He'd be repulsed by that she was sure. Maybe she'd have time to speak to her actress friend, Sarah. Maman wouldn't have liked this, but she wouldn't have kept back her practical advice.

Laura pressed her hands against her skirts. She hadn't done this before, so it was natural to feel nervous, but entirely unnecessary. Jasper wasn't a novice. Follow his lead, she told herself as she stowed her brown half-boots in the trunk. She repeated the advice again as she tidied away the brushes on her dressing table and a third time when she called for a servant to cord up her trunk.

Just follow his lead, she thought, summoned by the gong for dinner. Good advice probably, but it didn't help. Jasper wasn't there.

"Where is he?" Sophy said, repeating Laura's question. "Tom?"

Tom was succinct but unhelpful. "Gone out."

By noon the next day Laura was fuming. She'd told the Bagshots she was leaving, but if Jasper didn't arrive soon she would have to relent and tell Tom that she would, after all, be grateful for the use of his carriage.

"I wish you'd give up the idea of leaving," Sophy said with a reproachful glance at Laura.

"I may have to." Laura frowned through the window at the empty drive.

"Not such a bad thing," Jack put in. He wasn't speaking to her, but his scowl had faded the longer she delayed. Now he'd relented enough to address the room at large.

Curse Rushford. She'd get to London if she had to walk and find herself a different lover there. Protheroe or Willbank maybe. Someone who kept his appointments on time.

"We'll miss you," Sophy said. Her eyes darted back and forth between Laura and Jack.

"He's here," Laura said, spotting movement at the end of the drive. Jasper rode on horseback behind a large traveling chaise. She'd expected the curricle.

Sophy came to the window. "No—oh. It is him. How strange." Sophy looked again at Laura. "This is all very strange."

"A friend requested my help—" Laura pulled out her threadbare excuse again.

"Yes, you told me," Sophy said, unconvinced. For one who'd been confined to bed not long ago she made for the door with amazing speed. Laura caught up with her on the stairs, but outside Sophy swept past her into her brother's outstretched arms.

"Jasper this is quite provoking," she said. "I don't like you taking away Miss Edwards."

"She mentioned she had to return to London," Jasper said. "And I have business there of my own."

"Business," Sophy huffed. "What kind of business?"

"An actress," he said. "If you must know."

"Jasper!" She threw a worried glance to see if Laura had overheard. Laura pretended to be absorbed in the details of stowing her luggage—it was useful too, for quashing the sudden desire to strangle him. "You musn't—"

"Say such things?" Jasper interrupted.

"If you left actresses alone there would be nothing objectionable to say," Sophy muttered.

"Yes, but think how dull I'd be. Miss Edwards, may I help you get your things stowed?"

"Nearly finished," she told him.

"Excellent. We'll be on our way. It's a bit cumbersome to travel in this overdone fashion, but I should have you to London before seven o'clock."

"Thank you, sir. It's very good of you to take me. I fear you've gone to some trouble..." She didn't feel them, but that was no reason to abandon the niceties.

"Not at all," he lied grandly, surveying the cavalcade beside them: an elegant chaise drawn by four horses with mounted postillions and two more following behind.

"Does your mama know you are using her carriage?" Sophy asked.

"No, but I'm sure she won't object too loudly. I wouldn't wish to subject Miss Edwards to any impropriety and I didn't feel it was quite the thing to drive her all the way to London in my curricle."

Laura tried not to choke.

"I'm glad we needn't give up all hope for you," Sophy said. "But Georgiana will draw and quarter you if you damage it." She looked at him sideways. "She and Father don't seem to mind each other so much anymore."

"It won't last," Jasper said. "Just because you and Tom are head over ears for each other doesn't mean everyone else must be." He turned back to the chaise, his frown vanishing as a stout, sour-faced woman climbed out of it. "Miss Edwards this is Betty Burt. She'll attend you." He turned back to his sister. "You see Sophy, I've thought of all the niceties."

A maid? Why had he brought her a maid? This one looked ominous. Laura doubted she had ever worn a smile.

Sophy lifted her face so Jasper could kiss her. That duty completed, Jasper made his goodbyes. "My best to Tom and his mother. And you can give a kiss from me to that squaller of yours. Write me once she's got better to look at." Dodging Sophy's swift punch, he took Laura's hand and helped her into the chaise, interrupting her hollow-voiced thanks to her hostess.

"Not at all." Sophy waved Laura's words away. "I ought to thank you. If you get a chance today, smack him for me?"

"I will," Laura promised.

"Shall we go then?" Jasper asked as Betty took the seat beside her. Without waiting for a response, he signaled the postillions and they were off.

THEY HADN'T GONE FAR before Laura was wishing for the curricle. She'd had no chance to speak to him since yesterday and every minute he seemed more of an enigma. Her irritation over his absence at dinner and his late arrival today got lost in a tangle of other emotions. She wanted it to be like before, the two of them crowded on the high seat as he raced around corners. They would tease and laugh and fling quotes at each other and she wouldn't wonder like she did now what he thought of her. Today's silent, decorous procession unnerved her and try as she might she could pry no conversation from Betty, who answered questions dutifully with a minimum of words. When Laura did spy Jasper riding alongside, he smiled mockingly and tipped his hat, then gave his horse the spurs.

She was so full of questions. Where had he been last night and what did he think she would do with a maid like Betty and how could he speak like that in front of his sister? Alone with him in the curricle she'd have got answers—and roasted him soundly. She needed reassurance and a good laugh. Solitude wasn't good for her. It made her brood. She'd hardly slept last night, troubled with doubts, and now she was afraid they'd never get back the friendly flirting that had come so easily before. If only she hadn't been so hasty.

"I expect you'll need to know where I live," she said, forcing herself to have courage when they pulled up for a change of horses.

Rushford didn't answer immediately; he was busy with the innkeeper ordering her lemonade. He turned to her once he was finished. "Yes, I suppose you have things you'd like sent over," he said at last. "Just give your orders to Betty. She'll see that whatever you need is brought round."

It was a faultless and vastly unsettling answer. Laura accepted the lemonade, sipped through stiff lips, and wondered where they were going and how bad it would be. After her bold proposition he wouldn't guess she was a virgin—and if he did would he care?

The remaining miles slipped by like sand in a glass while Laura imagined ways to explain she wasn't ready—just yet—to sleep with him. She thought he'd understand, but what if she'd misjudged him? He might be a sensualist behind that faultless veneer. Suppose he brought her to a vault-like townhouse with rooms of red damask and velvet cushions, exuding the jumbled scents of other women's perfume? Licking dry lips, Laura wished she'd finished her lemonade.

"Do you know where we are going?" she asked at the outskirts of London, prodding Betty awake.

"Basil Street I think," Betty said.

That didn't tell her much. "Where is that?" Laura asked.

"I'm not certain." Betty sniffed. "It's not the best part of town."

Even the maid despised her. Laura felt sick—then even sicker as the carriage swayed and stopped. She wished for her lucky garters. Or Maman. Or Jack. He wouldn't even know how to find her. How foolish of her to keep back the truth.

"Miss Edwards?" He stood with his hand out ready to hand her down.

"We're arrived? So soon?" Her voice cracked.

"I think you'd be exhausted after such a long journey," he said and Laura seized her chance.

"I am. Exhausted, I mean. Perhaps I should lie down. And take a sleeping draught," she added for good measure, trying to see where she was without gawking. The street seemed respectable enough. Clean with newer houses. But maybe Rushford was one of those who liked seaminess under a white-wash—she'd learned from other actresses about those. Men who kept stuffy-looking houses with plain fronts and brass knockers and inside the rooms had peepholes and silken bonds. No. She wasn't going inside. She'd run. She'd kick him and Betty too and race to the theatre and confess all to Mr. Rollins and Peter.

"You didn't mention you were unwell," Betty grumbled.

"Come inside." Jasper tugged on her arm.

"I can't," she said, trying to pull free. Even though the house was loathsomely ordinary it wore a sinister cast—that vanished as a small boy hurtled out the front door. He was five at most with stained cuffs, grubby knees, and a head of black hair long enough to hide his eyes. Laura reached out and steadied herself on the handle of the carriage door. Was this—Rushford's son?

"Where are we?" she asked, her voice too harsh.

"Your new abode," Rushford said, bowing. As he rose he reached out to ruffle the lad's hair, telling him to talk slower, that he couldn't make any words out of such impertinent piping.

"Is he yours?" Laura hissed, sidling closer.

Rushford started. "Lord, no! This is my cousin's boy. Master Henry Morris."

"Why is he here?" she asked, each word pounding out the same note.

"He lives here," Rushford said, turning sheepish and

spreading his hands. "This is all just—a trifle fast for me. I thought...for the time being at least...I'd have you stay with Henry's family. Just until we decide where to put you."

Laura was about to argue that she wasn't a hat, but there wasn't time.

"Come, I'll introduce you."

She balked. On one hand she felt incomprehensible relief at the sudden reprieve. But this was not what men did with their mistresses and she was only capable of so much deceit. "Do they know?" she asked.

"That you've got a Lecroy-Duplessis tacked on to the Edwards? Yes, but Alistair at least won't hold it against you. His wife, Anna, wasn't so sure but she relented once I explained that you're also Gemma Holyrood. Anna," he explained in a whisper, "is dreadfully middle class. So watch you don't snub her."

"What about Saltash?" she asked. Had Rushford reconsidered the whole plan? If he had, was she sorry?

"We'll discuss him later. No time now. Anna will be waiting." Not pausing for a reply, he took her arm and ushered her inside.

ANNA BEAUMARIS, Laura discovered, was an alarmingly beautiful woman lost in a shamble of bits and pieces spread out on a serviceable-looking carpet. "You're here," she said, smiling up at them from the floor. She pushed her dark hair away from her face with the back of her wrist. A black, sticky substance adhered to her fingers. "You must be Miss Edwards."

She stretched out her hand then drew it back and wiped at the persistent grime with a man's handkerchief. "I didn't believe Jasper when he said he could have you here by suppertime, but I had your room made up and extra places laid just in case."

"No one gives me credit for anything," Jasper said. "I'm not nearly so loose in the haft as you all believe." He made introductions and they exchanged pleasantries until Jasper cut them off. "Still puzzling over it?" He gestured at the oddments littering the floor.

Anna frowned. "It's not fitting right. And the articulated ankle wasn't such a good idea. It drags and Alistair nearly tripped on it."

"She's making her husband a new foot," Jasper explained, as if that settled everything. Before Laura could ask if Mr. Beaumaris was a complete or partial automaton, the door opened and the gentleman in question appeared—handsome as his wife was beautiful, of middling height, with tanned skin. He used a walking stick and leaned on it a shade too heavily. He wore two boots, though. "Just leather over wood," he explained, interpreting Laura's confusion. He tapped his cane against the left boot. "There's no foot in here, but it works well enough. Anna, what a mess you've made." He crossed the floor, stepping carefully around pieces of carved wood, stiffened leather and some ugly metal buckles and hinges.

"Henry helped with that," she said. "Did you finish?"

"The stanza? Yes. I'm working on a translation of Horace," he explained to Laura.

"It's the only way he'll ever get me to read it," his wife said cheerfully. "And even then..." She spread her hands.

"Anna has little affinity for the classics," Alistair put in. "But she's very tolerant of my love for them."

She grinned. "You work with the beautiful and I keep to the useful—as I hope this mess will be eventually. I'm convinced these artificial feet can be better."

"She wants me to dance," Alistair said.

His wife snorted. "I just want the thing to stay on without such ruthless tightening of the buckles. Little things, Miss

Edwards. We deal with little things here." She said it so content-edly Laura suspected it was by choice.

Even with both his legs, Alistair and Anna Beaumaris would have made an unconventional couple—her blunt manners and unwomanly interests were striking. Alistair was a model gentleman: handsome, gregarious, charming, and yet they complemented each other. "He wants to ride." Anna smiled at her husband. "Insists on it. That's why I've begun working on the legs."

"They're a long way from crutches or my first wooden peg," Alistair said, leaning back on the sofa and crossing his ankles. "This one almost looks real. By next summer I'll be running."

When Anna left the room to tend Henry her husband also took the opportunity to excuse himself, wearing something akin to Jasper's smirk as he limped from the room and softly closed the door. Jasper, grim about the mouth, got up after him to open it.

"Anna's parents live here too," he said. "So no matter what Alistair thinks my plans are you're safe here."

Two couples, a boy and servants...it was a comfortably sized house, but it was no small imposition, adding her to the list of occupants.

"I have rooms near the theatre," Laura said. "I can stay there."

"Not anymore," he said.

"Mr. Rushford—" she began.

"Jasper," he corrected. "I'm not your solicitor."

"No, you're not. Will you tell me what this means?"

He bristled. "You'd rather I took you to a quiet house and hustled you under the sheets?" His words came with a look equally sharp.

"No, but—"

"I'll play along when you're Gemma Holyrood because I said I would. But I'm not going to sleep with you."

Laura dropped her eyes to her fingers, afraid they would betray her relief with a twitch or that he would hear her hammering pulse. "Why not?"

"Because you're Laura Eduard Leroy-Duplessis. I'd have to marry you. If my conscience failed to compel me I'm certain your brother would."

She swallowed. "You know I would never—"

"Pssshh." He linked his hands behind his head and stretched out his legs, crossing them at the ankles. "I like you just fine Laura, but I'd rather we never found ourselves forced to the altar. Simpler. Besides you're my friend. Ruining you would be a shabby thing to do and I know you don't wish it."

"I—"

He cut her off with a wave of his hand. "Don't tell me you haven't been worrying. I've never seen you so green and I know you don't get sick in carriages."

"Do you mean...all along? Why didn't you say something?" Laura demanded, angry now. "I—"

He laughed. "Were you frightening yourself all this time with visions of naked flesh and satin sheets?" His eyes twinkled, kindling an even hotter burn on her scorched cheeks. She felt about thirteen years old.

"Yes I was!" Laura snapped. "And it was beastly of you to let me. Why didn't you say anything?" It was mortifying, but the agony of her frantic escape plans still haunted her.

"You weren't exactly kind to my nerves, springing this on me. Needed a bit of my own back," he said. "You can't argue that. It's only fair. And I confess I didn't think of telling you right off—too tired. Didn't catch much sleep you know, jaunting last night between here and Sophy's."

Maybe. But he'd enjoyed himself at her expense. "You tricked me," she huffed.

"Yes, but aren't you glad?"

She was, but it was too humiliating to admit it.

"Oh, come on. You can't have really thought—what kind of fellow do you take me for?" He asked lightly enough, but his eyes studied her too intently.

"You put up a convincing front," Laura said grudgingly. "I didn't see past it."

"Pots and kettles, my dear. Be careful."

Laura laced her fingers together. He had a point. And though the laugh was at her expense, she couldn't deny it was funny. Already it was more work that it was worth to keep her mouth from smiling. "Very well, Mr. Rushford. Beneath the black you're rather a dear. You're right. I was afraid."

"Not half so frightened as I! Yesterday in the garden—I thought you'd gone wild." He laughed. "I was tempted to run."

Laura made a face. "You needn't be so brutally unflattering."

He snorted. "And what was your green face all day? A compliment? I must be a prospect indeed to make a female that ill at the mere thought of—"

"You got your revenge," Laura retorted. "You enjoyed watching me suffer."

One shoulder lifted, conceding the truth with a shrug. "Perhaps a little."

"It wasn't satin, you know. Red damask and velvet. You can't imagine how sordid it was."

He winced. "You have the lowest opinion of me. I'm sure my love nest is fitted up more tastefully than that."

"I'll never know now," Laura said, laughing.

"You certainly won't." He traced an upholstered leaf on the arm of the sofa, giving himself time to select words. "Don't worry. I'll come up to scratch in other respects—I said I'd play along and I told you once that if you were my mistress I'd get you beautiful horses."

"Don't. I shouldn't have asked you," Laura said, hoping to chase away the sudden awkwardness. "Let's forget about it." It was a mad, impossible idea. And it was too much to ask of him. "There's no reason you should. You aren't getting anything from me but trouble."

"What are you talking about?" he said, aghast. "I'm getting two hundred pounds, plus the satisfaction of watching Protheroe's face as I flaunt you about town. And I'll love watching you stick it to Saltash. You can't stop the game now.

"When must you be ready for the stage?" he asked, stretching a long arm along the back of the sofa. Something about the gesture made Laura's answer stick in her throat. He was beautiful. Impossibly kind. And completely uninterested in touching her, while she suddenly was so fraught with longing that her palms ached.

An hour ago she'd been afraid of him. Now given the chance, she might have followed him into a scented den layered with tasseled pillows and silks, for she knew that any woman would be lucky to be loved by a man like this one. He was exactly the type recommended by her mother, who'd said more than once that the best loving was with a man you could laugh with. "One who doesn't make you shy, Laure. Or understands shyness if you truly can't help it. Of course, I hope you know better than that."

Laura exhaled shakily. There'd never been such a fool as she. It hurt, more than she cared to admit, knowing he didn't want her.

"Soon," she said. "I must be back on stage soon. Mr. Rollins wants me next week." She'd have to act every minute until then to hide the things it was better Jasper never know.

17

THE PLAY'S THE THING

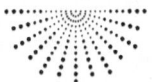

*J*asper didn't come the next morning. He arrived late, after luncheon and the arrival of a 'French' modiste.

"She says you sent her," Laura said, gesturing angrily at the woman and her samples of lace and muslin.

"Quite right. You're done with the white gowns and gold crosses." He dismissed her everyday costume with a wave of his hand. "I'm not dressing my mistress like a school girl."

Anna Beaumaris, who'd greeted the dressmaker warmly and dived into a discussion of fabrics and trim, chuckled from her seat on the sofa. Laura steeled herself. Someone had to stop this nonsense.

"Rushford—"

"That sounds dreadfully cold," he complained. "Why is it so hard to say Jasper?"

"Jasper—"

He shook his head at her clipped syllables. "Not like that. Worse than my mother."

Laura forced herself to soften in the face and hands, keeping tight in the middle lest her temper fly away with her. "Jasper."

He lost focus as she rolled the plummy syllables off her tongue. "I didn't say you could dress me."

"Better," he said, collecting himself. "Say it just that way in front of Protheroe."

"Jasper." She purred it this time, pulling from deep in the diaphragm, testing how far she could stretch each syllable. "You can't buy me clothes."

He blinked. "I'm not sure that one's for company. Save it for a special occasion. I'll tell you when."

Laura brought her glare from him to the modiste.

Jasper sighed. "Your scruples are commendable but misguided, I'm afraid. No one will believe this if I don't lay down the blunt for you. Mistresses are expensive. You are at any rate."

She could have managed a sound retort—if she wasn't choking in her haste to glance back and see if Anna'd overheard.

"He's right you know," Anna said. "No point arguing. Come, there are the prettiest things." She gestured to the row of laces she'd laid on the back of the sofa. "I like this one." She pointed to a discreet confection that looked sickeningly expensive.

"I can buy my own gowns," Laura hissed.

Jasper shook his head. "If you don't know how much Pomeroy-Jones spent on your competition last quarter you're not nearly clever enough to pull this off."

Mutinous, Laura grumbled. "I have some idea—" Sarah was never squeamish about sharing details and was shrewd and mercenary as they come.

"He dropped five thousand in six months." Jasper ignored her gasp. "The choosy Miss Holyrood can't settle for less."

Laura choked. "You aren't—five thousand—"

"I'm not setting you up in a house. There's a great cost savings there. No furnishings. No servants, save Betty. But the illusion—the illusion must be there." Nudging Laura toward the stool where the modiste's assistant crouched with tapes and a mouthful of pins, Jasper addressed Anna. "You know what I like. I don't want her dressed like some milk and water miss and I don't want anything vulgar. Short sleeves. And more décolletage. And get rid of this," he said as he flicked a contemptuous hand over Laura's gown.

"I know what will suit," Anna said.

Jasper grinned. "Laura, I've written to Rollins. I'll bring you by the theatre tomorrow. Madame assures me she can have a suitable dress ready by then."

The modiste clucked assent in her execrable sham-French. Laura winced. She wasn't reconciled to this at all and knew just how late the modiste's assistants would work piecing together a dress before morning. "I won't—"

"I'll see you at dinner," Jasper said and breezed out the door. Laura snapped her mouth shut, grinding her teeth.

"Infuriating isn't he?" Anna studied Laura's figure and compared it to the dress pictured on the card in her hand. "He's like a mosquito. Try to smack him and he buzzes away and all you've got for your trouble is a warm spot on your arm. You'll feel better if you just give in and spend a great deal of his money."

Anna, it seemed, wasn't entirely unconventional. She might spend her time dreaming up articulating hinges and fall in willingly with shocking deceptions, but when she gave it her attention she had a passionate interest in clothes. For an hour Anna worked, discarding fabrics, reserving patterns, quarreling with Laura over why she needed three day dresses instead of two.

"Fine. Does everyone know?" Laura asked, giving up on the

dress and turning to the other thing bothering her. "About Jasper and me?"

Anna's hand stopped in midair, hovering over a well-thumbed copy of the Lady's Magazine. "Alistair and I do, of course. And my parents. We didn't mention the plot to Henry. It won't go any farther."

It was shaming and ridiculous to stand like a doll with a virtual stranger reassuring her. "It's good of you," Laura said stiffly, "to keep my secrets."

Anna looked up. "Yours? I'm afraid I was thinking of Jasper." She smiled. "When he told us my husband couldn't stop howling with laughter. He said it was past time Jasper got himself into a fix and—" Anna broke off, perhaps wondering if she'd said too much. "It was rather precious to see Jasper of all people going red about the ears. At any rate your uncle sounds a perfect horror. I understand, you know, how it feels to hate someone so much you can barely breathe."

"Oh?" Laura smoothed her palms over her skirts, not sure she believed her.

Anna put down one pattern card and examined another, her face falling into a frown. "My first husband. He was..." She looked up and something in her eyes made Laura shy away.

Anna shrugged. "I understand. I'm in no position to give advice and certainly unqualified to judge, but...we'll be friends, I think. At least I hope so. You've got Jasper tangled so beautifully and you think for yourself and speak your own mind. Just do be careful. In my experience it's hard to know in the heat of anger if you're making your worst decisions or your best ones." She huffed a scarcely audible laugh. "And who can say? Life changes so fast, a single choice can even be both."

Laura didn't know how to respond. Anna rescued her. "You'd look well in this." She held out a card. "But I think scarlet braid and not the bugle trim?"

"Perfection," sighed the modiste.

"*Parfait*," Laura corrected. There was only so much artifice one could stand.

———

Jasper collected Miss Edwards early the next morning, pleased to discover she was suitably attired in blush muslin with a darker velvet pelisse. She was grimmer than Betty while accepting his compliments, but her aspect improved once they reached the theatre.

"How long shall we be?" Jasper asked. He must tell his groom when to return with the curricle.

"I'll be at least six hours—for rehearsal and I must catch up on the news."

Jasper scratched behind his right ear. Six hours was a frightfully long time.

"You needn't stay," Laura said, laughing at him. "It will be dull for you I'm afraid."

"Come back in an hour," Jasper told his groom. He bent over Laura and dropped a whisper into the chestnut curls decorating her ear. "I'll stay long enough for you to trot me around."

"Gemma?" A thick-bodied fellow with hands like bricks peered round the back of the curricle.

"Peter!" Laura exclaimed. "Did you get my letter?"

Peter sent Jasper an appraising glance. "Hmm, yes."

"Mr. Rushford, this is Peter Samuels," Laura explained. "He's been charged the last several years with looking after me."

"Yes, I recognize him," Jasper said, placing him as the lump of muscle who made threatening faces outside Gemma Holyrood's dressing room door. He wore a grubby leather vest today and was speckled with sawdust.

"How are things at home?" Laura asked.

"Well enough," Peter said. "You coming back to your own quarters anytime soon?"

"Not in the foreseeable future," Jasper answered for her.

"So I'm counting on you to keep an eye on things." Laura rested her hand on Peter's arm.

He grunted. "Fine feathers today," he said as he limped back to open the door.

"Me? Or Mr. Rushford?" Laura smiled at Jasper with a wicked gleam in her eye. It was true he'd dressed with care, but still...

"I meant you, Gemma," said Peter.

"It is a pretty gown, isn't it?" Laura didn't preen, but there was certain brazenness as she went on. "I adore the color."

Peter didn't ask why she was leaving off white, but he sent Jasper a speaking look. If Jasper wasn't minded to already, it was plain Peter intended to keep him in line.

As they passed through the door Jasper leaned over to whisper in the man's ear. "I'm concerned about Saltash."

"You know about him?" Peter asked, eyes widening.

Jasper nodded.

"I keep an eye out," Peter said.

With practiced ease Jasper slid a coin into his hand. "Keep two."

Better disposed to each other now it was clear they fought under the same flag, they followed Laura into a maze of back-stage clutter. Overall Jasper was pleased at having brushed through so far—a suitable place for Laura to stay and forcing submission in the matter of dressmaking were no mean feats—but there were still pitfalls everywhere. Should he step wrong Jasper felt sure Peter would happily punish him.

No good worrying. Tackle each problem as it comes. Whistling a flourish to keep his mood light, Jasper followed Laura around another crate into the wide cavern of the theatre.

In the vast space his whistle grew another set of legs and dashed to the ceiling. The sound silenced the murmurs of half-costumed players, toiling painters, fatigued seamstresses, and writers scribbling away with stubby pencils on cheap paper.

"Hello, George," Laura called, waving to a pair of feet dangling from the scaffolding. A long whistle from a grinning face decorated with a smear of yellow ochre answered her. The place smelled of lamp oil, sawdust, and turpentine.

"You've returned!" A man in a self-effacing suit that was nonetheless of excellent quality greeted Laura with outstretched hands.

"Mr. Rollins." She curtsied once, then lifted on toes to kiss his cheek.

"I didn't think you'd come back."

"But you're glad I have, I trust?"

"Supremely."

Jasper let his eyes wander. He'd never seen the theatre stripped like this, the mechanics exposed for all to see. The handsome Welshman Daniel Bowen, who often played opposite Laura, was deep in argument with a writer, reinforcing his opinions with profanity and emphatic gestures. A scrawny boy who moved like a monkey slid down the cables from the roof that held up rolls of painted canvases. The boy darted across the floor and pinched a seamstress's bottom along the way. "Gemma! Who's the swell?"

"Stephen. Your manners," she demurred, cuffing his badly trimmed head. The boy skipped out of reach, so Laura forgot him and turned back to Jasper. "Mr. Rushford, if you would allow me to present our manager, Mr. Rollins?"

Jasper nodded and smiled, unsure if he'd ever been the subject of such scrutiny. Every eye in the place was on him—the Welsh actor had the audacity to wink! A trio of musicians tittered and two actresses leaned together to confer behind their hands. They wore only the rudiments of historic costume, tall wigs and wooden panniers that looked especially ridiculous without the covering of an elaborate gown, but Jasper felt the urge to squirm and had to buttress himself with his own pride.

"Good day to you all," he said grandly. Rollins bustled to his side, bowed, offered refreshments, and sent the impudent boy to fetch him a chair. When Jasper had leisure to look about (before he could protest Rollins had summoned wine) Laura was talking to the Welsh actor.

It was a strain but Jasper caught their lowered voices.

"Nicely done, Gemma. He'll be good for your art."

"I'm glad you approve," she said.

"Perhaps not as good as me, but I'm taken," the actor said, glancing fondly at a copper-skinned girl busy dressing wigs set out on a table. Jasper tried not to frown.

"The rest of us must take what consolation we can find," Laura returned with a sigh. They were bantering. He didn't like it. Pointed repartee was what she did with him.

"No, really, I'm glad you're back," the actor said. "Alice does fine, but she's not as good at the back and forth patter as you. Holds herself back all the time to wait for laughs."

"She'll grow out of it."

"Let us hope." He glanced again at Jasper, nodding when their eyes met.

"I must change," Laura said, detecting the tension and moving between them. "Excuse me. I won't be long." Summoning a little girl with a hare lip, she vanished behind the scenery and made for her dressing room.

The theatre was different without the crowd, without his kind watching from the boxes. It was low, ribald, and vulgar, but...she looked so easy here and her liveliness shone. She didn't draw these friends with the same magnetism she used on the stage. The people here, from her lovely blonde rival to the boy

Rollins waved away, gave Laura smiles because they liked her. And she liked them, greeting everyone from the surly violinist to the scruffiest painter. Returning in half-costume, she thanked her understudy and the seamstresses, Mr. Rollins and the hare-lipped girl who'd helped her dress, and then sat beside him to read over her lines while the stagehands set up the next scene.

Intent on her script, testing variations of inflection and pitch, she was alive as he'd seldom seen her in Suffolk. It should have made him smile instead of feel unaccountably sad. She was part of this world and he would never be, other than playing a sleek, indulgent aristocrat who'd bought her attentions instead of winning them honestly. He was simply Gemma's patron, the first of many who would pass among them and be fleeced for every penny that could be got.

"You needn't stay," Laura told him, looking up from her script. "Peter will find a hackney for me and see me safely back to Ba—home." She stopped herself at the last moment from saying Basil Street. "Watching rehearsal will spoil tomorrow's show."

"I'm not sure that I've made a sufficient impression," Jasper said. They had an image to maintain—and he had a point to make with the Welshman. "I don't think I look devoted enough."

"I don't need you to fawn," she said.

"Is that what I've been doing?"

"No. If anything you're terrifying with your casual interest —so elegant. Sarah over there is starting to feel sorry for me. She likes her lovers in the doting style. You seem just a little too exacting. She's afraid you're too much for me."

"I hadn't realized you've had time to discuss it," Jasper said. The two of them had only exchanged a few words, but then it always amazed him how much meaning females could cram into the smallest things. "I didn't mean to come off like that. I've just never seen you in all this before." And it gave one much to think about.

"The off-hand style suits you. But I've work to do and it will be easier on everyone if—"

"I understand." He rose from his chair. Before she could protest, he pulled her to her feet and put his hands around her waist, ignoring the barrier of her wide skirts. "I'll go. But we can't have your friends feeling sorry for you."

It wouldn't do to overthink it. Besides, he'd seen her kiss men before: the Welsh actor, his predecessor Mr. Kean, and a handsome blade who'd only acted two seasons and then disappeared. She knew what she was about, even if this wasn't choreographed.

She drew a half-breath of surprise when she saw he meant to kiss her, but yielded without a twitch and let him close the last inches between their lips. She felt every bit as good as he'd imagined—better, he decided, as her arms slid up to wrap round his shoulders. "We ought to try this with you standing on a stair," he murmured. "Or in taller shoes." Perhaps then he wouldn't feel so tempted to lift her up and—

It was no good to torture himself. Even this was probably too much. Jasper moved back an inch, drew a shaking breath, and caressed her cheek with his own.

"Convincing?" he asked.

"Very." She sounded good and wobbly.

"Excellent." He raised his head. Behind her, the shrouded eyes of the company flickered away. Jasper reminded himself that patrons and purchasers didn't blush. He drew his hands along the curve of her waist—slowly, because he could and because he wanted to.

She smiled. "Not that you would ever need to, but I think you could have a wonderful career on the stage."

From her he knew it was a compliment.

THE ADVANTAGE of hurling yourself into serious rehearsal, Laura realized, was that you had no time to worry or answer questions, especially your own. She was preparing to perform and had no time to think about Jasper Rushford. Or his kiss.

Eventually there came a lull while Mr. Rollins fell to lecturing the stagehand who'd mishandled the mechanical thunder. It was the fifth time they'd interrupted this scene. Laura waved a fan over her face and leaned against the ballroom backdrop next to Sarah—Mrs. Rawlings, her blonde rival. They played it up for notoriety, but were good friends.

"Giving up the wings, Saint Gemma?" Sarah asked. "I was worried for a while there, but your Rushford looks nice."

"Nice enough," Laura said. "How are you going to play this one?" Her deception would affect Sarah, even if just in the quarrel they kept up for the gossip sheets.

"Scathing I think. The 'she's fallen at last' scorn should get me through the first bit. Maybe I'll say I pity Rushford for having to tutor you in bed. You don't mind?"

"No, that sounds good," Laura said. "It will set me up for some nice cutting responses." They shared a smile. Over the years Laura had watched Sarah string along half a dozen different lovers. She was beautiful, sharp, and completely mercenary, but had a good heart. None of Sarah's patrons ever knew that the little girl with the twisted lip who tidied her dressing room and combed her hair was her daughter. It ought to have been impossible; Sarah had birthed Kate when only a child herself. She was a careful mother though, keeping Kate close, but at a safe enough distance and depositing her patrons' largesse in three percents at a London bank.

"Now you've got yourself a man I'll have to find someplace

else for Kate," Sarah said with a sigh. She rubbed a finger beneath the edge of her wig.

"Oh, I'll—" Laura stopped. She couldn't tell Sarah she wouldn't have Mr. Rushford's company overnight, and she couldn't bring Kate to Basil Street. "You could ask Peter. He's staying in my lodgings," Laura suggested. Sarah didn't have the same friendship she had with Peter, but he might still be willing. If not, Sarah would have to find another place to hide Kate the nights she welcomed lovers. "Sorry."

"It's not your worry," Sarah said briskly, moving forward as the prompter signed for them to restart the scene. "So he's put you in a love nest already? That's good. You know you can come to me," she added, casting a tired smile over her shoulder, "if you ever need advice."

"Thank you." Sarah would know what to do when your heart skipped about too much after a bit of kissing. She would know how to control it and let the head take charge. Stretching her neck and aching shoulders (after a few hours, wearing the tall wigs hurt), Laura took her place on stage. Sarah would know what to do but Laura couldn't ask.

Pleasantly exhausted by the end of rehearsal, Laura tugged off the wig and set it aside to peel back the coarse layers of her heavy rehearsal skirts. Peter knocked on her door. "Mr. Rushford's here. Should I send him in?"

"I'm nearly finished." Laura turned so Betty, who'd arrived mid-afternoon, could button her into her gown. She was a competent maid but none too gentle.

"Are you ready?" Jasper asked, escorting her out the theatre's front door where a crested carriage was waiting.

Laura nodded. It would begin in earnest tomorrow night,

though the carriage drew plenty of eyes. They climbed inside, Betty taking the seat beside her.

"I was going to take you to Mrs. Reeves'," Jasper said, settling in the seat across from her.

"The gaming house?" It was almost as select as it was scandalous.

"Yes, but you're too tired for it," he said. "It will keep for another night. And we'll stun them tomorrow just as much as we might today."

Laura refrained from commenting on his own state of exhaustion—he couldn't have slept at all riding back and forth between London and Suffolk—and asked a question instead. "You'll come for me then, after the performance?" She expected it, but was tired enough she wanted to be sure.

"Yes," he said. "Protheroe won't know what hit him."

Unable to suppress her yawn Laura hid it behind her gloved fingers. Smiling an apology she asked, "What will you do with his two hundred pounds?"

He thought a moment. "Haven't decided," he said finally. "I suppose in the end I'll have to give it back. But for now what a joke it will be! I can hardly wait to see his face."

"Tell me about it tomorrow." Laura relaxed into the cushions.

They drove to a quiet alley where Peter waited with a second, unmarked carriage. Switching vehicles and bidding good night to Jasper, Laura then made her way back to Basil Street. She was used to these kind of precautions, but now she had to hide her whereabouts from everyone, not just Saltash. It wouldn't do for anyone to discover she stayed with Jasper's relatives.

The moment they pulled up Betty hustled her into the house. Caught between Betty, Anna, and Anna's mother (a true mother hen if there ever was one) Laura was clucked over and bundled into bed with injunctions to sleep well and soundly. Even if she were of a mind to, she was too tired to argue.

She woke in the morning to the sound of Henry bounding down the stairs. Venturing out in her dressing gown she learned there was no immediate crisis, only he and his papa were going out to sail his toy boat.

"I hope you have a fine time," Laura said, ruffling his hair in the split second before he ran off.

She spent the morning copying minutes from Anna's mother's Benevolent Society and tallying donations for their vaccination campaign. In the afternoon she walked with the Morrises and their son in the small square nearby. Anna was in high spirits, having persuaded her husband to escort her to a public dissection.

"I've seen enough gore for a lifetime," he said, "but Anna finds it interesting."

"Doctor Ferguson is so skilled, he's able to demonstrate how the hands work," Anna said happily. "You should come."

"Jasper's asked me to go driving," Laura said, grateful for the excuse.

"Maybe next time," Alistair said with a smile.

They waved Laura off in the early evening.

"Good luck," Anna said.

Laura grinned. "The correct thing to say before a performance is *break a leg*."

"Really?" Anna's look made her disapproval plain. "That's incredibly silly."

"We're a silly lot I'm afraid," Laura said.

"*You* aren't. I'll be watching tonight. Take him down."

"Saltash?" Laura clarified.

"Yes, but I wouldn't stop there. Go for the lot of them."

Laura laughed. "I'll certainly try." For a moment the empty space between them threatened to dissolve into a hug, but they held back a second too long. "I'll look for you at the curtain," Laura said, dashing down the steps to the waiting carriage. In a week or so perhaps a hug between them would be acceptable. Today was too soon.

IT WAS COMFORTING to forget herself in the familiar panic before a show—in last-minute checks, line revisions, frantic searches for stray props, and hasty costume repairs. Dan got in a towering fury when Rollins suggested trimming one of his speeches, and Alice, Laura's sulking understudy, was only partly mollified by an additional scene and Laura's assurance she was no longer required to act as her maid.

The bell rang and they hovered in the wings while Dan gave the prologue. He swept off stage to generous applause, his smile triumphant. The orchestra played a snatch of music to give them a few last seconds to organize their thoughts and take their places. Laura stiffened her spine, absorbing the voice and manners of yet another Maria—some playwrights weren't that imaginative with names.

The curtain rose and Laura plunged into brilliant light and heated air. Her heart jumped, then steadied. She was Maria, and her lines came like she'd thought of them herself.

"IF YOU'D GIVEN me more of a chance," Alice began bitterly as they exited stage left and raced for the dressing rooms.

"You'll get another," Laura interrupted. "I won't last. None of us do. You'd be wise not to forget it."

Be patient. You'd feel bad too after a burst of success that was suddenly snuffed, Laura told herself. If she wasn't careful, Alice might decide to lock *her* into a wardrobe.

No time to worry about it. Kate, hurrying from another

errand, helped Laura out of her breeches, which fit more snugly than usual. "Sorry. I've become thicker," Laura admitted. Soft living in Suffolk had downsides.

"I can let the breeches out a stitch or two," Kate said in her soft lisp.

"Don't trouble," Laura said. No harm in giving the audience a jolt. Most of them seemed to like it. Kate helped Laura into her gown and hooked her up the back, since Laura had offered Betty's services to Alice as a sop to pacify her. Laura was getting used to Betty, but Kate had gentler hands.

"Thank you, Kate." She kissed the girl's crumpled mouth, dropped a pat on her smooth hair, then slipped out and made her way back to the wings. She flashed a smile at Peter as she went and one at Dan, who lounged on a stool next to the curtain puller on the far side of the stage. No mistakes; Rollins was counting on her. The orchestra finished one piece and struck up another, so Laura took the chance to peer through a worn place in the curtain. Silly, imagining she could see clearly through that bit of ruined velvet when it was difficult to distinguish the pit from the boxes. Saltash hadn't been present in the first act but he was here now, she felt sure of it. The shadows in his box had different shapes. Her heart hadn't beat this fast during a play in years.

He was a duke; she, practically nothing, but she'd won this life of hers with skill and schemes and luck and wouldn't let some cold-hearted gargoyle steal it away. It was hers and worth guarding—even from her brother. She'd written to tell Jack of her safe arrival, but she didn't expect a reply.

Time for Maria's problems. Laura waited for a nod from the prompter, then gathered her breath as the curtain parted.

18

GOOD FUN

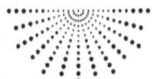

asper knew Laura's character began the second act; he even knew all the words. The orchestra's swell and dramatic crash into silence told him the moment was come. Still, as she flew into the speech he caught his breath. Foolish of him. She knew what she was about, winning them with words and gesture and feeling. Retreating behind a door in the set to generous applause, there came a check. Saltash rose abruptly, turned his back and left, followed by his baffled guests.

"Bless me, what is that scuffling?" Laura said, peeking out from the door, alerted by the stir in the audience. "Rats? Vermin?" She winked, the crowd laughed and the Welsh actor came on, starting with mock surprise at the sight of Laura, half out of her hiding place. Improvising, they fell into a discussion on rats—when the rat catcher must be called and what good people could do to convince them to leave on their own.

"Perform, my dear! Perform! Everyone knows the vile creatures can't stand good theatre," the actor said. Just as well Saltash was gone for the audience collapsed in a wave of laughter. Deftly, before they stopped crowing, Laura and her partner returned to the script. There was a comic miscommunication, a series of flying exits and entrances, then a shuddering scene change and the actors were parading back and forth in front of a painted forest. After a sword fight and Laura in breeches once again, fleeing the amorous pursuit of the rival actress Sarah Rawlings, the drama of Saltash's snub retreated, but Jasper knew the gears of speculation would be whirring again once the show ended. For such a gudgeon, Saltash had a real talent for magnifying things all out of proportion. Served him right.

Laura muffed a line late in the third act but turned the lapse in a blink and earned a laugh. "She's marvelous, Jasper," Anna whispered beside him, intent on the drama. "Are you sure you're as high-minded as you claim?"

Alistair cut in before he could reply. "If not he only has himself to blame. We'll see how long he sticks to his resolve. I warned him consciences are expensive." He looked smug.

Easy for Alistair. Anna hadn't taken too long to fall in love with him. Though they'd traveled a difficult road, at least they'd found one together. Anna adored his cousin; Laura saw him as merely useful. He'd like to see Alistair in *his* shoes—course, Alistair probably wouldn't mind being able to wear two of them. In his place, then. It wasn't a joke, bound by scruples to behave honorably while being tempted beyond what any man should have to bear. He shouldn't have kissed her. It was torment, now he knew how good it could be.

The only consolation he had was that everyone would think he was having her. A paltry satisfaction that grew feebler the longer he spent with her. Suppose the time came when he was no longer satisfied with just the illusion?

It was foolish to allow thoughts like that.

When the curtain fell the house shook with applause and not just for Laura. The company had been exceptional tonight.

"Quick," Protheroe said, rising behind him. "We'll never make our way through the crush if we don't hurry."

"Go ahead," Jasper said. He gathered himself slowly, apologizing to Anna for parting company.

"I expect we'll see you again before too long," she said, a stern slant in her brows.

"Naturally." He kissed her hand, bowed to his cousin, and struggled into the packed corridor, Boz lamenting at his heels.

"I wish you'd give over. Neither of you will win this bet. Even if she gives up that fellow in the mask."

Shaking himself free of gloomy thoughts, Jasper allowed himself a smile. True, he couldn't have everything, but that needn't stop him from enjoying this particular pleasure.

The usual sample of gentlemen clustered outside her door: tall, short, some young, some only wishing they were, specimens from the rich and titled, and some with only one of these two virtues. Even pride wouldn't let Jasper think he was Gemma Holyrood's natural choice. There was Smyth-Gordon, for instance, heir to an earldom with a reputation for indulging his mistresses. And Mercer, who, if he chose, might fill a lake with his money. Kind-hearted Protheroe was intellectual, easy with his fortune and...useless to go on, really. The point was she'd chosen him, no matter the reason.

Jasper fought his way through the press with a growing smile. At the time he'd been the only weapon to hand and she hadn't been thinking reasonably, but still...he would pass through her door and judging by the look on Peter's face, no one else would. It was something of a relief to Peter, Jasper realized. It was dangerous setting her in front of this pack of panting dogs night after night. No wonder Brother Jack was so lined about the eyes.

"Mr. Samuels!" Jasper called to Peter through the thicket of tailored coats.

"Mr. Rushford, sir! Excuse me gentlemen," Peter said, trying to clear a path to the door. "Yon fellow's—"

"Will my so delightful dumpling be receiving tonight?" Jasper asked. Ahead of him Protheroe gasped.

"Just you, sir," Peter said. The low-toned banter and jockeying for places ceased.

"What an agreeable girl," Jasper drawled. "Is she ready for me?"

In a perfectly timed answer, the door swung open.

"My, what a flattering horde!" Laura sparkled in a patterned dressing gown and the rest of her Holyrood attire. "It quite breaks my heart, having to tell you—"

"Darling." Jasper swept to her side and laid finger on her lips. "You are quite the sweetest rogue I've ever seen, but another word and you'll surely break mine. Don't make me wait any longer." He glanced back over his shoulder. Protheroe's jaw hung open. He was as dumbfounded as the rest of them.

"What happened to the other one?" some artless young pup asked.

"No others now," Jasper grinned. "Night, boys." Laura pulled him inside and he shut the door.

———

"Enjoying yourself?" Laura handed him a handkerchief.

"Exquisitely." Jasper broke off his suppressed laughter and wiped his eyes. "Even if I have to give Protheroe back his two hundred it was worth it." He chuckled again. "But maybe I won't. As a mistress you've made me exceedingly happy."

"Have you been drinking?" Laura asked.

"Only my own high spirits," Jasper retorted. "Congratulations. You were wonderful."

"So were you," she said. "That was quite a performance."

With false modesty, Jasper dropped his gaze to inspect his fingers.

"How long do you think before it will be safe for us to leave?" Laura asked.

"A few hours yet." Jasper said. "Betty, help her change into something inconspicuous so we don't draw any eyes when we bring Miss Edwards back to Basil Street." He reached into his waistcoat for a small packet. "Laura, my dear, I hope you like cards."

It was fitting, Laura supposed, that after all her frenzied imagining on the drive to London she and Jasper passed what remained of the evening squabbling like children over cards, winning and losing fortunes in hairpins while Betty nodded in her chair with her feet resting on a cushion.

"She should probably stay awake," Jasper whispered to Laura.

"I'm not making her," Laura said. "She's been up since before dawn. That's inhuman."

Jasper shrugged. "She's here and that's what matters I suppose." He didn't seem convinced.

Laura's eyes flew to the ceiling. "Aren't you supposedly impossible to seduce?"

"I'm a gentleman. I'd never say." He pretended to be wounded.

"You and I both know I'm quite safe."

"Your virtue at least. Not your pins." He laid a card that made her groan and push over her dwindling pile. "You're not very good. I'll have to watch you when we go to Mrs. Reeves'."

"Why not the one in Pickering Place?" Laura huffed, annoyed he'd tease her with absurdities. Both were gambling hells, but select for all that. He couldn't bring her there.

"Oh, we'll visit Pickering Place too," Jasper said. "Eventually. Climb our way up—or down if you like."

"Heavens. You'll be promising me a voucher for Almack's next." Laura said.

"Lord, no. I can't stand the place." Not that she'd ever under any circumstances be admitted to that temple of snobbery. "What is it?" he asked and Laura realized she was staring at him again.

"You're kind to me," she said, unwilling to hide her feelings behind a joke this time. He'd spoken in earnest—so far as he was capable at least—and you didn't expect that from scapegrace tricksters.

"Why wouldn't I be? I'm not an ogre—or at least I wasn't last time I checked. You must mention it, should you see me getting knobby round the knuckles and toes or if a hump sprouts on my back."

"I'll watch for signs." Laura dealt out the cards. "What about Saltash?"

He chuckled. "For someone so concerned about scandal he really goes about it the wrong way. If people aren't already saying you chose me over him, your bit with the rats was more than enough."

Laura smiled. "He'll be furious."

"A tight-buttoned fellow like that? He might just explode. Now there's a way to end to your difficulties. If I was a praying man—"

"Be serious," Laura said.

"Can he hurt Rollins?"

She considered. "I don't think so. Rollins has some debts from a failed show last year but trusts the man holding them. Saltash can't know of them."

"And you're safe in Basil Street with Betty looking out for you. We won't let out you are there."

"No, that would ruin things rather spectacularly."

"Not quite the sensation you were looking for? Me neither. So much more fun this way."

"You enjoy the notoriety?" Laura asked.

"Oh yes." He smiled and again swept away her cards. "Don't worry about Saltash. We'll just have to wait and see how he plays his hand."

19

HENRIETTA IS DISPLEASED

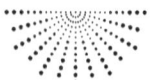

*J*asper slept later than usual after the long night at the theatre but woke to good news. There was a splashy piece about him and Miss Holyrood in the paper and a note with two hundred pounds from Protheroe. The terse phrases weren't quite provoking enough to quarrel over, but they were close. Smiling, Jasper stuffed the money into an empty mug and tucked the note into the frame of the mirror over the mantel. He had no intention of letting Protheroe call him out, but it would be amusing to look in on him. Tomorrow perhaps. Give the fellow a little time to drown his sorrows.

Jasper wasn't quite dressed when someone banged open the door.

"You!" His sister Henrietta marched toward him, flags of angry color streaming across her cheeks.

Jasper glanced at his valet and hastily reached for his coat.

"You were expecting someone else?" He struggled into the sleeves. "Really Hen, bad enough to come round here as it is, but not the thing at all if you aren't looking for your brother. I'm not even dressed. What will your husband say?"

"How could you?" Henrietta said. She wasn't as good at the

dramatic lines as Laura, but Jasper thought it prudent to move behind a chair.

"What did I do this time? Fawkes, would you—?" His valet, not needing extra urging, melted away.

"You know perfectly well. I thought you were better than this!"

Glancing at the door, Jasper wondered if it might have been poor strategy to send his servant away. Henrietta hadn't been the least inhibited by Fawkes' presence, but now that she had him alone there was no telling what she'd do.

"Calm yourself. What—"

Henrietta sucked in a breath through clenched teeth.

"Think of the baby!" Jasper interjected.

She scowled. "What do you mean, taking up with Miss Holyrood?"

"Is that all? You're supposed to pretend not to know such things," Jasper argued.

"An actress?"

"It's quite fashionable to have one of those. She looks good on my arm."

"And black eyes? Are they fashionable too? I'll make you a present of a fine one."

Jasper took another step back. If it was come to that, he'd rather she delegated the business to her husband. Percy hardly ever left his library. Though hard to rouse, Henrietta had a wicked temper and a good arm. She marched closer, fury crackling from her fingertips to her clenched chin.

"She's so alive," Jasper said helplessly.

Henrietta stopped, her chest heaving. "Merciful God," she said. "You're in love with her."

"I am not," Jasper retorted, a little too late. Laura was witty, brave to the point of foolhardiness, and dashed easy on the eyes.

She was a prize to flaunt in front of the world and a friend to tease in private. She wasn't...

"Of course you'd deny it," Henrietta said gloomily. "What's to be done?"

"You're quite mistaken. I have the situation well in hand," Jasper said quickly. Henrietta was simply overwrought by her condition and her love for melodrama. "It will be best for all concerned if you leave me alone. Go home. Some tabby may have seen you get out of the hackney."

"I drove my own carriage," she said.

"Henrietta!"

"I'm going," she said. At the door she paused, narrowing her eyes at him. "Just don't think you're going to get away with this."

From the window Jasper watched her groom hand her up into the carriage. She fixed him with one more glare, then snapped the reins. Jasper held himself together until she reached the corner when his repressed laugh finally fizzed out his nose.

If Henrietta was convinced of it the ruse was working perfectly. Nothing Saltash said could overturn his and Laura's story. Wiping his streaming eyes, Jasper sat down to record the incident in his diary. Henrietta, if she ever learned the truth, would no doubt find Turkish punishment too lenient for him, but her outrage today was priceless.

———

It was a strange and dizzying life, but Laura was used to scene changes. Mornings and afternoons she spent with the Beaumaris family in their haven of domestic contentment. It was never dull and Jasper often dropped in for a good-natured wrangle with Alistair and Anna, or to 'call on Master Henry' as he put it. Sometimes he and Alistair took themselves off for shooting or boxing or cards—despite his missing foot, Laura gathered that Alistair was a frightfully good shot. To Laura's surprise, she wasn't uncomfortable with only Anna and her mother, Mrs. Fulham, for company. Both ladies were nearly unshockable and enjoyed her stories of life in the theatre. Nor did they hesitate to enlist Laura's help with their personal causes. Between Mrs. Fulham's charity work, Anna's tinkering, and Laura's rehearsals the hours flew by. Evenings were even busier. When Laura didn't perform in the theatre, she and Jasper play-acted everywhere else, driving round the park at the fashionable hour and visiting the pleasure gardens at Vauxhall. They took in the opera and plays at other theatres, where she enjoyed the action from the vantage point of a box and the sensation she herself caused when she leaned against Jasper's arm. She wore silks and lace, plumes and jewels with pleasure, after Jasper made it clear they were only on loan. Decked out in that style it was no wonder they turned heads.

They hosted dinners for his friends at the piazza and though Protheroe initially kept away, he soon succumbed. Who wouldn't want to be part of those evenings filled with laughter? Sometimes Laura missed female company—Anna's acerbic wit went so well with her husband's, but Alistair refused to include his wife in entertainments with what he termed a pack of dissolute jackals.

"Prude," Jasper told him.

"Just so," said Alistair, drawing on the cigarillo in his fingers. He'd picked up the habit in Spain.

Laura didn't mind the smoke or the innuendo, the hair-raising language—compared to the green room this was mild. And since Jasper made it quite clear she was his, his friends acted more like, well, not brothers exactly, because she doubted their sisters heard jests like these but something like it.

Once, Alistair and Jasper journeyed together from London

to straighten some difficulties over young Henry's property. Quiet evenings in Basil Street were a welcome respite after so many nights of dissipation. Laura assured Anna she wasn't the least bored and took the chance to finally finish the novel she'd begun reading back in Suffolk. The next day she went out, accompanied by Peter, to visit Hookham's library.

She'd sauntered along Bond Street as Jasper's mistress before, but today was too cold to enjoy her notoriety, even dressed in a scarlet redingote and sables. No one lingered out of doors in this stinging wind that burned cheeks and pinched her nose. Keeping her fingers tucked in her muff while Peter held the door, Laura slipped into the welcome warmth of the library.

There were whispers from the other patrons as she cruised the shelves, but that needn't trouble her. Indifferent to stares Laura searched for something to interest her. Gothic romance? She had plenty of that already, thank you. And with Anna for company a surfeit of science. History? It couldn't be as good as Jasper's fabrications. Maybe she'd read something in French. It had been a long time.

"Miss Holyrood."

Laura looked up into a face that was almost familiar. Jasper's eyes and silver-blond hair, but dressed in ringlets. She knew instantly who this was. Jasper had mentioned his other, legitimate sister.

Laura swallowed and dipped a curtsey. "Lady Arundel," she said.

"My name is my own," the lady said. "I'll trouble you not to use it."

Laura bit her lip.

Lady Arundel didn't waste any time. "What will it cost to make you leave my brother?" Her voice, pitched too loud, trembled and summoned every glance. She looked on the brink of a lashing spurt of temper—or tears.

"My lady, perhaps we could talk somewhere—somewhere not here," Laura said. "This meeting, in such a public place, does no service to you or him."

"How else am I to meet you? Stroll down to your dressing room after tonight's performance? I won't be put off. I've been trying to catch you for over a fortnight."

Good heavens. But Jasper's family must love him. She should have expected this. "You've been looking for me?"

"You aren't hard to find on the arm of my brother," Lady Arundel snapped. "A private meeting has been more difficult to arrange. Now. Name your price."

Laura's breath left her. "My lady—"

"Whatever it is I will pay."

"I can't—" Laura began.

"You are not a fool. When will you get another chance such as this?"

"I don't expect one," Laura said.

"Oblige me then," Lady Arundel said. Her pretty mouth twisted into an unbecoming line. She had two small boys, Laura knew, and seemed to have an unfortunate eye for color. Like her brother she was distressingly beautiful. Jasper often spoke of her with exasperation or a bored roll of his eyes, but always with a strong undercurrent of affection he could never entirely conceal.

"I can't," Laura said again, feeling helpless. Even if she explained the truth it wouldn't satisfy Lady Arundel. No matter what their private arrangements were, Laura was trouble for Jasper. She felt sick.

"Forgive me." Laura curtseyed again and fled into the street.

"You all right?" Peter asked. Laura slowed so his limping gait could keep pace with her.

"Gemma wouldn't have run like that." Laura pressed her hand into her cramped side.

"You aren't her."

"Thank goodness," Laura said. It was a new feeling but she didn't question it. Pride and sneers she could withstand—easily. Love disarmed her. She knew how it felt to worry for a brother. She still hadn't heard from Jack, probably her own fault. Now she was hurting Lady Arundel. And Sophy and Lord and Lady Fairchild. Back in Suffolk they'd been so kind to her and Jack. She was hurting Jasper too, even if he denied it.

She mishandled two lines in the play that night and awaited Jasper's call the next afternoon with a hot knot of muscle bunched between her shoulders.

"Your sister spoke to me. She wants me to leave you," Laura said as they pulled away from the house in Jasper's curricle.

"And you're persuaded you should? Really, Laura. Don't let Henrietta's fidgets bother you."

"You've done enough. Saltash is beaten."

He hesitated. "He's on the retreat. But I had to buy up Rollins' debts. Saltash tried to acquire them."

There was no wind today but Laura shivered. "You shouldn't have to—"

"Someone must. Besides it's too soon for you to send me packing. Think of the gossip! When a pair is as in love as we are it should last longer than that."

She gave him an exasperated look, glad he spoke in jest. If he knew how her heart shuddered when he touched her, how tempting it was to believe his kisses were real...she was trouble for him on all counts. "I still think we should end it."

All along their circuit through the park he countered her objections—with sarcasm, with reason, and finally a blunt refusal. "No. Such a short affair is an insult to me. I'll never live that down. I want more time. Don't let Henrietta spoil our fun."

He was misguided—and not just over her. He ought to let himself be better to his family instead of shamming it and concealing his feelings behind needling and sarcasm. But he was her friend, even if he didn't know she was more than halfway in love with him. If he insisted on more time... "I will try," Laura said. "But we can't keep this up forever."

"I'm only asking for another few months! You haven't ruined me with your gambling yet. Every self-respecting man needs his mistress to at least try." He brushed a finger across her cheek. "There now. Enough frowns."

Her throat grew thick with something absurdly like tears as she lifted her face to his. He bent to kiss her. This time it was different than before. Her lips were hunting; his met hers almost fiercely. The hand she threw up to his shoulder clutched him with a nearly desperate grip—until the carriage lurched forward.

"Inexcusable," Jasper said, breaking away and tightening his grip on the reins. "Tempt me no more, darling. I must mind the horses."

20

LADY FAIRCHILD IS DISPLEASED

When her husband blew in from his morning ride, nipped about the ears and nose, Lady Fairchild greeted him from her place on the sofa, curled up in the cushions frowning over a crumpled newspaper. She'd crushed it in an angry fist earlier but now had smoothed it out, ready to tackle the problem calmly. She hoped.

"Cold?" she asked her husband, handing over her cup of chocolate without glancing up from the page. No matter how she stared the letters stayed the same.

"Thanks." He gulped it down and returned the cup to the tray. Georgiana moved aside long enough for him to fit himself on the opposite end of the couch, then put her feet in his lap.

Ugh, he had cold fingers. "Jenkins brought up your letters," she said. Generally she didn't care for informality, but she'd grown comfortable with this arrangement of sitting together in the mornings. William reached for her unfinished piece of toast.

"What news?" he asked.

"It's cold," she said—meaning the toast, not the outdoor temperature, which was hardly news. Pursing her lips, she smoothed the page again, trying to decide how to phrase this catastrophe. William couldn't know about it—he read only the racing news and political items, not the society pages.

"Miss Matcham is engaged," she said, deciding she needed to work up to it. "The elder one."

"That's good," William said as he chewed. He brushed the crumbs from his fingers, sprinkling them onto the carpet. Then he shucked off her slippers and began massaging the web of sinew and bone preceding her toes.

"That tickles," she said, toes curling.

"Don't be squeamish," he said, pressing harder. Once she softened it did feel good.

"Our son's found himself a mistress," she said, furious with herself for filling her days with William, Sophy, and the new baby. She'd been so busy it had been weeks since she'd glanced at the papers. A costly lapse. Gathering from today's tidbits, the identity of Jasper's mistress was a long-established fact. And she'd thought to ignore him for making off with her traveling carriage! A convenient mistake—for him.

"What? Let me see," William said, craning his neck to see the paper. "Who's Gemma Holyrood?" he asked.

"You've seen her. At least a half-dozen times," Georgiana explained. "She played Lydia in The Rivals last year. We saw it with Alistair."

"Brown curls?"

"Sometimes," Lady Fairchild said. "If I had to guess I think that's her real color." Hard to say when onstage she wore so many wigs. "We could ask Jasper."

Her husband snickered and Georgiana hit him on the arm.

"This isn't a laughing matter," she said.

"I know," he said, sobering instantly.

The news troubled her. She had keen social instincts, sensitive as cat's whiskers. Over the years Jasper's name had been casually linked with any number of dashing widows—but only in whispers. This flashiness was new for him. If she believed the paper he was besotted, gloating over her at the theatre, bringing her to dine with his friends at the piazza, and letting her squander money at a long list of gambling hells. Georgiana sniffed.

"He's too old to lose his head like this," Georgiana said.

"Come now. You wouldn't like it even if he was younger."

"Nor would you," Georgiana retorted.

His shoulders sagged. "Not now. I'm wiser than I once was." He shook his head. "I don't like this, but I've no right to condemn him."

He looked...defeated. She had to do something. "We don't know it's true. Maybe it's just talk," she said while thinking, *Talk?! My eye!* Even William didn't look convinced.

"I'll write," Georgiana said. "Going to London and reading him a lecture might be satisfying to imagine, but—"

"When has he ever listened to either of us?" William finished for her. He laced his fingers together. "Society will say he deserves what he gets if he's fool enough to let some actress get her teeth in him. But—" He sighed.

"I know." She pressed his hand. "Demanding the truth from him will only add fuel to his fire."

"Perhaps if I write and invite him to come home for the shooting—"

"No, he'll see through that. I'll write Alistair instead. He'll tell me how the wind blows."

It took the two of them four attempts to compose a satisfactorily-worded letter. And the tidbits in the paper only got worse each day they waited for a reply. Even Sophy was wise to it now —she didn't read the society pages herself, but her mother-in-law, Mrs. Bagshot, seemed to read nothing else. It was very trying, accepting the commiserations of that kindly, dumpy woman and worse still, when Georgiana found herself blinking back tears and biting her lip.

"Forgive me." She dabbed her eyes. "I should know better than to bother over trifles." It didn't feel like a trifle, though, not to her.

Apparently Mrs. Bagshot agreed. She clucked over Georgiana and held out a handkerchief.

"People say girls are easier. I wouldn't know. I had a hard enough time raising my boy. They are a trick to handle, even the best of them."

Georgiana composed herself. "I suppose I should ignore it or pretend not to know. Men have their foibles."

"Pssssh!" Mrs. Bagshot said stoutly. "You didn't stand for it from His Lordship!"

"Well, I—" Georgiana began weakly, but stopped, mesmerized by Mrs. Bagshot's wagging finger.

"Don't let fear stop you from saving your son's soul. He's a good sort but won't stay that way now he's allowed the devil to lead him astray."

"I—I'll try," Georgiana said, more awed than she'd admit by such vehemence. She avoided Mrs. Bagshot after that but did mutter a few prayers under her breath when she went to church on Sunday, trying not to feel silly.

No miracle came: Miss Holyrood wasn't struck down by a carriage, Jasper's name peppered the newssheets as much as ever, and he answered his father's letter saying he was too busy to come to Cordell for the shooting because '*London is so amusing these days.*'

"You should go there and thrash him," Georgiana said.

William massaged his temples. "He's not a child anymore, Georgiana."

"He is! Ours!" she shot back.

"I know." He took her hand wearily. "Let's go together."

But the next day Alistair's letter came.

Dear Aunt,

Naturally you're concerned for Jasper given the fuss that's in the papers. Don't be. I've seen the situation up close—

"Does that mean he's met her?" Georgiana asked.

"Presumably," William said, reading over her shoulder.

—and I can say the news you're reading is exaggerated. All is not as it seems.

He closed with his best regards.

"I don't want cryptic reassurances. Or regards," Georgiana fumed. "I want him to kidnap that trollop and put her on a ship to Australia!"

"We mustn't overreact. Alistair would tell us if there was cause for worry."

True. Georgiana tapped her fingers on the arm of her chair.

"These things don't last long," William assured her.

"Oh? What about the Duke of Clarence and Mrs. Jordan? Twenty years and ten children!"

"You're catastrophizing."

"Jasper's twenty-six. He's never shown more than an idle interest in a female."

He gave a defeated shrug. "Maybe we should be glad—he needs a heart."

She couldn't argue that but unlike William, she wasn't sure this was the way to grow one. Nothing good could come of it.

21

DEEP WATER

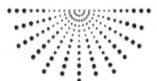

*E*verything was going beautifully, but Jasper still found daily occasion to curse his interfering sister Henrietta. Laura felt guilty, even though she hadn't said as much. If he wasn't careful she'd end it. He kept a smooth face but inside he was starting to panic.

He couldn't lose her. He hadn't even taught her to ride yet. Yes, there were advantages to the curricle—for one thing it gave him an excellent excuse to keep her pressed against his side. But he was very taken with the image of them riding side by side on horseback and it took time to train a competent horsewoman. At least a year. He must persuade her to try riding.

Perhaps he should marry her. She couldn't get rid of him then even if she wanted to, and if they married he could do more than kiss her without feeling guilty about lying to Brother Jack. Lust and guilt were horribly incompatible motivations. And exhausting.

For Laura he thought he could be an agreeable husband, something he'd never believed possible for anyone else. Apart from the growing temptation to bed her—the kisses in front of her friends at the theatre must stop if only for his own sanity—

he liked her. In fact there was no mood in which he didn't like her. When she was stricken with guilt over his siblings or hers, he felt tender. When she was cross about him buying her furs, he wanted to tell her just how fetching she was in them. When she slid her arms up his back as he kissed her, he wanted to hold her more often. Every hour would probably suffice. And when she trod the boards captivating hundreds...well, that was the problem. She was so good at it, loved it, and he liked her too much to take it away.

Marrying an actress was scandalous but not unheard of. Of course if his parents didn't expire from shame they'd shun him forever—but the title and Cordell Hall had to come to him. His father had no choice about that. Marrying Laura was an excellent idea if only to spite them, but he knew she'd never agree. Actresses might on rare occasions marry their noble lovers, but afterwards, without exception, they left the stage. No man of his class could let his wife parade in breeches in front of half of London and kiss villainous Welshmen. Jasper didn't particularly enjoy watching those kisses now, but some things one had to endure. Even if he could get her drunk on love words, blind her with kisses, and somehow get her to the altar she would regret it. Eventually she'd see him as another Saltash and the marriage would fail. He'd rather lose her than live that hell himself.

He'd known he would lose her from the beginning. It was coming—but please, not yet.

In spite of his resolve to spare himself the torment of kisses, Jasper lingered on her lips when he collected her from rehearsal that afternoon.

"Vauxhall tomorrow, I think," he said as they climbed into the carriage.

"With your friends?" Laura asked.

"I haven't spoken to them. There is some kind of gala, but we'll go to dance. Give the tabbies something to whisper about. You can show off your new Vienna green silk."

She agreed with a smile.

"And enough excuses," Jasper added. "I'm going to teach you to ride." He felt much better, knowing he had time.

THEY DROVE out to Richmond after rehearsal to argue the merits of the latest play and say admiring things about the changing color of the leaves—as if either one of them cared about that. Hopefully he wasn't serious about teaching her to ride.

Laura wasn't as troubled anymore, not since she'd decided to pretend. It wasn't real, this romance, but if the world believed it to be she too could suspend good sense for a while. If this imaginary affair was all she would get from Jasper, she might as well enjoy it to the full. Besides, you needed to pretend to act convincingly.

Yes, it was odd, night after night, having your lover return you to the care of his relatives after flirting scandalously all evening. But if you ignored that, and the ever-present Betty, you could convince yourself he was softening, that his gaze held real attraction, that he kissed you because he couldn't not kiss you, instead of just playing to the crowd. She could let herself be in love with him, so long as she kept the secret to herself.

It was so easy to like him. Jasper was in many ways her romantic ideal. He was fair, with crystalline blue eyes, and elastic wit. He was clever...and he was speaking to her. "Hmm?"

"If you like I could speak to Protheroe and the rest. Or

perhaps we could bring along Alistair and Anna." To Vauxhall, she realized, surprised he was still thinking about it.

"No, I think it would be marvelous to go alone," Laura said, meaning it. If they could just lose Peter and Betty... "But if you could put Protheroe in the way of my understudy, Alice—"

"She still jealous? It's an idea but no good, I'm afraid. Protheroe only wants the unattainable."

"Pity," Laura said.

———

THEY'D VISITED Vauxhall Gardens before but not through the water entrance. It was worth the trouble, Jasper decided. Even he was charmed by it: quiet boats nosing through dark water that reflected blossoms of lantern light from the gardens. Ashore more enchantments worked, strains of music and winking lights luring them in.

"Quite a picture," he said.

"Isn't it?"

She made a fine picture herself, but since she couldn't help being aware of that, he refrained from commenting. A moment like this couldn't stand too many words.

They disembarked, shadowed by Betty and Peter, and progressed along the promenade to one of the supper booths for chicken and ham, salads and punch. Jasper mixed the punch himself and though it wasn't as strong as the infamous brew served by the house, it must have fuddled him.

No other explanation for his actions. Even for the sake of their deception it was foolishness to feed her strawberries and let her dab away crumbs from the corner of his mouth. Without other company they drifted on the music, nibbled delicacies, and refilled their cups until she stopped and looked at him. Such tender eyes—though he knew the glance for the work of an actress, his heart stumbled. They were silent, like two skaters on the ice waiting for it to crack.

She could have asked him about horses; he could have searched out an acquaintance in the passing crowd. "Will you dance?" he asked without thinking, before the moment was gone.

It wasn't his best idea. Instead of distracting them, the music and chatter was muted by the clinging tension between them. As they moved through the set, his heart galloped to a precipice each time he stretched out an arm for her hand. Confronted by the thick gloss of her hair, the slope of her ivory shoulders, he hummed along with the orchestra to distract himself—a detestable gaucherie he'd never stooped to before. Perhaps she teased him, but she hummed along, smiling dreamily.

Let it be real. Or else let her not see so she won't laugh at me.

"Forgive me. I'm being an ass," he said.

"I like the music," she said as she floated away to the next gentleman in line. Jasper tried to smile at the new lady on his arm, but wished desperately the dance was a waltz.

All Jasper was prepared to say about the music afterward was that it was long and he was thirsty. He drank another glass of punch. "Let's walk," he said, setting down his glass and staring purposefully at the crowded promenade. Was she reluctant? At any rate she followed the pressure of his arm. As they cleared the last dancers she looked back, just as the violins in the orchestra raised their bows again. "Oh, may we—"

You couldn't deny a breathless request like that. They danced again: an old fashioned minuet, a boulanger, two waltzes, and a quadrille. After that, giddy and flushed and laughing, they escaped into the dark, forgetting to see if Betty and Peter were behind them.

"I've used up about six years' worth of dancing," he told her.

"I'm not sorry. You should do it more." She fanned her face

with her hand—what had become of the one she'd carried? Perhaps she'd left it on the table.

"Maybe I should." It was certainly one of the safer ways to end up spent and laughing with a woman. He glanced sideways at her as they walked. She looked warm. He liked the way color suffused her cheeks, the cadence of her quickened breath that made her skin flutter against the neckline of her gown.

She was chattering—something about the theatre involving Alice the understudy and a misplaced prop. He didn't hear. Her words were chimes, incomprehensible when he was lost in the expression of her face and the movement of her fingers. Above them marched a watchful moon, but they were shaded by scalloped leaves with the noise of the revels dwindling away behind them. He stopped walking. She turned to look at him and the words were gone, though her lips still held the shape of the last one to fall. He couldn't stop himself. Soundlessly, like a crocodile rising from torpid, silty waters, Jasper reached for her with his mouth.

She dropped one graceless sound, shocked by the sudden attack, but that was all. Then she sank into him, her velvety lips soft on his own. He wasn't sure if it was her arms or his, but they coiled tighter. Then tighter still.

"No audience here. Least none but me."

Shocked into stillness, it took Jasper a moment to turn his head sideways, confronting Laura's keeper, the breathless but implacable Betty.

"You promised, sir, that my work would always be respectable."

Jasper stepped back and passed a hand over his mouth. Laura was right in front of him, but he was afraid to look. He kept his eyes on Betty.

"You'd best tell me if things are going to change. I don't like walking into this," Betty said.

"Of course not. Forgive me," Jasper said, hoping Laura would know the words were meant for her too. He passed a grappling hand through his ruffled hair. "I wasn't thinking. Let the game run away with me after all the dancing."

"Too much punch, sir?" Betty offered.

"Betty..." Laura began.

"I dare say she's right," Jasper said with a weak laugh. He turned to Laura. "Are you as fuddled as I am?"

"I suppose I am," she said shakily. "Last time I let you mix it."

"We'll stick to lemonade," he said firmly. "Safer." He took Laura by the hand. "Best I take you home now. Sleep it off."

They kept up a brightly ticking clockwork conversation on the voyage back. Jasper attended with only half an ear. He was thinking and none of it was comfortable, so he dodged those thoughts and began cataloguing. He'd let the atmosphere confuse him. There couldn't be romance here. Not between the two of them. The enchantment he'd felt back there was mere intoxication, just as this was only Thames water and not a black, secretive sea. Their barque was a simple rowboat with creaking oars and this sky was one of a thousand others, even if it seemed immense and flat and sprinkled with dust-mote stars. Laura was Laura: Jack's sister, charming friend, clever actress, and only that.

22

FAULTS AND FIXES

*S*ome troubles didn't blow away no matter how aggressively you threw your horse over ditches. Though sticky under his shirt and sore in his legs, William didn't go back to the house. He needed the balm of his stables, warm with the smells of hay and horses.

The horse he called Mandana had velvet ears, a whorl of white beside her right foreleg, and she nudged fondly at his shoulder, lipping his sweat-dampened hair. Working a brush like it would smooth the turmoil in his mind and not just comb dust from his champion mare, William groomed her until his arms ached. The rhythm of his hands distilled his thoughts, as always, but today it did not comfort him. Georgiana was worried. So was he. Every day he heard more of Jasper's affair and every bit of it was troubling.

Easy to think, given this second chance with Georgiana, that the mistakes of his past were behind him. He had his wife's forgiveness and her love and was hopefully wise enough to keep both. The difficult chasm separating him from his youngest daughter was gone. Sophy was learning that he'd always loved her, despite his failings as a father. He was making ground with her and Tom; his past mistakes no longer cast such long shadows. But Jasper was in trouble—if not now, then soon—and there was nothing he could say to his son.

Almost as long as he could remember Jasper had used that curling lip and contemptuous eye. He wore it well, but it had been disconcerting on a ten-year-old boy. Even then Jasper never listened to sermonizing. He would laugh and remind William of his own faults, and none too gently either. Jasper wouldn't take correction any kindlier now. In the eyes of Society he hadn't done anything terribly wrong. Actresses were an acceptable pastime for gentlemen; William was the one who'd ruined an innocent.

A bead of sweat rolled alongside his nose into his eye. William rubbed his face against his sleeve and blinked away the sting. A man of twenty-six like Jasper ought to understand his father wouldn't wish him to repeat his own mistakes, but it would be easier, so much easier, if he could counsel his son from a blameless position. Bent double, brushing caked mud from his horse's fetlocks, William clenched his teeth and ignored John Whitsall's cough at the front of the stables.

He hadn't realized till now all he'd thrown away that day he chose to ignore his conscience.

As dirt crumbled away a different awareness intruded on his thoughts; it was quiet now, the only sound the sweep of his brush. John and the lads were silent, their feet and forks still. Puzzled, William threw a glance over his shoulder and straightened at once. It was Georgiana, holding up her skirts as she minced over the straw on the floor.

"Miss me?" William set down the brush.

"Yes, if you must know," Georgiana said, trying without success to protect her beaded slippers. "I expected you an hour past."

"Worried on my account? You spoil me."

"Why are you doing that?" Georgiana asked. "You're filthy."

William shrugged. "Helps clear my head." It wasn't his habit to worry but when he did, it was best done here. "Next time I'll send a message. You needn't fret yourself." Usually he remembered her need to know his whereabouts, but today unhappy thoughts had distracted him. William reached for the rag hanging over the edge of the stall and rubbed his hands.

"You're just making your fingers dirtier," Georgiana said. "What's the matter?"

He didn't evade. "Jasper. I want to make things right, but—"

"I know," she interrupted, lowering her voice.

"We shan't be disturbed," William told her.

Georgiana looked around. The stable boys were already gone. John vanished into his cupboard of an office. "Did you make them evaporate?"

"You did." He smiled. "They're smart enough lads. They know only a reason of particular importance would bring you here. I expect some of them have never seen you before." He leaned a shoulder onto the partition dividing the stalls.

"Yes, well—" Her face changed and she broke off. "I came only to find you."

"Normally you send for me. I expect," he said blandly, "they gather you've an important matter to discuss."

Georgiana turned a beautiful shade of pink. Mastering a grimace, she said only, "I suppose it would be foolish to expect them not to notice the change."

"Does that upset you?" he asked. She was skittish about scrutiny of their changed relationship. He understood. She was proud and didn't want to be humiliated again.

"It shouldn't. I've been thinking...well, there's no need to be a coward. I should like to visit Henrietta sometime soon. With you."

Coward? That was his flaw not hers. It had taken him so

long to move past old grievances. "It has l
we've seen her and Percy," he said in a neu

"You'll come then?" she asked.

"You know I will." It was no hardshij
side. The servants knew the truth and the
thinking Sophy and Tom hadn't winkled
visiting Henrietta—together—was differe
pretend nothing had changed if they did tl
—" William began.

"I'm not proposing to make a vulgai
anything. Let Henrietta discern the truth—
at least as clever as your grooms." It was l
obliquely over important things, but he cou
thing like this.

"Are you saying you trust me?" he aske
her directly.

Being Georgy she only nodded. "Henrie
already. Sophy would tell her I think. But I
like to see for herself and—"

He wanted to hold her but knew she wo
salt-stained face and grubby hands. Later, l
away plans to catch and disarrange her.

"—our children at least should know."

William abandoned his good intentions. Sl
seized her, but that was all.

"Come away from here," he said, trying to
of the crowded stall.

"I'd much prefer that," she said, breathles
go. "If we are to make a spectacle let it be just a l

He laughed. If they weren't going to worry a
talk, he must immediately carry her somepl
hygienic...

"Probably no one will notice us once we g

said. \
She fe

"I
and tl
wife's
but h
pullir

floor.

him,"

I
moth
troul
"Ma
prese
displ
son.
expc
but
didr

her,

her
to s
on
cor

of
my

William made a noise he hoped sounded like agreement. It so good in his hands and—

ondon already has Jasper to stare at," Georgiana finished en William was thinking again. About his son, not his perfume and her warm skin. Sober now, he let go of all er hand and thumped onto a bench by the tack room, g her down beside him.

What can we do? I don't like it," he said as he stared at the "Till now, Jasper's always been discreet."

He misses Sophy. And Alistair. And I think we've upset Georgiana ventured. "Perhaps he's doing it for spite."

was possible. He'd always had a keen instinct for riling his er, one of his favorite sports. But there was another more ling possibility, one that had driven him to the stables.

be he loves her," William said. It certainly was the image nted to the papers. He couldn't remember such a blatant ay of a couple in love from anyone—it wasn't at all like his Jasper was elusive, impenetrable as a blizzard. He did not se his feelings. Perhaps this was a game, merely for show, hat too was distressing. Even if she was only an actress, he 't like to think Jasper could be so false or cold-hearted.

I thought of that too. It will be a terrible mess if he loves but correctable if she's merely avaricious."

'Buy her off?" William suggested.

"Henrietta already tried. We could as well, but if he loves he'd never forgive us," she said. "I hope, though it pains me y it, that this affair is just a sordid thing of physical passion both sides. Even those, of course, can have unfortunate sequences." She didn't look at him.

William studied the straw stuck to his boots. "I've thought peaking to him—but how can I? He need only remind me of own mistakes."

"You could be perfect and he might not listen," Georgiana said. "We still must try. He's worth the trouble."

"Suppose he fathers a bastard of his own?" William asked. It was one worry, but there were others. Jasper might marry her. Or cast her aside and find a new ladybird to flaunt about town. Both possibilities felt like his own failures. He should have raised his son better.

Georgiana looked down at her hands. "Whatever happens, whatever she is—and I fear she's a female of the worst kind—she must not be ill-treated. If there is a child..." She stopped, rear-ranging her fingers. "I'll ask Jasper to give it to me. You won't be providing more bastards, but I could make heart-room for another if need be." Her chin fell, but after a moment she gathered herself and was brisk again. "A needless worry I expect. Don't women of her class usually avoid that?"

William stared at the wooden wall opposite. "She's an actress, not an innocent like Fanny was. If she's clever she'll get herself with child any way she can. Nice little pension for her."

Georgiana's hands tightened. "Then I don't think we can afford to wait. Better to do something, isn't it? Even if we get it wrong?"

William couldn't say. He wanted to believe her but knew how closely catastrophe could follow the slightest misstep. "Let's speak to him. We've sat on our hands long enough."

———

THEY SET out early next morning. Georgiana sat facing her husband, clenching her hands inside her sable muff. She reminded herself there was no reason why carriage travel should affect her. Then they lurched again and her stomach heaved in protest. She closed her eyes.

"Will a little air help?" William asked, reaching for the window.

She wished it wasn't necessary to concede, but— "Open it a crack." Hot bricks under the toes only kept their heat for so long and the day was too cold to have outside air whistling around the carriage. William hadn't dressed very warm. "You should have brought thicker gloves," she told him. "Come and put your hands in mine."

He switched to the seat beside her and it felt a little better to clasp his fingers and lean against his shoulder.

"Just keep your eyes on the window," William said. "Fix them on something distant. The horizon or faraway trees."

It helped. Somewhat. She hadn't eaten but still felt like she was on the brink of disgracing herself.

"Wish I could recall this girl of Jasper's," William said. "Then I could guess better if she's likely to be amenable to offers."

"Everyone has their price," Georgiana said.

William grunted. "Jasper appears infatuated. I'm sure if it comes to that the price of her leaving him will be expensive. You don't mind?"

"It can't be helped."

"Is she beautiful? It would be some consolation if she were beautiful at least."

Georgiana heaved a sigh. "Not tall. If it's not another wig, brown hair like I told you. Chestnut, really, with gold glints in the right light. Not sure about the eyes so I suspect they're of a muddy sort of color. It's the spacing that makes them lovely. Wide and with the eyelashes painted so they look even larger. Darker complexion but she remedies that with powder. She's quick on her feet and enviably graceful in her movements—has to be in her profession. You've seen her as Lydia Languish and Titania and in *School for Scandal*—as Maria I think—and I expect you've seen her as Viola in *Twelfth Night*—" Georgiana stopped. Viola, of course, made her think of her goddaughter, little Ollie, who would have come visiting today with her mother, except they were posting off to London...

She took a sharp breath. "Would you say Miss Edwards is tall? Dr. Edwards' sister?" Georgiana sensed she was on the brink of something important—something almost tangible, just beyond her buzzing fingers.

"Not especially. Pretty though. I like the way she moves. Restful in a sickroom."

Exactly. Georgiana steadied her breath. "I think we need to turn around."

William reached under the seat. "I thought I might need to provide for this eventuality," he said, pulling out a bucket.

Georgiana waved it away. "No, I don't need that. We need to turn around."

"I thought we'd decided on London?" William said, surprised. "Yes, I'm afraid of doing the wrong thing, but—"

"I just realized something." Georgiana kneaded her forehead with a thumb and two fingers. "I need to think." William rapped the roof with his walking stick and they rolled to a halt.

"What is it?" William asked her.

Miss Edwards had brown hair. She held herself beautifully and sometimes, when she troubled to, she could snare eyes with the way she walked and spoke and moved her fingers. She never put herself forward, but when you looked close you noticed the lovely eyes. And when she laughed it was music that filled a room—or something even larger. "Yes, we must turn around," Georgiana said. "I'm not feeling at all well. I need to see Dr. Edwards."

23
DESPERATE MEASURES

Jasper never cared for morning visitors, especially after finding his bed between the hours of three and four in the morning. "Tell Alistair to go away," Jasper groaned and hid his head under the pillow.

A moment later his valet returned. "Mr. Beaumaris says he'll wait."

"Clunch," Jasper muttered. There was no help for it. He reached for his dressing gown. Stumbling into his sitting room, disheveled and bleary-eyed, he glared at his cousin for daring to present himself neatly dressed with a cheery face at this ungodly hour. "What do you want?" Jasper asked.

"I've put off telling you, but it's been weighing on my mind. I've had a letter from your mother," Alistair said.

"Got her shift in a twist?" Jasper asked.

"Don't be rude." Alistair glanced at the valet. "I don't suppose you could bring Mr. Rushford some coffee?"

"I'll have ale," Jasper corrected. "And a beefsteak." He wanted to scowl and gnaw on something. In the meantime he must wait, so he crashed onto the sofa with the force of a felled tree. "What did you tell Mater?" he asked. He'd known she'd try to poke her nose in eventually. He just didn't want to deal with it today.

"No need to worry," Alistair said, limping to the window and fiddling a moment with the blind cord. "Yet."

"Don't be inhuman—" Jasper begged in vain, flinching as Alistair tugged up the blind and soaked the room in jewel-toned November sunshine. "Must you?" He threw up an arm to shield his eyes.

"We need to talk," Alistair said, finding a chair. Propping his cane on one arm, he laced his fingers together. "How do things stand between you and Miss Edwards?"

"Damned if I know," Jasper retorted. "If you want a reasonable answer come at a reasonable time." After that disaster the other night...

"You're always with her," Alistair replied. "I can't get you alone."

"No reason in the world why you couldn't ask when we're together," Jasper said, ignoring Alistair's darkling glance.

"Maybe I should just ask her," Alistair said, but Jasper wasn't going to be bothered by threats.

"Do that. And then tell me. I'd love to know what comes next." Jasper couldn't see Alistair, having turned his head towards the cushions, but he heard him shift in his chair.

"You could end it you know," Alistair said quietly. "Perhaps you should."

Jasper's eyelid twitched. Without a dark room and another four hours of sleep he'd find himself smacked with a blinding headache. It hadn't been an easy week since that unfortunate kiss at Vauxhall—not for him at least. Both he and Laura were pretending it hadn't happened, that it was no different from him kissing her at a gambling hell or at the theatre. It was though, and not speaking about it made it nigh impossible to think of anything else. Kissing her in dark corners wasn't part of their pact. He'd broken his promise to Jack and there weren't many remedies for that.

Perhaps Alistair was right. Laura had said she wanted to be done with him. Saltash was leaving her be—couldn't very well do anything else. It was time to end the game. Jasper knew it but stubborn fool that he was, he didn't want to say those words.

It was a troubling discovery, one that chaffed him as he met with his tailor and dined at his club. When he collected Laura after the performance and she asked, "Where to tonight?" he had to manufacture a smile.

"Jermyn Street." They'd gambled there once before.

Behind the prim facade of the house writhed a scintillating glitter of coin, dice, and flashing cards against a backdrop of scarlet hangings and green baize. Whatever the hour a forest of candles lit the rooms for gamesters drifting about, like ornamental fish trapped in a shallow pool. As before Laura was pinked out in jewels and lace, laughing as he swept her past the guard at the door, sheltered in the warm place at his side. They both knew what to do. He played with her fingers and she leaned on his arm as they ate supper, teasing each other as he cut her morsels of chicken and signed for more champagne. He sipped it slow, not emptying his glass.

The drink was delightful but the evening flat. He stood behind her at the tables, trailing his fingers down her back, reaching around her to place his counters on the wheel, with a perfect view of her breasts he couldn't even enjoy, so dogged was he by guilt. His responses to her sallies were late and it was work, doting on her for the benefit of the crowd. Jasper watched roués and desperate men, lacquered prostitutes and defiant ladies, all trying to fascinate and look invincible. He felt sick. For once he longed to admit life had trammeled him completely. Lowering his eyes against the glare, he tried to guess how much longer it would take to lose the stake he'd allotted for tonight.

"Aren't you feeling well?" Laura whispered, her breath sweet with champagne. Beneath her powder, a sun shower of freckles hid on her cheeks.

"Not particularly."

"Then let's go." When the delirious spinning of the wheel slowed and the ball clattered to a stop, she picked up her remaining stake and led him away, their fingers linked loosely at the very tips. "You," she said smiling back at him, "ought to be in bed." It was nicely pitched for the benefit of the uniformed major traversing the room beside them.

"Be gentle, Miss Holyrood," the major said. "Rushford looks fagged to death."

"Greenaway," Jasper said, acknowledging and dismissing him with a nod. As they parted ways he muttered, "Damnable man."

"Are you cross with me?" Laura asked, slowing again.

"No. I have a head tonight."

"You should have said something," Laura said. "We needn't have come."

Usually he liked this. Usually it came easy, laughing, touching her and making it look careless, acting like she was his own. God, what a mess.

"Pardon?"

Damn. He'd said the last bit aloud. "I need to be outside." He motioned away the attendant and roughly fastened her cloak. Pulling her by the hand, he broke through the door into the cooler dark, pursued by music and vapors of scent. Ignoring the nearest hackney he towed her down the street.

———

Something's wrong, Laura thought, stumbling after him. "You forgot Betty," she said.

Jasper swore. "We'd better go back."

"First you should tell me what's the matter." The nighttime chill whisked past her cloak and gown, snaking round her ankles.

Jasper pressed his hand against his forehead. "I think—have you heard from your brother?" he asked, changing tack.

"No." She'd written again last week, but forgiveness—or even a reply—hadn't come.

"You see?" he said. "This is no good. Why hasn't he written? I assume, under other circumstances, he's a regular correspondent."

"You must know why," she said. "He's angry with me. For coming back to London—and for taking up with you."

"Yes. It's wretched for him, for all of us."

She bit her lip. "I thought you were enjoying yourself."

He laughed, a sharp stone bouncing away down the cobbles. "Oh, very much. You think this is easy for me?"

He made it look that way, but—

"It's torture," he went on, "playing at seduction and returning you to Basil Street each night."

Fear left her in a rush. Her breath caught and her heart surged, borne by winds of hope. She could face anything, so long as it wasn't indifference. Stepping near, she laid a hand on his arm. "Torture? It needn't be—"

"It's impossible," he broke in. "Treating each other like pets, flirting like mad, pretending it doesn't affect me at all. I'm a patient fellow, but not bloodless, Laura. I've had enough. I can't do it." He hunched his shoulders against the wind and stuffed his hands in his greatcoat pockets.

Laura dropped her hand so it didn't hang stupidly in the air. He was talking too fast for her, his emotions galloping past too furiously to check. She stared at him, licked her lips.

"You'll just have to marry me," he said.

"What?" Laura reeled.

"You're too good at acting. I want you, but damned if I make a liar of myself to Jack."

As proposals went she couldn't have imagined anything as wretched as this. Who wanted love when it came with a white flag? You didn't love the overlord who conquered you—you fought, even in defeat. They would be miserable long before his heart turned against her. She must end it. Now.

"How romantic," she said, her syllables lubricated with disdain. "Marriage. Dare I hope my wishes come into it?"

"Don't tell me—I don't need to know if it's real for you or not. If you act like it is I won't know the difference, Laura. And if you pretend long enough, your heart will begin to believe. It's happened to me."

Her stomach turned. "I won't—"

"Try." His lip curled and she was almost glad. Anything was better than that hasty pleading. "Perhaps it doesn't work that way for professionals? Well, dear one, I said I wouldn't know the difference. Humor me."

"I will not." She stepped away and clutched her cloak tighter, fighting the burn in her eyes. "You've no right to be angry with me. I made it plain from the beginning that—"

"Yes. But I didn't exactly plan for this."

"I'm sorry. What you ask is impossible." He must see that.

A muscle in his jaw twitched. He looked away. "And what about my heart's bleeding?" Yearning words, but they came with a sneer.

"The last thing I wish is for you to suffer," Laura said. "I do not forget all you have done on my behalf. We must end this. Give yourself time and you'll find someone else."

"She won't be you," he said.

"You'll be thankful of that."

He grimaced. "I suppose I will. Give me my farewell. You'll

forgive me if I don't linger in London? This time, I don't think I'll be capable of joining in as the world laughs."

He reached out and she stiffened, sure she'd break if he touched her.

"Miss Edwards!"

"Ah, our faithful Betty," Jasper said, dropping his outstretched hand and turning to the white-faced maid jogging down the pavement. "What of your counterpart? Where is Peter?"

"Gone to fetch a hack."

"Excellent. You will convey Miss Edwards home—no, Laura, you needn't fear. I won't inflict my odious presence a moment longer than necessary. I'll see you into the carriage, but I shall walk."

A small mercy, but one was grateful for those after an earthquake. It took all her discipline to compose herself until she was handed up into the carriage. Even then, she couldn't slacken, not even the smallest joint of her fingers. It took an age to drive back to Basil Street, but Laura knew she'd be straining to keep a smooth face for many days to come.

24
MAKING REPAIRS

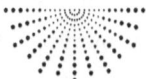

ool. You should have planned it better.

Watching the hackney vanish into the night, Jasper knew he would have ample time for the cruel pleasure of reliving this moment and pretending he spoke better words. He might win her in his imagination a hundred times and it wouldn't matter—he'd failed when he had the chance.

He stumbled and caught himself on the stone coping of someone's front steps, pausing so his breath would settle. He knew better, but hoped that a quiet spell would dim the light dancing in front of his right eye—making his way home was impossible when he couldn't see. He'd get lost or wander into the clutches of footpads. In London they were never that far.

The invisible band ringing his head tightened. Jasper squeezed his eyes shut, wishing for darkness but instead getting an explosion of light that sparked from one side of his head to the other. Staggering, he retched until he trembled, then wiped his sour mouth with sweat-dampened hands.

Fool. He could do nothing else, so Jasper sagged against the steps and let himself sink down to the ground.

———

LAURA HADN'T CRIED—MUCH. But she looked like a fright and her throat was sore when she finally braved the sitting room.

"Good morning," Anna said.

"Sorry," Laura replied. She'd accidentally let in the cat.

"He goes where he wills, that one," Anna said, unperturbed by her mother's cat, but frowning at the stack of illustrated pamphlets in front of her. Laura was afraid they might have something to do with digestion. She'd done her best with a roll and some butter, but thinking about it wasn't helping.

"It's time for me to go home," Laura said.

Anna glanced at the back of the chair nearest the fire, then to Laura again. "You can't!" Seeing that Laura's expression didn't soften, Anna tried again. "Why?"

"Jasper asked me to marry him," Laura said.

"That's wonderful!" Anna forgot the pamphlets and the cat and jumped to her feet. Yowling, the animal streaked to the farthest side of the room.

"I said no," Laura said.

"Oh." Anna reached behind her, hunting for the chair she'd heedlessly pushed away. She sat down. "Why?" Her hands reached for a bit of wire she'd left on the table, twisting it unconsciously.

"It's impossible. You know what I am," Laura said, choosing the simplest explanation.

"Rubbish," said someone from behind the chair. Alistair. Laura turned scarlet.

"Laura believed we were private!" Anna hissed.

"Aren't I allowed to say anything?"

"No," Anna told him.

"I think it's a pity you refused him," he said, rising to address Laura, laying aside a battered book. "I quite fail to understand this sudden attack of conscience and surrender to convention. Really Laura!"

"We wouldn't be happy together," Laura said. She hadn't expected to fight a rearguard action, which must be why she was doing it so badly.

"I suppose not since you've decided it. Shall I walk round and stop him from blowing his brains out?"

"Alistair!" His wife tried to frown at him.

"It's kind of you but quite unnecessary," Laura said stiffly.

"He'd do no such thing," Anna added.

Laura pinned her lips together, not wishing to say that if she hadn't sworn never to set eyes on him again she wouldn't mind inflicting some physical harm. Alistair broke the silence by reaching for his walking stick.

"Well, I can tell I'm not wanted. Anna, dear, try to persuade her," he said, managing in spite of the limp to stroll from the room.

Persuade her to stay? Or marry Jasper? Probably both, Laura thought sourly. They were lunatics, the whole family. Self-sufficient, dictatorial...and since she had no intentions of marrying—or speaking with Jasper again, it was impossible to remain in Basil Street. She was still wrangling with Anna when Alistair came back into the room.

"I haven't changed my mind," Laura told him. Why was he back so soon? "Did Jasper shoot himself already?" Alistair had only absented himself a few minutes.

Alistair ignored her sarcasm. "He's sent a message for you." He stood aside so a grave-faced Peter could enter the room.

"Mr. Rushford sends this with his apologies," Peter said, holding out a folded note. "But Miss Laura...you should know he's not well."

"How so?" she demanded crisply, unwilling to muster sympathy.

"I went round to his lodgings last night after bringing you home. He wasn't there. Found him not two blocks away from Jermyn Street, weak as a baby bird and casting up his accounts."

"He hadn't drunk that much," Laura said, disgusted.

Peter shook his head. "Not drink. He's down with a megrim."

"A migraine," Anna, ever one for details, corrected. "Thank goodness you found him."

"Lucky he wasn't robbed. I helped him home, but he's still laid out in his bed and no signs of getting out of it."

Blood drained from Laura's face.

"It will pass," Anna said, glancing at Laura. "They do. But in the meantime," she glanced at her husband, "I should go look in on him."

Alistair nodded, explaining for Laura's benefit, "He gets headaches, you know. Has since he was a boy. Recovers after a day or two in bed, but in the midst of an attack even scents make him vomit. He can't stand light in his eyes and sometimes he can't even see."

But he's safe now, Laura reminded herself, shutting out the picture of him in a dark street, blind and crippled by pain. There was a tinny whistling in her ears, but she shook it away. Thank goodness he hadn't been angry with her—some of that outburst must have been pain. If he'd been himself, he would never have proposed. Never. Yet even as she thought it, hope trickled into her. Perhaps if he'd been well he might have asked better, with the words and the gaze—and the kiss—that would have convinced her.

Stop. She mustn't imagine anymore. No matter how he asked, her answer must remain the same. She'd burdened him enough. It was wrong to permit him to shoulder her troubles for a lifetime. She couldn't ruin any man, let alone one she loved. Used to love, Laura corrected, forcing herself to remember the spiteful words—that had been forced out of him, she knew now, on the point of intense pain.

Enough. Thinking wouldn't make this better. "You said there was a note?" She stretched out her hand to Peter. The sounds of her breaking the seal and unfolding the paper were the only ones in the room.

Laura,

 Forgive me for last night. I wasn't myself—in fact, I'm quite unwell this morning.

Laura snorted, furious at him for diluting the facts. Quite unwell? She hoped Anna did physic him. He deserved every one of her teas and leeches.

"This isn't his writing," Laura said.

Peter grunted. "He dictated it to his valet."

Anna gave a displeased hiss. "I will see him at once."

Laura turned back to the note.

Please don't allow my behavior to rush you into any decisions. My offer still stands, but I'd like another chance to put it to you. Perhaps in a week? I shall be better in a day or so, but expect you'd prefer more time than that before we consider the future once more. It's not much time, but perhaps if I am lucky my worst gaffes will be forgotten—or at least the pain I've inflicted on you will have worn off. In a week I shall put my case to you, if not eloquently, at least rationally.

 Yours always,

 Jasper

Silently Laura folded the letter, remote from the hasty arrangements Anna made with her husband and son.

"I will meet you at the theatre," Peter told Laura as Anna

trundled him out the door. Laura nodded, but couldn't say exactly what she'd settled with him. It was a relief two hours later to leave Basil Street for the theatre. Troubling, though, that she expected less drama there.

"I HOPE you aren't thinking of Rushford," Sarah said after afternoon rehearsal. "It's no good when you start wearing that look."

Laura looked up from the props she was fruitlessly rearranging, sorting by size, by color. The paste jewels marched across her velvet-lined box neat as a row of cabbages. "I'm not pining for him."

"Sure." Sarah dragged over an oval-backed chair of faded brocade, sitting herself sideways on it so she could rest her clasped hands and her chin on the back. "It generally helps if your men believe you've fallen in love with them, but actually doing so isn't very kind to yourself."

Laura glanced at her out the edge of her eye. "Does everyone know?"

"Dan and I expected it right from the first. Rollins didn't say so, but I say that's just his wishful thinking."

Laura gave a wan smile. "I'm in a fix, aren't I?"

Sarah was too kind to agree. "Maybe you shouldn't have waited so long. When dreams grow too long, pruning is hard, never mind uprooting. I want you to be all right."

"I will be." Laura tried to displace wistfulness with a deep breath. "I've cured myself of love before." It was just as well, Laura decided, that she wouldn't see him for a week. She'd need at least that long to think of a way to refuse him. She probably shouldn't let him ask. It was kinder to both of them.

"I know you have." Sarah rolled her cheek onto her soft arm, pale except for a scattering of golden freckles. They were the tell that gave away the relationship between her and her daughter Kate, but with Kate the freckles glittered like the kiss marks of angels across her snub nose. "I don't blame you for losing your heart to him. If you hadn't got him first, I wouldn't have minded him myself."

Laura gave a weak smile. "How is Sir Eustace?"

Sarah wrinkled her nose. "Adequate. I'll keep him around. For the time being I've no better prospects."

"Trouble?" Laura asked. It would be a relief to think about Sarah's problems instead of her own.

"He wants to see me more. I'm not sure if it's the prelude to an extravagant gift or the end—sometimes I think I wouldn't even mind." She sighed. "He likes to stay overnight."

Sarah was expert at begging favors without asking, so Laura knew what came next. She didn't mind. "Rushford's gone for a week. Let me look after Kate for you."

"You certain?"

Laura was. Sarah looked tired. She never slept well when her gentlemen insisted on resting in her bed too. "Of course I'm certain. I've missed her. Unlike you I like the sound of someone else breathing in my room." She'd missed it since her mother's passing, but Sarah would think she meant Jasper.

"You're an angel," Sarah said.

Laura just smiled and told her to make sure Kate brought her toothbrush. It would be a relief to mull things over in her own rooms instead of Basil Street, with Anna and Alistair trying to prod her round to their way of thinking. She might be already partway to forgiving him, but she could never accept him. She should begin as she meant to go on and use this week to put distance between them. By then Jasper would be in his right mind and her refusal should come as a relief.

It wasn't hard to send Betty with a note to Basil Street to let Anna and Alistair know she would spend the night in her

rented rooms not far from the theatre. As there was no performance that evening she and Kate slipped out the back door with
the stagehands, peeling away from them in the bustle of the
market and walking the half mile to Mrs. Goodwin's trim
boarding house. Relieved to find everything as it should be,
Laura spent the evening crouched beside Kate on the hearthrug,
cutting dolls out of paper and toasting bread and cheese over
the fire. Thank goodness for Kate. Laura knew she'd be
surrounded by damp handkerchiefs if she'd had to sit here
alone.

"Will it be safe for me to go home to Mama tomorrow?"
Kate asked. She spoke quietly because of her malformed lip, but
Laura was used to leaning close.

"I expect so. If not I'll keep you here with me." Laura set
down the scissors and unfolded a row of ladies in wide, old-fashioned gowns. She had red marks on her thumb and finger from
so much cutting, but Kate's laugh made it worthwhile. The girl
sprawled out on her stomach, chin on one hand, coloring gowns
and faces on the ladies with some of Jack's old drawing pencils
that Laura had rummaged out of the back of her desk.

When at last sleep began dragging the long fronds of Kate's
eyelashes, Laura peeled her out of her rumpled dress and
wrapped her in the heavy nightdress Sarah had sent along in her
basket. The hour was late; Laura decided this once they could
forgo conversing with the toothbrush and slid Kate into her
mother's empty bed, her cheek round and golden as a bun from
the oven. Soon the child was asleep. Laura sat in her own bed
thinking of Jasper and missing her mother. And Jack.

Her bed felt small after Chippenstone and Basil Street;
she'd become used to more and thicker pillows. Piling them
behind her back she tried to read, propping her book against her
bent knees until her stunted candle flickered a plea for mercy.
She snuffed it with her fingers and let it live for one more day.

Wishing Jack's new home was not so close to Jasper's, Laura fell asleep.

KATE WAS an early riser and a sturdy eater of Mrs. Goodwin's oatmeal. When her bowl was emptied down to the shine, Laura offered to walk out and get the child an orange since she'd already dispatched Peter to fetch her things from Basil Street.

"Stay put, mind. You can draw in the rest of your dolls."

Kate promised so Laura got herself buttoned and bonneted, tucking back her hastily pinned hair as she ventured into the street. It was good to be back in her own rooms, Laura decided. The same fruit seller hawked wares at her usual corner, so Laura lingered, telling as much of the truth as she could to explain her absence—she'd been in Suffolk with her brother, who was setting up his medical practice there. Bargaining merely for old time's sake, Laura left with three oranges instead of two. She'd have one herself and tomorrow, when she collected her things from Alistair and Anna's home, she'd give the last to Henry. Clutching the bright globes to her stomach because she'd forgotten to bring a basket, Laura hastened home, her boot heels marking time on the pavement. The errand had taken longer than planned and she didn't want Kate to worry.

She glanced down the street and saw no traffic but a wagon heading the other way. Laura cut across the road, jumping over the clogged gutter onto the opposite pavement. Ahead of her a smocked laborer trudged along. "Pardon me," Laura said, darting past him. She was nearly home, just three more houses, busy imagining her apologies to Kate, when something slammed into her shoulder. Her arms flew wide, one hand catching the wall. Before she could steady herself, she was shoved into the brick, fire igniting her palms and right cheek. The oranges rolled like toys down the street.

"Wha—" A thick hand—none too clean, for she tasted dirt and salt—silenced her and cut off her air. Heaving against the wall, she writhed and twisted, trying to catch his palm between her teeth or jam an elbow into the bulk behind her. Pulse hammering, desperate for air, her thoughts grew loose and thready. She kicked again and was answered with another shove. Feeling for his feet, trying to gouge a heel into them, she crunched into bone, but won nothing. Panic rose in her throat and black fog curled in front of her eyes. She shoved again and the seal over her mouth broke long enough to her to gasp and fire a strangled cry. She flailed again with her elbows. "Help!"

Dim above the pounding in her ears, she heard footsteps.

"Hold there!"

Thank God, she thought, as the grip around her slackened and was gone. She fell away from the wall. Hoarse and gulping air, her eyes cleared and she swayed into the arms of her across-the-road neighbor, Mr. Perkins, a solid man who kept a cheese shop. "My boys are after him," he said, nodding after his two pursuing sons. They tore after her assailant and vaulted into the traffic on the next street. "Are you—"

"I'll be all right," Laura interrupted him. She forced her fingers to let go of his shirt and tried to rub feeling back into her arms.

"He didn't steal your purse." Perkins stooped to pick up her dirty reticule. It was torn and looked like it had been stepped on. "I hadn't much in it," Laura said. A few coins. A handkerchief. Rouge and a hairpin or two. She swallowed.

"Nice thing, young ladies being assaulted in the light of day. What's the world coming to?" Perkins' glare scoured the street. Laura tottered forward, her feeble steps recalling him. He slipped an arm beneath her shoulders. "Let's get you inside."

. . .

LAURA TRIED to minimize the fuss. She didn't want to alarm Kate. But Perkins repeated the story twice to her astonished landlady, Mrs. Goodwin, and then his sons returned sweaty and red-faced to say the ruffian had got away.

"I'm just glad you saw and came to help," Laura said, wincing as Mrs. Goodwin pressed a wet cloth to her bleeding cheek. "Thank you."

"We'll watch for him. You be careful now." Perkins left her to Mrs. Goodwin and her pot of salve.

"Smells but it works a real miracle," she said, dabbing the greasy ointment over Laura's cheek bone. "Give it a few days and no one will know what happened."

Steadier now Laura realized she had a problem she hadn't considered. "Kate, dear, will you fetch my mirror?" Solemn and round-eyed, the girl complied. Laura raised the glass and winced. Well, Alice would be pleased. There was no way she could go onstage tonight.

Aided by the sympathetic Kate, Laura changed into a clean dress and sat down to write a note to Mr. Rollins, ignoring her unsteady fingers. She spattered the sheet and had to start over twice. She was rattled but it would pass and sooner the less she attended to it.

She'd talked herself into quite a state of fortitude by the time a liveried messenger arrived. Puzzled, Laura opened the note. Her confidence shattered.

It was from Saltash. She read it again, her damp hands leaving spots on the paper. Kate, sensing her distress, went still as a startled rabbit. Laura looked up. The footman was gone. She raced to the window, but already he was halfway up the street, his powdered hair and gold-crusted coat clearing lowly maids, draymen, and errand boys out of his way.

"What's wrong?" Kate asked, her voice quavering.

"Nothing." Laura said, suppressing a shudder as she heard Saltash's cultured vowels reciting the note.

It's a pity you are too indisposed for tonight's performance. The crime in this city is shocking. Just think...suppose he'd carried a knife?

She must send for Peter.

PETER CAME BUT NOT ALONE. Jasper and Betty were with him.

"He needed to know," Peter said, cutting off her protests.

Jasper reached for the note. "You can't stay here." He folded it away into his pocket.

She didn't want to, not now, but returning to Basil Street was unthinkable. What if she brought danger to Anna? To Henry?

"Perhaps a hotel," Peter suggested.

Jasper shook his head. "Too public. Too easily found."

"Then where?" Her voice was high and tight.

"The theatre for now. Give me a few hours. I'll think of something."

"And Kate?"

"She'll be safer with her mother. We'd best go," Jasper said.

"Wait." She and Kate were mostly packed. It had helped pass the time as they waited for Peter. Some few things remained, but it would take only moments for Betty to add them to the baggage. "I must do one thing more."

Jasper didn't understand at first when she sat down and picked up her pen. "Letters? Now?" he asked.

"It's for Saltash," Laura explained, scratching against the page.

My dear uncle,

Bruises heal. Forewarned is forearmed. A pistol will take care of any ruffian with a knife.

"That's the spirit," Jasper said and she felt a little better. But not much.

25

CROSSING SWORDS

*T*heir arrival backstage, with Laura in bandages and a hair-raising story besides, added a new measure of havoc to the preparations for the evening performance, but Jasper was pleased to see Rollins took the matter in stride.

"Alice will go on for you tonight, don't fret yourself," he told Laura. "The prime concern is your safety. Mr. Rushford is right," he told her. "Stay here until we have a safe place to hide you."

Unless he coerced her into marrying him first, his lodgings were out. Given his way he'd take her to Suffolk, but he wasn't sure how that would play out. "I'll sort it out," Jasper promised her. "I won't be long."

Squeezing her hand, he took himself off. Since he had no better ideas, Jasper went to Basil Street. After hearing the news, Anna and Alistair, like any pair of brave fools, said there was no reason Laura couldn't stay on.

"No one knows she's been here. If she stays in and avoids the theatre, no one will find her. Meanwhile we'll soften her up for the Grand Apology. I trust you're working on it?" Alistair asked.

Jasper stopped pacing. "Right now it's the last thing on my mind. She'll never agree to come here. Think of the risks. You might not mind on your own account, but what of Anna's parents? And Henry?"

"How's your head today?" Anna asked.

He waved away her sympathy. It didn't hurt, not exactly. He felt the strain and distress of Laura's bruises and her defeat, yet had no solution for any of them. He'd like to slap a glove in Saltash's face, or better yet, mill him down in a flurry of fists, but —"I'll come up with something. I'll let you know. Thank you for all you've done. A thousand times over."

"Tell us if you change your mind," Anna said and they let him go.

He drove to his rooms on St. James Street without an answer presenting itself. Wearily, he let himself in, glad at least to see there were lights in his windows. If he was lucky his valet had put out supper on the off chance he came home to dine. Thinking would be easier on a full stomach. Jasper stepped inside, reaching over to put his hat on the sideboard.

"Good evening."

Jasper jumped, his eyes darting to the chair by the fire. "Father?"

Lord Fairchild was there, but not in the chair. That was occupied by Jasper's mother. She didn't look pleased.

"Mama." Jasper bowed, ignoring his dry throat. "To what do I owe the honor?"

"Your mother and I—" Lord Fairchild began.

"William. Please allow me," Lady Fairchild interrupted. "We are concerned—" Seeing him forming a retort, she broke off and tried again. "Jasper. Lord knows your father and I have done everything wrong, but I thought you had more intelligence. Must you?" She uncurled her fist from a crumpled newspaper. It was a scandal sheet with his name on it.

He would have laughed if he wasn't stung by the sight of it. He didn't have time for his mother's social agonies today. He must find sanctuary for Laura. If he could. He must get rid of his mother. Fast.

"Mama. How ungenteel. You know as well as I do that everyone has a fancy piece. No harm in it."

She snorted. "We can debate morality later. The weaknesses of your sex aside, I doubt if the gentlemen you refer to make a habit of recruiting mistresses from their family's circle of friends."

Jasper froze.

"Yes, I'm talking about Laura Edwards, or Gemma Holyrood as she calls herself. I've spoken to her brother and I know the truth. You can stop gaping at me."

He closed his mouth.

"I take it you've really done this thing?" Lord Fairchild asked, more stern than Jasper had ever seen him. He hesitated too long. His parents exchanged a look.

"It's not what you think," Jasper said. "And at any rate, it's not your concern."

"Not my concern? Why, pray—" Lady Fairchild's eyes narrowed and her mouth contorted in a minatory twist. "Miss Edwards is a friend of your sister's—*a guest in her house*—and you—"

Lord Fairchild reached out a restraining hand, but Lady Fairchild pushed him away. "William, may I speak to him alone?" she asked, drawing steadying breaths.

"I think I should stay."

"Very well. But you will both have to endure some plain speaking. The thrashing, if it comes to that, I leave to you."

Lord Fairchild bowed.

Before his mother could unleash the promised fury, Jasper sauntered to the liquor tray. "I'm being inhospitable. Forgive me. Father? Mother?" He offered it to needle her, but she only shook her head. "You both came up to London, I take it, on my account. Lord, but it's touching. I'm amazed you didn't kill each other on the drive."

"Jasper," his father warned.

"What? It's a bit rich, this lecture from the two of you."

"Neither of us is perfect," Lady Fairchild said. "But you are our son. We want you to be happy."

He laughed. "Happy? How vulgar. And terribly uninteresting. We are above such things, surely? Misery can be so elegant. Just look at the life you've made with Papa."

Her nostrils drew together. "I was selfish. I didn't think—at the time—that my quarrel with your father would make more than ourselves unhappy."

"You could have seen if you'd cared to look."

"I'm sorry. I know your father is too. Don't make our mistakes."

Jasper peered into his glass. "Remarkable. Am I to understand you've forgiven him? After twenty years?"

She fixed Jasper with a steely eye. "I have."

Jasper pushed his lips together. "Why?" he asked, bracing himself.

"Because I love him."

"We may have been fools," Lord Fairchild said. "You don't need to be."

"Wonderful." Jasper turned to the fireplace to spare himself the sight of his father actually possessing himself of his mother's hand. It wasn't an escape—he could see them watching him through the mirror over the mantle. Jasper dropped his eyes to the fender. "And what about Fanny Prescott? I expect you loved her too—or told her so at least."

His father started, but Lady Fairchild stilled him by squeezing their joined hands. "That's a matter between him and me." Rising from her chair in a rustle of silk, she came to stand at Jasper's shoulder. "I'm sorry. I know you loved her."

He snorted and brought up his glass to gulp down the rest, but she stopped him with a hand on his arm. Drops sloshed over the edge, slapped onto his fingers, marred her skirt, and fell with a hiss into the fire.

"Of course you did," she said, forestalling denials. "How could you help it? You were eight years old. Fanny was merry and pretty and loved both you and your sister for she missed her own siblings terribly. Did you not see the fat letters she wrote them, week after week?"

"I was eight," he said, half-strangled.

"Yes, and you would have outgrown it quite naturally, given time. It was a charming way to first lose your heart, don't you think? You were such a dear boy. I didn't realize until after Fanny left what her disappearance meant to you. I'm afraid—" She took a breath and then another. "I was jealous. Even my children wanted her more than me."

Jasper said nothing, but he felt her struggle to frame words.

"I was lonely," she said finally, her voice low and dull. "Everything I did pushed you further away. I told myself I had no right to complain—much—when you pushed back. I've been a wretched mother, but I didn't always want to be."

Cruel retorts, a good half-dozen of them, jostled on his tongue. He knew how to make her flinch and he relished it. But looking round he saw there were tears rimming the roots of her lashes and her voice was thick in a way he couldn't remember hearing before.

"If you've turned hard-hearted," she said, "it's because I forced you to be."

Jasper set his glass on the mantle with a click. "You flatter yourself," he said. "Give me the credit. I'm exactly the person I wish to be."

His father, cutting in on an admonitory tone, fell silent at a look from her. "I don't believe you," she said. "You are better than you let on. What about your sisters?"

"What about them?"

"You suffer agonies over them. You let Sophy badger you into bringing her to us. You helped her elope and made friends with Tom for her sake. You write Henrietta every week. And every year there are new flowers planted on your brother's grave." She turned away, hiding her face to wipe the wet from her eyes. "I know it's you," she said. "Who else would bring Julius pebbles and empty robin's eggs? Who else but you knows when poppies bloom and when it's time for meadow saffron?"

Jasper let out a trembling breath and fixed his eyes on the frame of the mirror. "Why should that matter?" he asked.

"You are too good for such sordidness, Jasper. Besides the fact that Laura Edwards is Tom and Sophy's friend and that we may very well owe Sophy and Ollie's lives to Dr. Edwards, you are too good to dabble in the dirt."

"Laura isn't—"

His father stepped forward. "We're talking about what you are doing with her, not the girl. She's Edwards' sister. You can't trifle with a girl like that, no matter—"

Jasper laughed, dodging past them both to the other side of the room. "You've got this wrong. It isn't a tragedy. It's a farce."

Lady Fairchild steeled herself. "I don't care what you think it is, I just want it to stop. You cannot be so selfish. I don't care if it's actresses or widows or whores, but I won't have you using any woman and breaking her heart, especially when the woman in question has taken tea in my drawing room!" Her voice rose as she lost control, loud enough to rattle the lamps.

Jasper glanced at the ceiling. "A little more gently, if you please. You'll bring down the chandelier."

Her hands convulsed at her sides and she let out a groan of frustration unlike any sound he'd heard her produce before.

"Better now?" Jasper asked.

"Not at all. I—" She broke off, shaking her head, closing her arms around her chest. "Never mind. William, I'm going to speak to Miss Edwards. I recommend you join me. While it's satisfying to imagine, I don't imagine thrashing him will do any good."

"He deserves one," Lord Fairchild said.

"He doesn't think so. That's the trouble." She moved to the door. Her sorrow, tinged with contempt, stung him.

"You've got it wrong, you know," Jasper said. He didn't believe her when she said she didn't care if it was widows or actresses or whores. No one was a stickier stickler than his mother—if you overlooked her affection for Sophy, that is. Less sure of himself now, Jasper licked his lips.

"Oh?" She glanced back, one hand resting on the frame of the door.

Flushed with defensive anger, Jasper scowled. "I haven't ruined Laura Edwards. She's been chaperoned this whole time. And as for breaking her heart—well, hers is quite intact." Jasper swallowed. "In fact—"

"Yes?" his mother asked, the sculpted eyebrows rising.

She'd begun it—this time for disgusting confessionals. The truth would serve her right. Jasper took a breath. "I'm afraid she may have broken mine."

If he was expecting pity, he didn't get it.

"Chaperoned?" Lady Fairchild asked. "How?"

"I don't believe it," his father said.

"Ask Alistair. Laura's been staying with him and Anna. You say you've spoken to Jack—well, I told him from the outset I wouldn't harm her. It's not my fault if no one believes me. Ask

Betty, the maid I stole from Cordell. Why do you think I needed her?"

"I don't presume to understand your doings," Lord Fairchild said, his face hardening into a shard of ice. "Why you would trifle with an innocent woman of gentle birth after seeing the wreckage of my own mistakes—"

"Enough, sir!" Jasper could do flint faces too. "I'm perfectly conscious of your errors. I have scruples even if you don't. The world thinks Laura and I are lovers. We aren't. I haven't bedded her or any woman."

Shock washed all expression from their faces, turning them into twin effigies. Jasper swallowed. "Fondled a few, but I haven't ruined a single one."

Lord Fairchild's eyes narrowed. "What about Mrs. Forsythe?"

"No." They'd stirred up talk two years ago, but despite her determined pursuit, he'd escaped with his honor intact.

"Mrs. Delacourt?"

He shook his head, surprised his mother had heard about that one. It had been a near run thing.

She tilted her head, intensifying her scrutiny. "Lady Foote-Harding?"

"Mama!" he said, revolted. "No, no, and no. I told you there hasn't been anyone! May we leave it alone now?" He had things to do—like figuring out where on God's green earth to put Laura. "I'm afraid I must ask you to excuse me. I'm rather busy," he said.

Ignoring his folded arms and pointed glance at the door, Lord Fairchild settled himself into a chair. "All right. I believe you. But why the pretense?"

"Miss Edwards asked for my help." Jasper explained about her feud with Saltash.

"Yes, but how did you plan to end things? Surely you must have thought—" his father said.

"I wish you'd grant me a small measure of privacy. I'm seven and twenty, you know."

"Not until April," his mother retorted.

Jasper glared.

"You honestly didn't think how it would end? Well, more fool you. There's no decent way out of this for either of you," Lord Fairchild said.

"There's one. I already asked her to marry me—save your hysterics," he said, frowning his mother back to her post on the arm of his father's chair. "She refused me." He waited for the sky to fall but neither spoke. Impatient, Jasper went on. "Mortifying for me, naturally, but that's neither here nor there. At present the larger issue is Laura's safety."

His father cocked an inquiring eyebrow, forcing Jasper to hastily explain about the stranger who'd attacked Laura this morning in the street outside her home. "So you see," he finished, "I really can't bandy words with you any longer. I've got to find her some refuge, if she'll accept even that much from me."

"Don't be obtuse, Jasper," his mother said, with an impatient wave of her hand. "The solution is simple. You must bring her to me."

Jasper stared but his father didn't even twitch. "It's the only way," Lady Fairchild went on, with a placidity Jasper couldn't believe, let alone trust. "No one will harm her at Rushford house and her virtue," she smiled thinly, "will be quite safe. It will certainly confound the gossips."

"There will be talk—" Lord Fairchild began.

"We'll suffer it," Lady Fairchild said. "You said yourself there's no decent way out of this. Given his promise that he will play no more tricks, I'm quite willing to assist him in his suit."

"She is an actress," Jasper said, still unsure if he heard right.

"I can't say I'll relish the scandal, but you are right. The best alternative is to marry her. You do like her, after all?"

"I love her," Jasper said, trying not to suffocate.

"Well, you'll never again be the darling of society, but you should have thought of that. At least she is the daughter of a Comte. Edwards was reluctant to mention that," Lady Fairchild said.

"He doesn't believe in titles."

Lady Fairchild sniffed. "Just bring her to me, Jasper. The rest will sort itself later."

For perhaps the first time in a decade Jasper decided he should obey his mother. With wary eyes, lest she shed this new skin and revert to form, he crossed the room. It felt confoundedly awkward, but he took her hand and kissed it.

"Thank you, Mama."

"Don't be long about it. I've had a tiring day and if I'm to have guests at Rushford house—"

"Let it rest, Georgy," his father said.

Pet names? It was too much. Jasper fled.

26

CURTAIN

*J*asper's presence was painful but even when he left, Laura felt no relief. Of course, she did have the wretched work of restoring Kate to her white-faced mother.

"I'm sorry," Laura said. "I didn't know—"

"You aren't to blame," Sarah said, holding Kate tight.

Not directly, but still...Laura watched Sarah and Alice ready themselves, saying little because of the lump in her throat. The warning bell, the audience's mumble and the muted strains of the orchestra were distant cacophony, so absorbed was she in her thoughts. Alice came in to change after the first act, breathless and flushed.

"How is it so far?" Laura moved aside so Kate could help Alice out of the breeches.

"Perfect," Alice said, leaning into the mirror. Determined not to appear jealous, Laura held out a dish of face powder, conscious of her own throbbing cheek, hoping the scrapes would heal without marks and worried they wouldn't. Saltash was right. She couldn't act with a marked face. It unnerved her to know how easily he made that happen. She loved the stage but was it worth her safety? Or risking the people close to her—suppose she'd brought Kate with her this morning?

If Saltash fought without scruples, there was little she could do. She couldn't allow him to hurt Mr. Rollins or Sarah or Dan —even Alice didn't deserve that. The defiance which goaded her to pen that note to him was gone. She couldn't start carrying a pistol, even if she was afraid. And Jasper and Rollins and Betty, even the neighbor across the way—she couldn't expect them to protect her.

She could take a different name and go to a provincial theatre, a second-rate playhouse in Leeds or Ireland. Saltash probably wouldn't trouble her there, yet the notion held little appeal. It wasn't just that she loved the stage, Laura realized. She loved this one where she worked with her friends.

"Where are you going?" Betty asked, moving to block the dressing room door as Laura pushed to her feet. "Mr. Rushford says I'm to keep you in my sight."

Dear Betty. Always so zealous. "I'm just going to take a walk backstage," Laura told her. "I won't be long."

Betty allowed her to pass, albeit with a frown. Keeping her footsteps silent and slow, Laura drifted down the corridor, past timber castles and plastered mountain tops, edging into the grotto-like darkness behind the lighted stage. She could see Dan and Alice silhouetted against the backdrop canvas. Alice was doing well. Dan, a nit-picker if there ever was one, wouldn't be satisfied, but so long as Alice learned to treat him as a partner and stopped trying to outshine him they probably would do quite well together. It hurt to see it happening, but then Laura had always known she was replaceable.

The stagehands moved, surefooted and soundless, preparing for the moment when they'd flip the world round and convert a fashionable parlor into a craggy forest. There had to be pieces from fifty shows cached back here: a throne with flaking gilt, a mechanical moon, the rippling lengths of silk they used for the sea. She was lucky to have had so many adventures.

Laura took a perch on the battered throne. Whether she gave it up now or next year, the adventures were still hers—no one could take her past triumphs away from her. The ones she might have yet simply weren't worth the toll Saltash would exact. Yes, she loved being an actress, but she could exist without applause; she was pragmatic enough for that. Leaving the stage didn't mean she'd have to shut herself in a box. Take Anna—she had interests. Safe, if unconventional, ones but Anna didn't give two straws for any opinion but her own. In the matter of Alistair's leg, she and her husband adapted to circumstance, finding happiness with what they had instead of pining for what used to be. Not a bad way to live, if one was wise enough to take it.

She could try new pursuits and not think of them as inadequate substitutes. Yes, gardening and reading and keeping house for Jack seemed vapid, but—

Laura rested her chin in her hands. Right now it would be the next thing to wonderful, being with Jack. If only she hadn't handled things so badly. He blamed her and she deserved it, but it would be such a relief to reveal to someone the bruises on her battered heart. If she went to Jack surely they could mend the rift between him. She was sorry and it wouldn't be hard to say the right things and own up to her foolish mistakes, now that she'd run herself to a standstill. Jack was a good sort. He'd forgive her.

If only Jasper didn't live in Suffolk. They needn't move in the same circles, Laura decided. It was the only way they could coexist. It was a problem, but not the most pressing one. Just now, she must tend to other matters.

Promising herself that if she had to, she could shed a few

tears later, Laura returned to the dressing room. She smiled at Betty. "I think we'd better pack up my things."

Thank goodness for Betty. Without her, Laura knew she'd have cried over the packets of letters from Gemma Holyrood's admirers and the playbills she'd saved—here was the first one to ever bear her name. There was a box of trinkets, her lucky garters, Gemma's gold chain and cross.

"It's good of you, continually looking after me," Laura said to Betty.

Betty grunted as she bent over to put another packet of letters in a box. "I don't do it for you. Got to keep you and Mr. Rushford safe from each other, don't I?"

"True." Laura smiled. "I won't cause him more trouble, Betty. You should know that." Heavens, but she'd already given him plenty.

"Well, I will miss you," Betty said. "You're really done with the stage?"

Laura didn't know how it happened, but she laughed. "Yes. Best do it now before it's done with me. I'm not sure what Mr. Rushford has in mind for me just yet, but I think it's best that I take myself to my brother. I can make arrangements tomorrow."

She'd do it herself. It wouldn't be hard to get passage on the mail coach. She could walk the rest of the way once she got to the village—a style of travel suited for penitents. She must take care to arrive suitably woebegone. Jack would forget his anger and they would both have a laugh about it.

They were to the fifth act now. Laura sent Kate to bring her another box and filled it with the remaining bits and pieces: Denmark lotion, rouge, silver-backed brushes, hair ribbons and pearl pins, a silk dressing gown patterned with butterflies. Gathered like this they looked insignificant.

She heard the curtain and the final applause swell as Sarah or Alice or Dan or all of them came out again for another bow.

She found Rollins in the hustle afterward, as the stagehands hastened to put things away and the actors sponged their faces and blinked their way back to reality.

"Rushford back for you yet?" Rollins asked.

"I'm expecting him soon," she said. He'd been longer than she'd expected, but he wouldn't leave her to sleep here. "Thanks for sheltering me one last time." Laura put her hands on Rollins' arm and rose up to kiss his cheek.

"Is this it then?" He gave her a level glance.

She opened her hands half-heartedly. "Better to concede now. I'd rather not be pummeled again. It wouldn't be fair to the rest of you."

"We'll miss you," he said.

"I'm sure you will. But you know the address of my banker. He'll be waiting to know the tally of this week's receipts."

"Gemma—" he said, rolling his eyes.

"Just so you aren't tempted to cheat me." Rollins never would, but she couldn't do this if they didn't keep the conversation light. "I'll miss you. And I'll write."

The corner of his mouth tugged up. "You're really done?"

"I have to be. You know that."

He sighed. "It's been a good run. Visit when you can."

Laura nodded and went back to packing while Rollins went back to work, putting his theatre to bed. It only took moments to hammer her boxes shut and put them next to her valise at the door. Then she broke the news to Sarah, who wept and hugged her.

"What are the boxes for?" Alice asked, arriving late and breathless to the dressing room.

"What's kept you?" Sarah snapped. "Detained by admirers already?"

"Perhaps," Alice said, sullen but blushing.

"I'm packing my things," Laura explained, anxious to avert a quarrel.

"Oh. You're leaving?" Alice looked skeptical.

"Yes," said Laura. Alice made a noble effort to look disappointed.

"I'm off," Sarah said. "Once you're settled, let me know."

Laura promised. "Will you find Dan and his wife for me?" she asked Betty. "I want to tell them goodbye."

She wouldn't mind a moment alone in the room, but Alice lingered, perhaps as stunned as she was by the naked room. It's been a good run, Laura repeated to herself.

"Gemma?"

Laura started at the name. It didn't seem to fit, now that everything was packed away.

"I meant to tell you," Alice said. "Mr. Rushford's here. He asked me to fetch you, but I forgot in all the excitement."

Laura winced. "I hope he's not been waiting long."

"Not long," Alice said. "Come on, I'll bring you to him."

"But Betty. And Dan—"

"I'll send them after you." Alice reached for the box.

"I can carry that," Laura said. "If you wouldn't mind bringing the valise?"

It was harder to thread a way through the backstage bustle with burdened arms, but they kept out of the stagehands' way and didn't knock anything over. "He's out the back way," Alice said. "Didn't want to be conspicuous."

She stopped Laura at the door. "Careful. Let me look first. Yes. It's safe. You can go. I'll run and fetch Betty."

"Wait." Laura fumbled in her reticule. She'd meant to give these to Kate, but she'd probably be happier with something new and pretty. Alice would appreciate these more. "Here," Laura said. "I want you to have these." She stuck out her hand

and dropped a tangle of faded blue ribbons into Alice's hesitant palm.

"Your lucky garters?" Alice asked.

"You should have them."

"You shouldn't—I can't—well, thank you," Alice said. "And good luck."

"Break a leg," Laura wished her in reply. Hefting her bag, she stepped outside. It was dark. A hackney waited. She couldn't see Jasper, but since he didn't want to be seen, she supposed he'd be waiting inside the carriage. Ahead of her, outlined by the lights at the end of the alley, stood a pair of broad shoulders. Peter.

"I left a box upstairs," Laura said, walking up to him. "Would you fetch it for me?" She might as well save Betty from carrying it down.

He turned. Laura realized with dry throat and widening eyes that these shoulders were too high and clad in lighter cloth. His face was masked in shadow, but the eyes weren't kind, the mouth wasn't smiling. She wasn't sure if he was the tough from this morning—but he certainly wasn't Peter.

27

ON THE HUNT

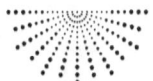

*J*asper returned to the theatre in hopeful spirits. If his mother wasn't going to object, Laura couldn't refuse him on that score. Even if she didn't love him, she liked him and plenty of marriages began with less. Once he explained how his life would be a colorless void without her...she would laugh, no doubt, but was too much of a friend to let him suffer. A break wouldn't be easy for either of them. She would miss him too...wouldn't she?

The theatre still hummed with the usual ruckus that always came after a show. Elbowing past the draymen crowding the back door, Jasper was negotiating the labyrinth backstage when Betty found him.

"I can't find Miss Edwards—Miss Holyrood, I mean," she whispered.

"What do you mean?" Jasper asked.

"What I said. She's not here."

"You must be mistaken," Jasper said, talking over a ripple of unease. "She's here somewhere."

But she wasn't. Not in her dressing room, not backstage, not with Rollins or that other actress. No one had seen her.

"She said she was finished," Rollins said, worry spelled out in hieroglyphic creases on his forehead. "That it was time for her to go away. I thought she was going away with you."

So did I, Jasper thought, anxiety fiddling above the increasingly ponderous bass of his heart. She wouldn't—couldn't—be running from him. "Her box is here," he said to himself as much as Rollins.

"But her valise is gone," Betty said. It hurt to look at the room stripped of her gimcracks. Laura's replacement was already studying the walls and trying different places for the chair.

If Laura was hiding—ludicrous idea—it must be because of Saltash. Even if she couldn't bring herself to accept his proposal, surely she knew he wouldn't press his suit if it was painful to her. She wouldn't run from *him*. He had obligations—to keep her safe, to protect her from shame and from Saltash's louts. For crying out loud, how many times had he reminded her he'd given his word to Jack? That infernal, fettering promise ought to have driven him to bedlam long ago. Keeping it was nigh impossible and now she was missing.

All his life he'd been blessed with a glib tongue. To mishandle a marriage proposal so badly that the lady he loved actually fled from him—

Jasper felt a touch on his arm. He looked left, then down. It was the hare-lipped girl, the quiet one who flitted about the theatre fetching props and tidying dressing rooms, who'd been with Laura this morning. "What is it, Kate?" Jasper said, producing the name just in time as he crouched to his knees. She looked frightened enough without him looming over her.

"Will you come, sir?" she asked, taking his hand.

He followed her away from the dressing room. "What is it?" he asked again.

Kate threw a worried look behind him. "Miss Gemma. Miss Beaton knows."

"Who's Miss Beaton?" Jasper asked.

Wordlessly, Kate pointed at the dressing room door. Ah. She meant the understudy, Alice.

"I saw Miss Beaton come up and fetch Miss Gemma and take her out the back way."

"You saw her leave the theatre?" Jasper asked.

Kate nodded. "But only Miss Beaton came back."

——

THREATS, shouts, and fists slammed against tables—both his and Rollins—soon extracted Alice's tearful confession. "I don't know who he is, but he's got money. He wanted to know anything I could tell him about Gemma."

"And you sold her out," Jasper snapped.

"I have to fight for my own chances," Alice whined, roused to defense.

"And you've had your last," Rollins said. "How could you betray her?"

"He said he wasn't going to harm her," she muttered.

"And you believed that—after they tied her up and threw her in a carriage?"

"How was I to stop them?" Alice said sullenly.

"By shouting for us," Rollins snapped. "Or summoning help. Just get out."

"But my place," Alice gasped. "I've got no—"

"I might be willing to help you," Jasper cut in. "If you can tell me where they went."

She looked up, face stricken. "I don't know, sir. Honest, I don't." She fell to weeping while Jasper ground his teeth. He had no time to waste. His chances of tracking Laura dwindled the more time passed. He glanced at the sniveling understudy. She must have seen something that could help, but how to persuade her... She was a spiteful little fool, but a desperate one and the world was hard.

"My sister may be able to find work for you," Jasper said and passed her his card. Henrietta would make him pay for this, but he couldn't think of anything else to do, pressed as he was for time. Though still weeping, Alice was grateful enough to give him details of the coach, driver, and the tough who'd mistreated Laura. It wasn't a lot to go on, searching for a battered brown coach with mismatched horses, one chestnut and one black, driven by a man with broken teeth, but it was all he had. He must find her.

Summoning Betty and Peter, he dispatched them to his parents. "They'll be at Rushford house. Tell them everything. Tell them Laura's taken. I'll send word once I find anything." God send that he did.

————

KEEP YOUR HEAD. You've done this before, Laura told herself, quelling her clamoring heart. She'd been kidnapped by villains dozens of times. Unfortunately the real experience differed from the stage variety. It hurt, for starters.

Her hands and feet were tied, she had raw knuckles and a bashed knee, and probably a bruise to match the scraped cheek she'd got earlier. She had blood in her mouth and hair in her eyes and only the vise-like action of her teeth on her tongue kept her from gibbering—a humiliating and useless response. She wouldn't do it. Someone would find her. Jasper and Mr. Rollins had to know she was missing by now. Jack would learn soon enough. They wouldn't let her disappear.

But it was dark, the hour was late, and she was trapped in a carriage with a boulder of a man with punishing muscles. His accomplice, a broken-toothed coachman with a phlegmy cackle, wouldn't help her—he'd held down her legs and tightened the knots. Neither man would say where they were going and she'd lost their direction after the first few turns. Unlike the heroines she played, she didn't have a concealed knife or a loaded pistol. These weren't trick bonds either. They held fast no matter how she twisted and the cords—

"Keep that up if you want to rub off your skin," her captor said mildly. He didn't speak like a lout and that scared her, almost as much as the flask in his hands that gleamed in the dark. The price of screaming, he'd told her, was to have it poured down her throat. If nothing else, she must keep her wits about her.

"I'm cold," she said, hoping he'd throw his cloak over her, giving her a chance to pick unseen at her bonds.

"You're welcome over here." He gestured to the place beside him.

Laura retracted further into the seat on her side of the coach. Shivering wasn't so bad.

No matter how she turned her head, she could see nothing outside. It was dark and the shade was down. The blind jolting made her queasy and every so often a tremor escaped her as she quailed against the forces of fear, shock, and cold.

He laid a stilling hand on her fingers. "Just a swallow," he said, unstopping the flask. "It'll settle you but not put out the lights."

Laura jerked her head no.

"Please yourself." He put it away with a shrug.

No turns or stops anymore. They were out of the city, Laura realized, glancing at the latch on the door. O'Trigger (she didn't know what he was called, but he looked like an O'Trigger to her, with his smarmy manners and cheap finery) had taken his fingers off the handle, but they were close by, resting on his knee. At this speed even if she got through the door she'd only succeed in throwing herself under the wheels. If by some miracle they missed her, she was no better off out there, trussed like a game bird on the side of the road. O'Trigger would only stop the carriage, walk back, and haul her inside, taking the opportunity again to feel her breasts. He should be grateful she didn't carry a knife because she'd have done her best to gut him.

Twice they slowed for tolls, but she didn't know the roads well enough to guess their direction.

"There were shawls in my valise," Laura said through clenched teeth. By now her bag must have been filched from the gutter—she'd swung it hard into O'Trigger, but that hadn't stopped him, only made him stumble.

"There's a rug under your seat," he said.

Bastard. "May I have it please," she said. If this kept up much longer, she'd grind her teeth to stubs.

"Since you ask so nicely." He leaned across and made a show of tucking the rug about her. "Anything else I might do for your comfort?"

"Thank you but no." Her chance for escape would come. Until then, she must wait.

———

LONDON HAD countless hackneys crawling like roaches through the streets, but not many had ventured beyond the metropolis. None had been seen at the posting inns on the westward roads, but an ostler at an inn on the Great North Road said he'd seen a brown coach with mismatched horses.

"Didn't stop or nothing. Tore down the road like he was outrunning the devil."

Though uncertain that he'd caught the scent, Jasper decided

to follow. The description matched and Saltash's seat was in the north. Dispatching a message for his father, he begged him and Peter to check the posting inns on the other roads in case he was wrong, then galloped north.

He had a grand start. The moon was full, both he and his horse were in good condition, and he had the additional confidence lent by pistol and sword. The first tolls all reported seeing the carriage and at Alconbury, the tollkeeper told Jasper his quarry was little more than a quarter of an hour ahead of him. Spurring forward, Jasper careened down the road to the next halt and found calamity: the keeper, surly at being woken hours before dawn denied seeing any carriages at all. "Haven't had any since ten in the evening," he said, his glare telling Jasper what he thought of persons who chose to conduct business abroad in the infant hours of morning.

"You're certain?" Jasper asked.

"Quite. Went to bed after the ale wagons passed at eleven. Haven't woke till now."

Laura's captors had turned off the main road then. What did one do with a kidnapped actress between Alconbury and Peterborough in the middle of the night? Stop at some quiet hostelry? Impossible unless they'd found a way to subdue Laura, and that possibility was terrifying.

"Can you tell me where a carriage like that might go, if they were leaving the main road and wanted to change horses?" Jasper asked.

"No, I can't," growled the toll-keeper before he slammed the window shut.

Jasper remounted, grim but resigned. He'd have to go back and try the side roads and check with the local inns. Hopefully he could find where they'd changed horses. If he didn't learn what the new pair looked like he'd never find them. Assuming he was tracking the right coach in the first place.

Ignoring the suffocating urge to despair, Jasper booted his horse to a canter. Time was precious and slipped fast through his spendthrift hands. He visited one village, then another, pounding on smithy doors and closed taprooms, but came up with nothing. His horse nearly spent, his mouth dry as dust, his face and fingers numb with cold, Jasper rode back to the main road and turned south again filled with doubts. Suppose they had ridden through that last village? The innkeep was a heavy sleeper—Jasper had yelled for a good five minutes before the fellow dragged himself to the door. A carriage could have passed without rousing anyone. But they would have had to change horses. By now the beasts would be dead in the traces if they hadn't been exchanged for others. He must find out where and what the new horses looked like.

Jasper's spirits rose at the next stop where a lighted window summoned him through the dark. Again, he found only disappointment. The grey-whiskered man who cautiously poked his head round the door explained he'd seen no one come by. The light was only so he could read.

"I'm sorry, sir. Haven't seen a soul."

Jasper declined the offer of a bed and the door shut. Too weary to curse, Jasper bowed his head against the frame, afraid to guess how far Laura and her captors might have traveled by now. They were hours ahead in God knows what direction. He pressed his fist against the rough wood and flaking paint until the bones in his hand creaked, then spun away to chase faint hopes down the empty road before him.

28

A CURE FOR TROUBLE

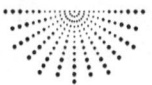

*L*aura huddled in the corner of the coach, damp with icy perspiration, her thoughts a discordant jumble of twanging nerves. And still they rumbled on. After an age they changed horses, but her captors didn't let her out of the carriage to relieve herself or offer her anything except O'Trigger's flask. Her mouth was dry and sour, her legs cramped, and she was growing worried about the increasing pressure in her bladder.

"I need to get out," she said, looking at O'Trigger.

"In a bit. We'll find you a hedge."

They did, but they only untied her feet, not her hands, snickering when she gasped in disbelief.

"I'll manage," she said and strove for haughtiness, no easy thing while stumbling into the branches where she'd be better concealed.

"How much is my uncle paying you?" she demanded, climbing back into the carriage.

"More than you can." The coachman smirked as he pared his nails.

Leaning against the carriage wall, the ache in her legs

spread to her shoulders and back. Laura watched the window and checked the color of the sky each time the shade bounced away from the glass. Soon they'd have to change horses again. When at last the pace slackened she got ready to scream and spring. If she could just get herself past the carriage door, the ostlers would see her and her bound hands. They'd have questions. But as they rolled into the yard O'Trigger jumped on her, squashing her face into his armpit and clapping his hand over her mouth.

"A change, quickly now," said the driver. Laura struggled, but the ostlers were swift and moments later they were rolling away.

"Pardon me." O'Trigger smiled as he removed himself and settled back in his seat. "Can't have delays or interruptions."

Laura scowled and wiped her mouth on her sleeve. She'd give anything to have Dan or one of the other actors swing onto the scene flourishing a sword. Were they looking for her? Surely Jasper must be in pursuit by now. Even though she'd refused him, he must know she would never run away without a single word... Hadn't he seen the truth in her kisses, in the talk and the lingering glances? There was a difference—she couldn't be the only one who felt it—in the way she spoke to him and the way she played to Dan. If Jasper didn't know he was a blind fool.

But not as fool as she.

Idiot, Laura thought. You should have told him. She might die... No, she would not. Thoughts like that were not allowed and it made little sense to drive her miles out to the country just to kill her. Why make a night's work out of a task that could be done in half an hour? Easier by far to slit her throat and slide her body into the Thames. Though it was meant to be a soothing thought Laura shivered. She wished she was sure Jasper knew she loved him.

Jasper would come. Even if he didn't know he'd won her

heart ages ago, he was the sort you could trust—she must have known that instinctively when she'd chosen him, though she hadn't guessed how much. He must be close now...mustn't he? Her head sagged and her eyes drooped, but though she snapped herself alert again and again, he didn't come.

———

"WE'RE ARRIVED." O'Trigger startled her awake as he unfastened the bonds at her ankles. "Not worth the trouble," he said, putting an end to her fumbling efforts to straighten her hair with her bound hands. Leading her by the wrists, he brought her out of the carriage.

Screwing up her eyes against the sunshine, Laura saw pasture, scythed fields, empty road...and a carriage, perhaps twenty yards ahead, waiting. It wasn't a vehicle like the one she'd journeyed in—it gleamed with scrollwork and new paint, and had a crest on the door. A footman stepped off the back of the coach and snapped the door open. O'Trigger pushed her in front of it.

"Here she is, Your Grace."

"You're late." She could scarcely see him in the shadowed interior, except for his hand, the heavy signet gleaming between his bony knuckles, the fingers clasping a gold-headed cane.

"Pardon, Your Grace."

Maybe he'd punish O'Trigger. Laura hoped so.

"Get in, get in," Saltash said, the hand beckoning.

O'Trigger pushed her into the carriage. "Uncle," Laura said, stumbling into the seat, her eyes mutinous.

"My dear, unfortunate niece. How lucky I am to have found you." The door shut behind her and the carriage dipped as someone, O'Trigger presumably, climbed up beside the driver.

"You can't do this," Laura said.

"It pains me to disappoint you, but I'm afraid you'll find yourself mistaken."

"Jack will find me." Someone would. Please God, let someone find her.

"It is possible," Saltash conceded with a tilt of his head. "But unlikely." Leaning forward, he rapped the side of the carriage with the cane and they rolled forward, accelerating so gently there wasn't even a lurch.

"Where are we going?" Laura asked.

"Down this road about a mile to meet an interesting gentleman. I hope you'll like him. He's looking forward to meeting you."

He glanced at her bound hands but did nothing. Laura pressed her lips together, unable to speak. She mustn't cry or beg or snivel. Saltash didn't deserve that pleasure. She must keep her head and think a way out of this. Run? She had no money, never mind her bound hands. Kick him? Satisfying but unproductive and she didn't want to face the retaliatory strike of that ringed hand. Just looking at him made her thoughts scatter like minnows whose sand has been stirred.

They swept past bare trees, haystacks, and fields of frost-rimmed stubble. Neat farms and shoddy ones too, but nothing that could help her. She was trapped here with the smell of Saltash's musk and only a hint of the smoke from a distant pile of burning leaves. Fear threatened to close up her throat and she didn't know whether to stare or close her eyes. Both were unbearable. She held on to her hands like her heart was in them, beating so fast it might burst.

This was real. She couldn't talk it away by comparing it to some play or pretending that—suddenly remembering, Laura realized she had lived this before. Not in a costume. Not in front of the lights.

In France. She'd seen her mother weep, but never once had

she given into fear. Not when mobs fired their home, not when they dragged away her father. Not in hiding when they trekked along unfamiliar roads with soldiers in pursuit or when they had to slip past guards to get onto the ship that promised escape. Swallowing, Laura steeled herself. Whatever Saltash planned couldn't be worse than what her mother had faced and overcome before. It might take time and she might be terrified, but she was the daughter of Marguerite Leonie Edouard Lecroy-Duplessis. She would not be any less than her mother.

Heart steadier, Laura watched the hedges pass. The carriage turned into a side road, then into a smaller lane, then through a gate. A house came into view, square as the bricks that built it, the untidy autumn gardens bounded by a low wall. The footman hopped down onto the gravel and opened the carriage door.

"Go on," Saltash told her.

Laura climbed out. The trees were bare, the borders dug out, but in the summer—in the summer, the place would be beautiful. The glossy black door of the house opened and a tubby man in a dark coat came out, attended by a female servant in a white apron and cap. The servant was taller than he was and her grey wisps of hair looked tired next to his bristling side whiskers.

This wasn't so bad, Laura thought. It was better than a brothel or a ship to Australia or a workhouse...or any of the dozens of places she'd feared.

"Your Grace," Tubby bowed, struggling over the *r*. It came out sounding more like a *w*.

"Dr. Matthews."

The crackling leaves under her feet sent a shiver over Laura's skin. She glanced again at Matthews, who didn't seem surprised by her bound hands.

"Is this the patient?" he asked.

249

"Yes, this is my unfortunate niece," Saltash said. Laura snorted, but Saltash didn't heed her. "It began when she was small," he said. "She never quite recovered after escaping the troubles in France."

"Most unfortunate," Dr. Matthews said, tsking and shaking his head. "All too common, I'm afraid."

"I've tried to keep her away from anything that might upset her, but since her mother died she's become even more unbalanced. Thinks she's an actress—the famous Gemma Holyrood. You understand, I'm sure, how embarrassing it would be if..."

"That's a lie," Laura said. "I am Gemma Holyrood and there's nothing wrong with me."

Matthews frowned. "I see the trouble, Your Grace. Naturally, you're beside yourself. And with your own dear daughter making her debut, you won't want anyone thinking such troubles run in your family."

"Precisely," Saltash said.

"He's lying." Laura started forward, but the female servant was beside her in an instant clamping stout hands on her arms. "Don't touch me," Laura said, pulling away.

Saltash and the doctor exchanged a look.

"Mrs. Stoke," Dr. Matthews said. "Will you help the young lady?"

Nimble as a spider in spite of her bulk, the woman seized Laura, twisting her hands over her head until her bound wrists rested behind her neck and her feet scrabbled on the gravel. Laura yowled in pain, but Matthews and Saltash didn't blink.

"Quiet," the woman whispered. "It'll go better for you." She looked past Laura to Matthews. "I've got her in hand, Doctor. No need to worry."

"Good." He eyed Laura closely, rocking on his heels. "Take her inside. If you'd come with me, Your Grace? I'd like a few more details of your niece's history."

Prodded along by Mrs. Stoke, Laura had no chance to break free. She floundered up the steps into the house and up again to the next floor. No pretty carpets here. The doors lining the corridor were all shut.

"What is this place?" Laura demanded, twisting to look at Mrs. Stoke. "You can't—"

"Shh." The woman leaned into her ear. "The talkers always get longer treatments. You don't want that." Her hands, Laura saw, were red and chapped.

"Treatment?" Laura's voice was as well-tuned as a virtuoso's violin, but now it scraped.

"Water," Stoke said succinctly, like that explained everything.

"You won't give me any?" Laura asked, horrified.

Mrs. Stoke chuckled. "Other way round, dearie. Poured over you until the fits stop and you promise to be docile."

Laura was too afraid to speak. "I don't have fits," she managed, finally.

Mrs. Stoke grimaced. "I expect you will by the time he's finished with you. They're like putty in the end. Say whatever they think he wants. Come along."

Laura tried to break free, but a heavy hand cuffed her hard.

"Don't start wrong. I've warned you twice now. Won't do it again." The woman dragged her down the hall. Beneath the sound of her scrabbling feet on the bare floors, Laura heard whimpering. It wasn't her own. Somehow that was even worse.

———

Cursed by innkeepers from piddly villages who didn't keep decent horses, Jasper pounded doors and prodded his borrowed horse until noon when he finally found the right turning. They'd changed horses in Egglington and driven west. Jasper followed on yet another horse, a skittish grey with execrable manners that at least was fresh. His pace was slow with frequent stops, lest he lose them again in this thin web of country roads. They hadn't been seen at the next inn and there was nothing off these turnings but farms, grimy hamlets, and a few manor houses. Dismal and heartsick, Jasper went back to knocking on every door, questioning everyone he saw, convinced the longer he was at it that the world was populated entirely by blind half-wits. Someone must have seen her.

At last he chanced on a laconic farmer in a darned smock with a clay pipe jammed into his craw. "Well?" Jasper demanded, tired of the man's silent deliberations.

"Didn't see the carriage you want, but there was a fancy one waiting at the bottom of my rye field for a good two hours. My Sam ran down to see it but the coachman chased him off."

"Where's Sam? May I speak to him?" Jasper asked, afraid to hope.

"Sure, an' you don't mind fetching him. He's in yon barn."

Jasper stumped across the field, leading his ill-tempered horse. The barn was more of a tired-looking shed with sheep, a pair of goats, and a serenading cow.

"Sam?" Jasper called, stepping inside.

"Here," the boy said, from the back of a stall.

"I'm looking for someone. She was taken from London last night." He described the carriage. "Your father says—"

"Yep, that was the other one," the boy said.

"Other one?" Jasper asked.

"Yessir. There was the shiny one rigged up for the nob inside skulking for a good spell at the bottom of yon field. Towards midmorning that one you'rn looking for rolled up. I din' go close. That chaffer on top had chased me away once already."

Jasper reached out a steadying hand to the partition

dividing the stall. "Did you see anyone? A lady? With chestnut hair?"

The boy shrugged. "Could've been. Didn't see close enough to tell."

"But there was a lady," Jasper said, his heart quickening.

"Unless it was a man in skirts," the boy said. "Got out of the shabby one and into the other."

"Where did they go?" He gripped the partition hard, resisting the impulse to take the boy's arm.

"Don't know where the shabby one took off to, but I expect the nob went down to Dr. Matthews' place."

"A doctor?"

The boy nodded. "Looks after them that aren't right in the head. A mile or so down the road. Not much else this way."

She was close. Thanking the boy with words and coin, Jasper flung himself into the saddle.

29

BEDLAM

The room Stoke brought her to was small with bare walls. Ironwork barred the window. The only furniture was a low bed and a chair with leather straps hanging from it.

"You must believe me. I'm not mad. The duke lies." Laura's voice was hoarse.

"Some do," Stoke conceded. "That's not so much the point. We take folk who are problems. Dr. Matthews fixes them, you see."

"But I'm not ill," Laura said again, growing desperate as Stoke brought out a pile of sacking that was apparently to serve her as clothes. "You must let me out of here, I can—" She had nothing. No jewels, no money. No weapon and even if she did, her hands were tied. At least on the flight from France, Maman had carried jewels and a pair of pistols.

Be calm, Laura told herself, but she felt lightheaded as if she'd bled without knowing it.

"Don't faint," Stoke said, as Laura swayed. "The doctor will say it's a fit."

"I haven't eaten," Laura said.

"I'll bring you something, if you go easylike," Stoke said, nodding at the coarse nightdress in her hands.

"Nothing's wrong with my clo—" Laura stopped. It wasn't in her interest to argue. She'd be in a fix without real clothes, but if Stoke was to get her into this shabby excuse for a garment, she'd have to untie her hands. Laura dropped her eyes and proffered her wrists. "I'm sorry," she said as she watched Stoke struggle over the knots with her cracked fingers.

"Done their job a little too well, haven't they?" Stoke said.

"Perhaps—"

Stoke shook her head. "The doctor doesn't allow me to carry knives or scissors. Keep still." She winced but finally succeeded in loosening the knot. When Laura's hands fell to her sides, she almost staggered at the pain as blood rushed back into them. Stoke frowned at the welts marking Laura's wrists. "Maybe I can find some salve for those," she said. "If you're pleasant, mind."

It was her best chance. "Thank you," Laura said. "I will be." She stood docile as a lamb, so Stoke could unbutton her, letting silent tears spill down her cheeks. It wasn't hard, producing them. When Stoke moved round to the front of her, Laura glanced up, woeful and wet-lashed. "I'm sorry," she said again and hiccuped.

"Just be quiet and agreeable," Stoke said, unfolding the ugly nightdress. "It needn't be that bad."

"But I'm—I'm so afraid!" Laura whimpered, choking back a sob and knuckling her eyes. "They'll hurt me!"

Stoke clucked. Swaying like a blossom whose petals are about to be torn off by the breeze, Laura held up her arms so Stoke could pull the nightdress over her. When the coarse cloth was round her head she let out another sob.

"There, now. Sit yourself down, quiet yourself, and I'll get that salve I promised. Wouldn't hurt to put some on your face, either."

Laura obeyed and Stoke left the room. As soon as the key turned in the lock, Laura was on her feet running her hands over the bare walls, testing the bars. The door was the only way out. Mrs. Stoke's footsteps sounded in the hall; in an instant, Laura was back sitting on the edge of the bed and drying weepy eyes with the edge of her sleeve.

The salve was grey and greasy-looking, but Laura held out her hands. "It won't be so bad," Mrs. Stoke said, smearing the stuff over her wrists. "Let me see your face, dear."

Laura lifted it obediently, fixing Mrs. Stoke with imploring eyes. The only way out was the door, if Mrs. Stoke could be persuaded to let her through it.

"You'll be all right. Just be quiet and do exactly as he tells you," Mrs. Stoke said.

"But I already did!" Laura's shoulder's heaved. "Uncle said —Uncle said—" She snuffled incoherently. "When he finds out he'll kill me."

Mrs. Stoke gave a relieved smile and patted her knee. "I meant the doctor, not your uncle, dear. We don't kill people here."

Laura wasn't going to quibble about half-drownings, now she had Mrs. Stoke's sympathy. "I know *you* won't," Laura said, "But once Dr. Matthews discovers the truth..."

Her leading pause hung only an instant before Mrs. Stoke filled in the right line. "What truth?"

She had some momentum now. Time to use it. "About the duke's baby!" Laura hid her face behind frail hands, fluttering like a helpless flag of surrender precisely into Stoke's arms.

For a moment in the horror-struck silence, Laura feared she'd lost Mrs. Stoke, but then a hand came up to rest on her shoulder. "Hush. Hush, my dear," Stoke said, glancing back at the closed door. "Not so loud." She helped Laura to the bed, sitting her on the edge and kneeling beside her. "What baby?"

"Another month and Dr. Matthews will know," Laura said, wiping her cheeks with trembling fingers, "And then—"

"No," Stoke interrupted. "Did you say the duke's baby?" She was caught.

Laura nodded. "I've been so afraid. For years. But my mother kept me close. She even slept each night in my chamber, holding me as we listened to him tread back and forth outside my door. Of course my aunt, the duchess, refused to believe anything. I tried to run after my mother died—my fiancé, Rushford—Captain Rushford," Laura added for good measure, "was going to help me escape. I had his letter pressed next to my heart when the duke caught me in the chapel—"

Stoke's mouth fell open, the blood draining from her face.

"Praying for my mother," Laura pushed on. "He—he—" She broke, letting her head fall again into her hands.

"He what?" Stoke croaked.

"He forced me," Laura said, sobbing into her hands. "There on the stones before the altar. After that, what could I do? I couldn't give myself to my dear Jasper, ruined as I was." Blindly, she swiped at her eyes. "And the duke wouldn't let me go. He said I was unwell and locked me in my room, permitting none but himself to come to me." She shuddered again, knowing Stoke's imagination would do the work for her.

Silence stretched. Laura waited until Stoke's other roughened hand came to rest on her shoulder. She glanced at her then with pitiful, weepy eyes. "I—I managed to get a letter to my aunt, the duchess, through one of the servants who'd been kind to me and my mother."

"But she didn't believe you," Stoke breathed.

"No, she did! That was the trouble. She insisted my uncle get rid of me. So he brought me here. But he'll never allow me to give birth to his bastard. He'll kill me first. And once Dr. Matthews knows, he'll tell him."

Stoke glanced back at the door. "Once he learns of it I'll ask Dr. Matthews not to say—"

"Oh, would you?" Laura let herself brighten to incandescence. "Would you, for me?"

Stoke's face fell. "No. He wouldn't keep something like that secret. I could tell him your story but he might not believe it. He'll be inclined to believe the duke." She glanced at Laura, then at the door. "Knows which side his bread is buttered, he does."

Laura fell again to soft weeping. "Then there's no hope. No man would ever believe me, not when the duke declares I'm mad—" She straightened and dried her eyes. "None would, none but my Jasper. I'm fated to die, but at least he believes me."

"He knows?" Stoke said.

Laura glanced at the door and dropped her voice to a whisper. "I told him I didn't love him so he could leave me and love another. But he didn't accept it. He crept past my uncle's guards and climbed to my window and begged until I gave him the truth. And then—"

"Yes?" begged Stoke.

Laura dropped her gaze humbly to her hands. "He forgave me," she said. "But alas, his planned rescue came a day too late. My uncle brought me here and now Jasper will never find me."

Stoke rubbed her nose.

"If I wrote a letter," Laura said, "swearing my undying love, even though it is too late, would you—"

Stoke stared at her hands, the wrinkled skin of her chest rising and falling against the neck of her gown. She was deciding, Laura knew, if she could face the cost of helping her. Crossing her fingers, praying to the Virgin and St. Genesis, Laura waited. If she had acted well, perhaps this would work.

And if not today, then she must keep it up until it did, because eventually they would discover she wasn't pregnant.

It was tempting to add more, to sniffle and lay a hand on her belly, but instinct told her no. She must wait and let Stoke decide what part she would play.

"It's not too late," Stoke said. "I can help you."

Careful now, Laura told herself. Stick to your script or you'll wreck everything. "Dear Mrs. Stoke. You mustn't. I can't let you disobey your employer. You mustn't suffer because of me."

Mrs. Stoke took Laura's hands and gave her a look that was almost pleading. "Dr. Matthews isn't so bad. A decent master and I need the work. But I may be able to help you. I think I must."

"How?" Laura stuffed her own ideas back where they belonged. Stoke must give hers first.

"Is there a way you could get a message to Captain Rushford?"

Laura let her chest swell, then bit her lip, deflating. "His ship leaves for the West Indies in three days. There is no time for a message. But I know where it is berthed. If I found him, he would marry me and take me away and we'd be hidden from Saltash forever."

"But you'd have to get away," Mrs. Stoke said, her shoulders falling.

"And Dr. Matthews knows I can't do that without an accomplice," Laura filled in for her.

It was a setback, not the end, Laura told herself. Eventually she'd think of a way that would keep Mrs. Stoke blameless. She must watch and think and...

"Unless," Mrs. Stoke began. "You got violent? Perhaps if I told him I let my guard down..."

"And I struck you and bound you in that chair," Laura improvised.

Mrs. Stoke looked uncertain.

"No one could fault you for my escape if you were confined there," Laura said, hoping to convince Mrs. Stoke before she could think it over too closely. She locked eyes with her, daring her to look away.

"It's not perfect, but it's the best way," Stoke said. "And best we do it now before they can say I've taken your measure. You'll have to get out of the house on your own—take the back stairs and step quietly when you pass the kitchen. It's a good two miles to Whitecross, but you can catch a stagecoach there."

Laura didn't mention that she had no money or that she planned to remedy that problem before leaving the house. "Do you think I can?" she asked.

"You must," Stoke said, firming her jaw. "Don't stop until you get to Captain Rushford." Hastily she dressed Laura back in her own clothes, all the while whispering advice—to stay clear of the road but keep it in sight and make straight for Whitecross. "If you find yourself in trouble go to my sister. She's a weaver in a cottage on the east side of the village. Tell her I sent you and she'll help you on your way."

Laura clasped and kissed the warm hands, real tears pricking her eyes. "How can I ever thank you?"

Mrs. Stoke colored faintly. "'Tis nothing. Look after the child and yourself." With a grimace she sat down in the chair. "Come on now, buckle me in quick. I can only give you a few minutes and then I'll have to call for help. You won't have much lead and you cannot let that beast find you."

Laura nodded. She wouldn't have much time.

With Mrs. Stoke's instruction Laura soon had her strapped into the chair. Gently, she tugged off Mrs. Stoke's cap and tugged loose a few strands of her hair. "To make the idea of a scuffle convincing," she explained.

"It wouldn't be the first one—just the first where I ended up beaten," Stoke said. "I try my best, I do, with the poor creatures here."

"I know," Laura said. She didn't like to think who might be behind the closed doors, but she had plenty of evidence of Stoke's kind heart. "I'll always remember I owe you my life."

"Don't forget the keys," Stoke said. "It will slow them down if they have to break open the door to get me out."

It hadn't occurred to Laura, but she didn't hesitate to grab them.

"Quickly now," Stoke told her. "And God bless you."

Laura stifled a twinge of guilt. It wasn't all lies—Stoke was saving her, even if from a less gothic fate than she supposed. Beneath her apron she hid a romantic soul. Laura hoped she'd look back and be grateful for the chance to play heroine. "I will," Laura promised and slipped out the door. "But not for the next two minutes," she added.

Laura tiptoed down the hallway and unlocked all the doors. Three were empty, but she turned grimmer than ever at the sight of the fragile-faced women confined in the others, garbed in those coarse nightgowns and with straggling hair. "Quickly!" Laura whispered. "You can get away if you slip down the back stairs." The first two took the offered escape without a word, but the third shook her head and trembled, refusing to get up from her chair. "You can get out of here," Laura hissed, losing her patience.

"I won't get far," the woman said. Her skin sagged and her hair was streaked with grey. "Leave me be."

Laura left, but she wouldn't lock the door.

The next one was a mistake. As soon as she nudged it open, the wild-eyed girl inside began screaming. Laura cringed, but despite the swiping arm and flailing feet, the girl couldn't reach her—one of her hands was bound to the bed post. Sick inside,

Laura closed the door and fled down the hall, cursing herself for ruining her own chance.

She raced down the stairs, but halted on the landing, warned by grumbling coming from the first floor. Grateful the doors were thick and the hinges oiled, she ducked into the corridor and crouched in the corner to wait for the grumbler to climb up and investigate. She'd be lucky to escape and had lost any chance to pocket valuables or exchange her clothes. Pressing her back against the wall, she waited for Dr. Matthews or her uncle to discover her.

Neither man appeared. No one moved at all, except the grumbler, banging for quiet on the upstairs door. Laura waited, dumbfounded. Perhaps her pounding heart had deafened her ears. Afraid to move, at last Laura gave in and opened the stairway door, listening. Not a sound. And the screaming upstairs had stopped. Perhaps screaming wasn't cause for alarm in this house.

If she didn't get out soon she'd vomit or her heart would burst. Maybe both—within seconds.

Keep your nerve, she told herself. She wouldn't get far equipped like this and couldn't risk being recaptured. She'd only fool Stoke once. Darting down the hall she tried the first door, looking for Matthew's chambers. No luck, but she guessed right on the second try, scratching softly before opening it in case he had a valet. The room was empty, but the clothes well kept, so perhaps the valet was down in the kitchen. Laura rummaged through the clothes press, yanking out breeches, stockings, and shirt. She bundled them into a coat, snatched up the pound notes she found rolled beneath the stockings, and grabbed a gold snuff box just for good measure. No time to change her clothes. Someone on the floor above was banging and shouting—not the wild girl this time. It was Stoke sounding the alarm.

Clutching her bundle and struggling for air, Laura cracked open the door and peered down the hall. There was more shouting upstairs and doors slamming. She heard someone pound up the back stairs.

Quick, while they're still in a panic. Laura flew down the corridor to the main staircase, then swerved to a stop. She'd forgotten O'Trigger and her uncle's carriage waiting outside. Convulsing with fear Laura turned back, stopped again by the sound of more feet on the back stairs. She'd have to try the front. If she burst out the door and ran through the garden and over the hedge fast enough, she'd gain a few seconds head start on O'Trigger at least. Steeling herself, Laura launched out the door, sick with relief when she discovered no carriage standing in front of it. No footmen either—they must be inside or in the stables. Off the gravel and onto the grass, she was just rounding the corner of the house when she saw O'Trigger with his back towards her sitting on an upturned pail with a mug of ale in his fist. For a moment she was still as a rabbit, waiting for him to turn.

Don't wait! Go! Prodded into action, Laura wheeled around and bolted in the other direction, tearing through the hedge and cursing the shorn fields. She needed trees. Haystacks. Cover. There was none. She must run and hope they were busy at the back of the house.

At the end of the field was a stone wall. Lungs burning, Laura dared a glance back. Nothing. Clambering over, she ducked behind and peeled off her dress, tearing it in her haste. Her slippers had holes already. Laura slithered into the breeches. They were big and she had to gather the lacing as tight as she could. Nothing she could do about the baggy knees, but at least the length was right. Stockings next and shoes—big, again, but that was better than the alternative. They stayed on all right if she wore her slippers inside them. Shirt, waistcoat...

she knotted the neckerchief and jammed the hat low over her forehead before peering over the wall. There was a commotion now in front of the house, but no pursuit. Yet. If she didn't run for it now, it wouldn't take them long to find her. Dredging up Mrs. Stoke's instructions, Laura looked about and tried to remember which way to go for the road to Whitecross. It was no good. The only thought she could hold was to run far and fast. Keeping low, she bolted, sick with fear that she wouldn't hear pursuit over her own breathless gasps but unwilling to risk the hindrance of glancing back.

A SCRAMBLE

*J*asper galloped recklessly down the road, trying to measure the time by the height of the sun in the sky, unwilling to pause and take out his watch. This pursuit seemed to have gone on forever, but at last he had a real lead and hope of finding her. So long as he wasn't too late...

The boy's directions were good. Before long he was in sight of the house, a geometric non-entity, just as the boy Sam had described. Stones flew as he raced round the corner and through the gate, speeding like an arrow up the drive. He was still a good ways from the house when he heard the screaming.

Heart in his throat, he set his spurs, reining in so hard at the end of the drive that he drove the horse onto his haunches. Leaping from the saddle, he vaulted up the steps, ready to smash through the door.

"Are you Jasper?"

Twisting round like a drunk tinker, he stumbled, righting himself with the doorpost just in time. "Yes?" He found the whisper coming from a haggard-looking servant in cap and apron, just coming round the corner of the house. "Yes, I am."

"Laura's Jasper?"

"The same," he said, afraid to hope.

"Thank God." She closed her eyes. "Quick," she said, seizing his hand and hauling him away from the door. "You can't be seen. The duke is still here."

"But what about Laura?" he asked, pulling free. "I've come to rescue her." The shouts—the pitiful screaming—"What are they doing to her?" He would kill them.

"Bless you. Your lady's not been harmed. That's one of the other patients who your lady set free. The duke's men found this one and brought her back, but there's still another loose. This one—that can't stop yammering—is mad as they come, but no one's hurt her. They'll lock her in her room while the duke and Dr. Matthews decide who's to blame. They're about ready to murder each other."

Hence the shouting. A fitting end for them both, but Jasper wouldn't bet on it. "Where's Laura?"

The harried woman rubbed her forehead. "It's such a tangle. She's on her way to Bristol to meet you."

"Bristol?" he asked, sure she must be mistaken. Not only had he never mentioned the place to Laura, he'd never had any desire to go there. Moreover, while he had just cause to be in a right fury, he couldn't see why this woman should be on the brink of tears.

"Yes, to your ship," she said.

Jasper looked about, unsure if it was wise to be so close to her. This was a madhouse, after all. Perhaps she was another escaped patient? Not that he was complaining, exactly, but it seemed irresponsible to let real lunatics wander about.

"I'm so glad you've come," the woman sniffed. "You must hurry and catch her. If anything should happen to her or harm the baby—"

"Baby," Jasper echoed, stunned and flat.

"Yes." She glanced again at the house. "But the duke doesn't know yet. I had to help her, when she told me he would kill her once he discovered she was carrying his bastard." Eyes shining with frenzied zeal, she babbled on. "Dear Captain, she is so fortunate in you. To be so understanding, willing to stand father to that villain's child...bless you, sir. Bless you forever."

Poleaxed, Jasper reached for his pocket, but found to his chagrin that he was without a handkerchief. No matter. This woman was content to weep all over his hands.

"Did Laura tell you...everything?" Jasper suspected this tale was too involved to be the creation of a weakened mind.

"Yes, everything. Your secret engagement, how the duke raped her, the failed escape..."

Good heavens.

"But you must not delay. Any moment the duke will finish shouting at the doctor and then I expect they'll both rejoin the search. She is alone and on foot—"

"I'll find her," Jasper said, stepping into his appointed role. "And if Saltash dares follow, I'll beat him as he deserves."

"Bless you," the woman said again. Emboldened by his words or perhaps his gallant pose, she planted her hands on his shoulders and kissed him.

"No, bless you, madam," Jasper said, bowing and drawing a smile from her withered lips. "I owe you my life."

"That way," she pointed, before he rode off in the wrong direction. Saluting her, hoping he'd got the gesture right, he spurred his horse and bounded through the gardens and over the hedge. Now to find Laura. He hoped—most sincerely—she wasn't really going to Bristol.

———

LAURA WAS THIRSTY. She had a cramp in her side, her wrists smarted, and she couldn't remember what she'd last eaten.

Whatever it was, her stomach was long finished with it. Shifting her bundle to ease the burn in her shoulders she ducked into a thicket of trees, straying a little further from the road in the hope of finding some water.

She didn't dare stop. Fearing pursuit, she started at every noise. The pebble on her tongue wasn't working any moisture into her mouth, yet she felt like laughing aloud. She'd escaped. Yes, she would have a devil of a time getting back to London and Matthews' shoes were no doubt giving her blisters, but she wasn't trapped at his Home for the Emotionally Disturbed chained to a chair and being doused with water. No one had applauded, but Laura was convinced she'd just given the performance of her life. The euphoria of it sped her steps over the rough ground, freshening her when she knew by rights she should be weary. She must find out where she was and how to get back to London.

Using a man's voice and keeping her hat pulled low, she stopped at a cottage to beg a drink of water and directions to Whitecross, then hurried on, moving closer to the road. Hiding every time she saw a rider or a carriage, she made steady progress, passing farms and a squalid inn. This time she didn't stop. Safer to ask for directions again once she'd put more ground between her and Saltash. She couldn't have walked more than a few miles, but if she kept to the road she was sure of ending up somewhere.

After stopping again to adjust her shoes, Laura strode on, keeping a wary eye on the road. Spying a horseman, she stuffed her hands into her coat pockets and slouched, wishing she wasn't caught out in plain sight. She ambled along, telling herself that at this distance she'd look like any country gent out for a wander. Except the horseman slowed. Stopped.

"Laura!" he shouted.

She shot a panicked glance beneath the brim of her stolen

hat, ready to run but knowing she'd never escape a mounted rider, not in this open field. Already he was off the road and halfway to her.

But it wasn't Saltash, riding straight as a ramrod on a suitably magnificent horse. It was Jasper, coated with dust and riding like a man half-asleep on a horse even she could tell wasn't quite second-rate. Her bundle dropped to the ground.

"Laura!" he called again, hastening over the dry stubble, his shadow rippling behind him. Suddenly, though Laura knew she hadn't an ounce of extra water inside her, her eyes dripped tears —hot, fast ones that streaked down her cheeks as her legs went wobbly, succumbing at last to the strains of fear and fatigue. Speech was impossible; mere breathing required a conscious nudge, her lungs heaving into action again like rusty ironworks.

He was hatless, reddened by the wind with baked runnels of salt and grime lining his face. Drawing rein, he was off his horse in an instant, catching her before she tottered—she was bruised enough without slicing herself up on this field of stubble. Without meaning to, Laura found herself crying into his dusty, sour-smelling coat, pressing her hands to him like she could soak him up through her fingers.

"Steady, my girl," he said and she realized he wasn't talking to the horse. She dared a glance up. His eyes were suspiciously bright. "What a heroine you are. Shh—shh. All's well."

Laura shook her head, helpless against the flow of tears and the sobs shaking their way out of her. "I'm thirsty, I've had the fright of my life, my feet are covered in blisters—"

"Ah," Jasper said and smoothed her hair. "It took me such a long time to find you. I was so afraid." His arm tightened about her shoulders and her sudden cloudburst lightened to feeble sniffs.

Pressed into his chest she mumbled, "I didn't want to cry."

"I wish you wouldn't," he said. "I'd hoped to kiss you, but

even I'm not heartless enough to try it while you're watering my shirt."

"I expect my tears are among the least of the damage," she retorted. The way he looked, no wonder she hadn't immediately recognized him.

He raised her chin to study her. "Very well. A moment, if you'll forgive me." He raised his sleeve, using it to wipe her wet nose. "I seem to have lost my handkerchief." Hot with embarrassment, Laura felt the air solidify around her.

"May I kiss you now?" he asked.

"Please." Still mortified, the word came out a trifle crisply, but Jasper wasn't put off. The arm at her waist tightened, his mouth closing on hers with an obliterating focus that told her something of his desperate search.

"You—" he began, but Laura wasn't ready for talking. Her fingers traversed his shoulders and slid into his sweat-roughened hair. His bottom lip—she must make it clear she possessed it, though he could keep it for her when she had other things to kiss, such as this ear. As she nipped the edge his breath ran down her neck in a frosty shiver.

He tried words again. "You—are like to be the death of me."

"*Le petite mort?*" she asked, feeling that nothing could be sweeter than this urge to flame and extinguish together.

He gave a shaky laugh. "That also I hope. Laura, never in my life have I passed such a span of worried hours."

She swallowed, focusing on a patch of unshaven jaw. "I know." Just now, she'd rather not think of it.

"I can't let you go. You know that." He closed his eyes, pressing his forehead to hers. When he spoke his words rose up on notes of poorly suppressed triumph. "And I've been informed by one Mrs. Stoke that we are engaged—in fact, that you are counting on me to make an honest woman of you."

Laura shifted. "That was only—"

He shook his head, which rubbed their noses together, then pulled away so he could smile at her. "Unless you're willing to go back and tell that woman how shamefully you've deceived her, I'm afraid you're going to have to keep your word."

"Jasper—" He couldn't possibly...

"I never imagined you conveying your acceptance of my proposal in such interesting fashion, but you'll notice I am good enough not to complain—think what an agreeable husband I'll make! Besides," he glanced down at her, widening his smile as he spun her in his arms. "This is terribly compromising. What a picture we must be."

She let him swing her around, rollicking over uneven stubble and clods of earth. "But there's no one here." Laura laughed. "Not for miles."

"I'll summon that haystack as witness, if necessary," Jasper said. "And don't forget Mrs. Stoke. You must have spun her quite a yarn, my star. Sometime you'll have to tell me the entire story. I regret that I can't fulfill your wishes for a sea captain, but I am willing to marry you and stand father, if need be, to Saltash's baby."

Sea Captain? Baby? "Oh—" Laura blushed scarlet and dropped her chin, but he was too quick for her, ducking in to kiss her ear. "I'm hoping all you fancy is the uniform. I could arrange that for you privately, I suppose, but I think I'm ill-suited to a life at sea. Besides, I've no wish to be parted from my wife."

"You mean me?" she asked, struggling to keep up with him.

"Indeed," he said. "And I warn you, if you attempt to break our engagement, I'll take you to court and sue you for breach of promise. Mrs. Stoke will testify to that."

"You leave me no alternative," Laura said. He would only take one answer and it was the one she longed to give. "Very well." Smiling, she let him pull her in. Heavens, but she could kiss him forever. Maybe she would.

"There's just one thing..." Jasper reached for her bottom. Laura started, but recovered quick enough to squeeze his right back.

"My dear, I've been wanting to do that for the longest time. I had no idea you felt the same." He pulled back a bit and frowned at her. "Except I'd always imagined you in better fitting breeches. We could both fit in these ones—an intriguing idea, but we'd best save it for later. Come, I'd rather not explain myself to any farmers. Antics like that are sure to draw a crowd."

He mounted his horse, then pulled her up behind him and they set off for the road and the village. It was a tiny hamlet, boasting little more than a smithy and a ramshackle inn. "No help for it I'm afraid," Jasper said. "We'll have to stop here."

Laura hid a yawn. "Doesn't matter. I'm so tired I could sleep under a hay wagon."

He kissed her. "We aren't sunk so low as that. Here." He helped her off the horse, then turned to the host who'd emerged in the door, drying his hands on his apron.

"Meals and a wash," Jasper ordered. "The bath first, I think —can you stay awake for it?" he asked, turning to Laura. "It will be a stretch for me. If I'm not down to eat in half an hour, you'll have to come and save me from drowning."

The host eyed them suspiciously—no wonder, they looked so dirty and disreputable—but his face cleared at the sight of Jasper's coin. "Very good, sir. And a second bath, I take it, for the other—gentleman?"

"If you would," Jasper said, not turning a hair. "I intend to have the pleasure of scrubbing her back, but it can wait for a day or two. Meanwhile I hope you'll take the opportunity to do something with our clothes? A good brushing should rescue them, at least temporarily, from the rag bag. As for our dinner, you should know that I never eat mushrooms."

The innkeeper just stared. "Sir, we are not accustomed—"

"That will be all," Jasper said.

"Of course! Forgive me, sir!" And with an amazingly delicate tread for a man of his bulk, the man motioned them to follow him into the inn.

THE RIGHT WORDS

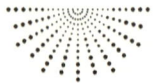

*S*ending up prayers of thanks for the divine relief of a tub of hot water, Jasper gave himself up to the pleasures of a good scrub and a clean towel. Laura was quicker than he. When he descended to the dining parlor, Jasper found her making inroads into a plate of roast chicken, potatoes, dumplings, and peas.

"I'm sorry," she said. "I couldn't wait."

"Nor can I." He lifted the covers and spooned food onto his plate. For a time neither spoke. At last Jasper passed between bites from starvation to the discomfort of gluttony and leaned back in his chair. Laura was still cleaning her plate, looking for all the world like a child dressed in her grandfather's clothes. Jasper couldn't hold back a smile. What a pair they were. He mustn't lose her. Not ever again.

"Pardon?" Laura said, looking up, and Jasper realized he must have murmured his last thought aloud.

"Sleep in my room tonight. I promise, no face-making," he said.

Her brow puckered. "Does that mean what I think it does?"

Jasper's ears burned. He couldn't think what to say. Clicket, dancing a blanket hornpipe...it all meant the same thing, but maybe he should have chosen something more genteel.

"Like bread and butter?" Laura asked.

He let out a choked laugh. "Yes, exactly. I'm too tired for it even if you're not, but I don't want Saltash taking you away from me again." He'd worry too much if she were out of sight. Or out of reach.

"All right," she said.

He swallowed, hesitating, but it needed to be said, no matter how awkward, so he hedged by dropping his eyes and playing with his fork.

"We'll marry as soon as we can—tomorrow if I can get my hands on a license—"

Laura stared into her empty water glass and turned it round on the table. "Jasper, are you certain?"

Not again. He stared at her. "I should hope so! After all this—"

"But what will your family say?"

His pulse slackened. If that was all that troubled her... "Oh, the Mater knows everything. Came with my father to London to browbeat me into doing the honorable thing." Jasper smiled. "Which we will."

"Lady Fairchild knows?" Laura looked stunned.

"Yes. So no more objections. I'm finished with them Laura, really I am." Considering everything, his parents had been rather wonderful. He should probably apologize for being such an ass. "What was I saying before?" he asked.

"No bread and butter." Her composure cracked and let a grin slip through.

"Not yet," Jasper qualified. Why hadn't he just let the subject alone? He must be bright as a beetroot. "We're both tired. The wedding isn't far off, thank heaven, and it's tradition, you know...virgin bride and all that." He spun his fork between his fingers. "It's a gift. And...well, you might not know...but I can give you the same."

She didn't blink. Almost as if she couldn't help it, her smile grew, but she didn't speak until his anxious fingers twitched and nearly dropped the fork. She shook her head. "How like you, Jasper—" Breaking off she hid her mouth with her fingers. "Treating your honor like a guilty secret! I hope you're not a prude!"

He flushed deeper but didn't have time to reply because she was out of her chair, walking around the table and taking possession of his lap. "How wonderful you are." She smoothed his hair. "I am not the least surprised."

It shouldn't be possible, he thought, to be so sensitive to the cadences of one voice or for the touch of her fingers on his freshly shaved cheek to completely hypnotize him. "I shall be the first then." She sounded pleased.

"The only," he said, liking the way she fit in his lap and the way it put her face level with his own. "That's what I've always interpreted marriage to mean. Don't you?"

"Unequivocally. Why didn't you tell me?"

"Well, it was a little embarrassing, with you so set on being my mistress."

Laura laughed. "You kept your secret very close."

"Only wanted to share it once," he told her. "And who would believe it? Come on. Time for bed."

———

He had ordered a separate room for Laura across the hall, but at this point he didn't care what the staff at the inn might think.

Servants were such a suspicious lot—may as well give them something to chew over. Ignoring the maid trundling down the hallway with an armful of freshly folded linen, he captured Laura's hand and pulled her into the room after him, winking when the maid gasped. It was most satisfying to shut the door and turn the bolt. "Come here," he said to Laura. He could kiss her once more. He had strength, but only enough for that.

Not for long, though. "Time to sleep," Laura said, drifting away.

"Yes, I think so," he agreed with a yawn. He helped her out of her coat. Perhaps it should have felt erotic, but in his current state it was more a sleepy promise of pleasures to come. Laura, too fatigued to pay much heed to whatever currents he might be feeling, merely stretched, toed off her shoes and, still wearing her breeches and shirt, rolled onto the bed, the musty smelling mattress deflating beneath her.

He let out a strangled sound, so she looked up, taking in the horrified expression on his face. "The bed's not so bad," she assured him. "If you're as tired as you say, you won't be uncomfortable for long."

True enough. "Might I—?" Jasper began.

"Beg help with the boots?" Laura asked, seeing that he wasn't budging from his spot on the braided rug. "You may." Laughing, she wrestled them off and dropped them in the corner.

"What did they fill this with? Clay?" Jasper asked, trying to beat the lumps from his pillow.

"I'm just glad I'm with you."

Yes, there was that. Jasper reached over and brought her into the crook of his shoulder, pulling his greatcoat over them both. Her hair tickled his nose, but even that couldn't keep him from sleep.

———

LAURA WOKE ALONE, but there was a well in the mattress where Jasper had been and it was still warm. Rolling into it, she shut her eyes again, but he reappeared moments later and informed her he'd seen to their breakfast. It was hot and substantial; by eight o'clock they were settled in a hired post chaise on their way to London.

"It'll take a week before I attempt riding again," Jasper told her. His joints did look stiff any time he had to stand up or sit down. In spite of his assurances, she dreaded breaking the news to his parents, but even these worries didn't keep her awake. She slept the last half of the way until Jasper shook her awake at the outskirts of London.

He was rumpled and even more travel-stained than she, but that was little comfort—she was still in breeches, having discovered this morning her dress was torn past mending.

"Don't fret yourself," he told her as she rubbed the grit from her eyes. "There's plenty of time to change before dinner. We can send a servant for some of your clothes."

Laura looked at him. "And you think I can hide until then? Or are you hoping my garb will send your mother into a spasm?"

He grinned. "That would be something to see."

Laura groaned and hid her face in her hands.

"You've just been abducted," Jasper said, slipping an arm round her shoulders. "Even my mother will grant you some license in what you wear. I told you. They know everything. And they don't seem to mind."

"I expect they've gone senile," Laura said. Nothing else could explain it.

"I don't think so," Jasper said. "Though they are probably too lovestruck to be fully rational—I never expected that, let me tell you. But you see, Mrs. Stoke isn't the only one who expects me to make an honest woman of you," Jasper said. "You should hear the Mater on the subject."

Laura tried not to squirm. "They must despise me for trapping you—and Henrietta, what will she say?"

"Something polite if she knows what's good for her. Leave the apology for our deception to me."

Laura pressed her damp hands to her knees and wished she didn't feel so sick.

"This can't be as hard as what I had to say to your brother," Jasper said.

"You told him?" Laura twisted to look at him.

"Course I did. First he thought I wanted a cure for pox." Jasper kissed the top of her head. "I know it doesn't come easy, but I insist you turn respectable."

"You—" Well, you couldn't scowl at someone who was kissing you, not unless you wished to go cross-eyed. Laura didn't.

———

Laura would have liked to postpone the reckoning a little longer, but Jasper didn't allow any lingering on the pavement and brought her promptly to the door. A butler ushered them inside. "Mr. Rushford. And..." The butler paused, unsure what to say. Laura burned scarlet. These breeches!

"This is Miss Laura Edwards," Jasper informed him. "But she's also been known as Gemma Holyrood, of Covent Garden fame."

The butler bowed low. "Welcome, Miss Edwards. Lord and Lady Fairchild are expecting you."

No reprieve. Heavy-footed, Laura let Jasper lead her to the drawing room where they waited as crisp and upright as if they sat for a portrait.

Jasper bowed. "Sir. Madam. You remember Miss Edwards." Laura curtseyed.

Lord Fairchild bowed. Lady Fairchild, who was seated, gave a tiny nod. "Sit down, Miss Edwards," she said, beckoning to a nearby chair. "You've had quite an ordeal, but it looks as if my son has returned you intact?"

"Perfectly," Laura said. "Thank you for receiving me. I'm sorry about my appearance."

Lady Fairchild smiled thinly. "I've sent for your brother. He'll be with us soon. You will want him to look over your bruises I expect."

"Thank you, ma'am," Laura said, stopping midway across the room, the muscles tightening around her throat. Jasper was wrong. His parents were making the best of a bad situation—they couldn't want this, no matter what they'd told him.

"I should tell you that Miss Edwards has agreed to marry me," Jasper said. He didn't mention Mrs. Stoke.

"Very sensible," Lady Fairchild said. "I should like a moment alone with Miss Edwards if I may?"

Laura stiffened, holding the Lady's eye. Yes, it would be better this way—to hear her opinion unfiltered by Jasper.

"That is up to Miss Edwards," Jasper said.

"Your mother has the right," Lord Fairchild began.

"I don't object," Laura said. She'd rather hear the truth, even if it flayed her.

"We will leave you then." Jasper bowed. "I won't be far," he whispered as he walked past her and followed his father from the room. The door shut. Laura felt marooned.

"I do wish you'd sit down," Lady Fairchild said. Obedient, Laura walked on legs as stiff as planks to the nearest chair.

"Do you love him?" Lady Fairchild asked.

"Painfully," Laura said, stung into theatrics. "Such fevered workings of my heart—"

"Don't be flippant," Lady Fairchild interrupted. "I'm in earnest. I want him to be happy."

"Why shouldn't he be?" Laura snapped.

"I know the quality of his affections. You must know by now that he will do anything for you." Lady Fairchild's eyes raked over her. "I've had no opportunity to judge the quality of yours. He will marry you whatever I say, but I hope very much you'll be good to him."

"You may be sure I will, ma'am," Laura said, wishing her throat weren't so dry.

"I should like your word," Lady Fairchild said.

"You have it," Laura said. "But for his sake, not yours."

Lady Fairchild sighed. "That's as it should be. Forgive me. I couldn't be sure—but I think you do love him."

Laura understood in a rush and the frost spikes around her melted. "Too much," she said. She offered a faltering smile. Lady Fairchild's ogress act was well-intentioned. She, too, loved Jasper. "Our marriage will be something of a scandal, but—"

"I'm quite aware of *that*," his mother said. "But he made himself very clear and he doesn't reveal his heart so easily. Why all the bristling on your part? Was it so hard to tell me your own?"

"Do *you* like being interrogated?" Laura asked.

Lady Fairchild frowned. "I shouldn't think so. You see, I'm usually the one with the questions—"

Laura laughed. "I see that. I am sorry if you are disappointed with the match. I did try to change his mind, but he thinks marrying me is worth ruining himself, no matter what I say." Her voice fell to a mumble. "I don't take that lightly."

Lady Fairchild tilted her head. "Ruining him? How so, my dear?"

Laura snorted. "Please. Don't pretend. I know what I've done to him. You don't need to grind it in my face that I've annihilated him as far as society's concerned. All London knows me as his mistress and—"

"It is, of course, regrettable that you children were so convincing with your charade," Lady Fairchild said. "But I think your time on the stage has confused you." The blue eyes, so like Jasper's, held her with intimidating strength. "You are Laure Seraphine Edouard Lecroy-Duplessis and you have never been anyone else."

At first Laura could think of nothing to say. "And if I wasn't?" she asked.

Lady Fairchild shrugged. "My son loves you. I dare say we'd have thought of something. But you must admit this makes it much easier. Your father's rank was higher than Jasper's ever will be."

Laura looked at her. She couldn't mean it.

"I'm only reminding you of some pertinent facts," Lady Fairchild said.

"There's a few notable omissions," Laura said. Her father may have been a count, but he was long dead, their lands lost to them.

"You have no trouble embracing the identity you built for yourself as Gemma Holyrood—you clung to it in the face of some remarkable opposition. Why this reluctance to be who you really are?" Lady Fairchild asked.

Laura hesitated, unsure she could explain even to herself. She'd followed her mother's lead—keeping calm as their home torched and their dear ones snuffed quicker than candles. You worked through each day one at a time and when memory threatened to capsize you, you looked to the future. Even there you framed everything with realism: only things you could accomplish with what you held now in your hands.

Distancing themselves from the world that was had freed her and Jack to test their abilities, to try and succeed—and yet,

Maman had never buckled when it came to teaching Laura her own worth. It gave her confidence and courage and sometimes made her foolhardy, but it was a fine birthright nonetheless. By Lady Fairchild's reasoning she was the same as she ever was, so why start feeling inadequate now? Maman wouldn't have blinked at this. Her Laure would be a fine Mrs. Rushford—and a Lady Fairchild too, one day—not because of a pedigree, but because of her own worth.

"I see," Laura said.

"Good. Naturally your marriage will be something of a wonder. I can't say having my son labeled for life as an eccentric was my first wish, but—" She smiled and Laura understood the rigid posture didn't mean Lady Fairchild was putting a brave face on things. It was her manner; she wasn't making concessions from a castle of ice. "Now we've bettered our understanding of each other, I'm pleased. My son loves you and I believe you will make him happier than he deserves to be. Which is all to the good, since I wasn't entirely sure what I was going to do if I'd found you couldn't be trusted."

This last came with a calculating look. It was a skill worth learning, Laura decided, uttering threats with such gentle simplicity. She might practice it sometime, if it didn't remind Jasper of his mother too much.

"Then you truly don't mind?" Laura asked. Even though women of worth didn't depend on approval, within a family it certainly helped smooth things over.

"Well, I think it ridiculous that this whole mess sprang out of a quarrel with Saltash. But justice will be served. Really, I can't think of a better way to punish him."

"How do you mean?" Laura asked.

"It's possible, however ignoble, for a man of Saltash's rank to punish actresses and neglect impoverished relatives. It's much harder for you, as a social inferior, to teach him the lesson he needs. Consider, my dear. If you could snap your fingers at him as my son's mistress, what will you be able to do as his wife? We will never be duchesses, you and I, but the Rushfords are a much older—and I would say better—family. Now you and Jasper are engaged, you are quite untouchable. Naturally it offends me that violence and threats should be visited on any female, but it is a sad truth that the lower orders suffer more in this regard. You will find, my dear, that assuming your true station affords great protection. And thank heavens for that. This business of your abduction—I haven't passed such an anxious night since Sophy went missing. We shall put it from our minds. I was thinking of a town wedding. Six weeks? At St. George's on Hanover Square?"

Before Laura could shape complete astonishment into some sort of answer, she heard a scuffling and Jasper burst into the room. His father, caught at an incriminating angle, straightened and tried to pretend he hadn't been listening through the door.

"Six weeks! Absolutely not. I won't have it!" Jasper said. "No more of your scheming, Mama. We'll be married this week if I have to do it in the fleet!"

His mother blanched.

"Jasper, I was just explaining," she began.

"Don't explain. Laura and I manage well enough on our own. And it won't be St. George's because Laura is Catholic." Lady Fairchild winced. This was almost as bad, Laura knew, as being an actress.

"Six weeks then, at St. James," Lady Fairchild said, like it pained her, but Jasper didn't notice.

"I'm not kicking my heels for six weeks while you waste our time with nonsense about dress fittings and decorating a church."

"Is there some reason to hurry?" Lady Fairchild asked coolly. "You said you brought her back intact."

"I know what I said. But six weeks!? No. We may as well have fornicated in that ridiculous inn, and never mind the poor excuse for a mattress."

"Jasper!" Lady Fairchild turned white with mortification, but Laura—and Lord Fairchild—both got caught in a laugh.

"Really!" Lady Fairchild huffed, glaring at them all. "I won't excuse such crude language. A six-week delay will prove to the world that Jasper and Miss Edwards have no need to marry—"

Jasper snorted. "Prove! Hah. I'm not waiting six weeks to play along with absurd social niceties that insist on pretending there's no such thing as contraception!"

"Jasper!" she said again. Afraid of her own stifled laughter, Laura buried her face in the cushion. She emerged wiping her eyes, but Jasper wasn't finished.

"Enough, Mother. If you haven't informed yourself on the matter, I suggest that you do. The way you and Father carry on these days you might just need it. I don't intend to endure the mortification of you presenting my father with a child younger than his own grandchildren."

Lady Fairchild, utterly immobile and completely scarlet, tried but failed to speak. Her husband stepped in. "That's out of line, Jasper. Your mother and my concerns are no one's business but our own."

"Yes, and so are mine and Laura's," Jasper retorted. "I'm glad of your help and your blessing, but I won't have any meddling. Laura and I have decided to marry and as I've held off taking her to bed thus far, I think I've waited long enough."

"Your bride may have something to say on the matter," Lady Fairchild said acidly. "My dear, wouldn't you prefer to enter into marriage with your head held high?"

Laura turned pink. "I can do that as well tomorrow as six weeks from now."

"Excellent," Jasper said. "Mama, in the spirit of compromise I give you until Tuesday."

Lady Fairchild cast her eyes heavenward, but no vindication came. The only sound was her husband clearing his throat.

"Georgy," he said. "Everyone can be here by then. Tuesday will be fine."

32
TYING THE KNOT

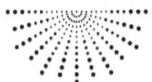

Thwarted in matters of calendar, Lady Fairchild fought for her own way with the rest. This might be a slapdash, hasty wedding, but she would go to her grave before she let it look like one. Laura was busy from dawn until long after dusk with fittings, confectioners, and florists. She might as well be tethered to Lady Fairchild's side. Jasper complained bitterly, accusing his mother of taking advantage of his good nature.

"*I'm* about ready to kidnap you. I haven't seen you since yesterday," Jasper grumbled to Laura when they drove out that evening. They were going, appropriately enough, to the theatre, now her bruises had faded enough to be hidden by powder.

"Don't whine. It'll soon be over," his sister Henrietta said in an uncanny likeness of their mother's voice. Laura wasn't sure it was intentional but was glad Henrietta was speaking to Jasper again. She'd been in high dudgeon ever since learning Laura hadn't really been his mistress—and that Anna and Alistair had been in on the secret all along.

"I hope so," Jasper said. He patted his sister's hand. "If you want to add your mite to the festivities, I could take your boy Lawrence to—"

"He'd love to see the beasts at the Royal Exchange," Henrietta put in. "Percy doesn't care for it and in my condition I can't tolerate the smell."

"How delightful," Laura said, seeing that Jasper was too stunned to reply. "I'm sure Jasper would love to take him."

They jolted around a corner. "Turncoat," Jasper whispered into her ear when the motion made her sway into him.

Henrietta beamed at Laura. "Come over tomorrow afternoon. Anna is coming. We'll visit over tea and I'll tell you everything about my brother."

Her husband, who generally seemed to follow a policy of non-interference, went so far as to cough.

"A little less temper all around, I think," Lord Fairchild suggested. "Or Henrietta's baby might come out with red hair."

"That wouldn't be so terrible," his wife said.

———

LAURA MISSED BEING ON STAGE, of course, and couldn't help mentally correcting a few of Alice's poorly delivered lines. Jasper had gone round to the theatre earlier at Laura's request to intercede for her with Rollins. In exchange, Laura demanded her lucky garters back. She wanted them for when she married and felt if there was any luck left in them, she deserved it, not Alice.

It was perhaps a small consolation that her presence in the box overshadowed the initial action on stage. It got so bad that Sarah and Dan took to improvising a cheeky dialogue—at Laura's expense. But it was only friendly jesting. She acknowledged it by blowing them a kiss. "I have been so fortunate in my friends," she whispered to Jasper.

She could scarcely breathe for the rush of visitors they had at the interval and she didn't intercept a single leer—perhaps not unsurprising with Jasper, Lord Fairchild, Henrietta's husband Lord Arundel, and Alistair Beaumaris watching, ready to retaliate.

The first attack didn't come from the men. "Miss Edwards," tinkled one of the ladies, a slender matron of an age with Henrietta. "You aren't by chance also the celebrated Miss Holyrood?" As one, the ladies turned their eyes on her expectantly.

"Of course I am," Laura said. "I have such a love for theatre." She could have added something about it being a passion of her late father's and drop in that he was a French count, but they could work that out for themselves. She needn't resort to thrust and parry tactics. She felt safe surrounded by Rushfords. If they accepted her, who else mattered? Not a one, according to them. There were advantages, she was discovering, to Rushford pride. It insulated her—until she noticed Saltash. He must have entered his box during the interval. He was staring at her.

Lofty pacifism was beyond her now. The indignities of being assaulted in the street, trussed up and bundled in a carriage, jolted across the country, and desperately conniving for her freedom flooded over her. She'd eviscerate him. Her fingers tightened around her fan as she rose from her chair, heedless of Anna's restraining hand.

"You wish to visit him?" Jasper asked, following her eyes.

"I'm going to corner him. Not cower here," she said. Jasper stood and put his hand in the small of her back.

Lighting her face with a sparkling smile, Laura waved artlessly, moving in for the kill. "Uncle!" she called.

The sharp-fanged ladies beside her hushed. "Uncle!" Laura called again, letting her voice carry. He could cut her, but even so, the damage was done. Tonight these ladies would go home and pull out their peerage, searching out the page where it informed all and sundry that the Duke of Saltash had married a Frenchwoman. It might even say that the duchess had a sister, one Marguerite Leonie Lecroy-Duplessis, widow of a Comte of the Ancien Régime, who was survived by two living children, Jacques-Marie Phillipe and Laure Seraphine. Even if it didn't, they'd uncover the truth before long.

A mottled flush rose to the duke's cheeks; beside him the duchess made frantic work with her fan. He nodded.

"Excuse me," Laura said, beaming at the shattered ladies as Jasper swept her out of the box. "It would be unkind not to give my regards to my uncle."

By the time they entered his box, Saltash's face was bright as raw beef. In perfect contrast, his wife was pale, her gauntness only accentuated by her gown of ivory lace. A young girl with a square chin sat beside them, leaning forward, her hands tight on the arms of her chair.

"Is this—"

"Your cousin," the duchess answered.

"We haven't met before," Laura said. The five of them exchanged courtesies, every smile as hard as chipped granite, but Laura scarcely noticed. Her attention was fixed on the duke.

"I see you've landed on your feet," Saltash muttered.

"In spite of you. Again," Laura said. "We will invite you to the wedding, but I advise you to absent yourself. Find a reason to take yourself out of London. I'd hate to let slip anything about my recent journey. It wouldn't look well at all."

"You—"

"Ah." Jasper raised a hand. "Enough, sir. It is sufficient for you to nod and look as if you are pleased to see us. Yes, yes, a little wider—that's the dandy!"

Saltash growled. The duchess crumpled her handkerchief.

"Madam, you are so very good to put up with him," Jasper

said, glib as ever. "I've always said it's a mercy you've not given him a son—I hope he thanks you often. Not because he's mean and a bounder and his bloodline deserves to die—but it's proof, madam, of your wonderful fidelity. I dare say, if you'd had your sister's spirit, you'd have cuckolded him years ago."

He dropped the insult as casually as a gunner lighting a fuse —but it was the girl who reacted, starting in her chair. Saltash and his wife were motionless as tombstones.

No son...and Saltash had a long-standing mistress. Who was also childless. "Jasper—" Laura began, as the duchess turned even paler and closed her eyes.

"You'll stand for this, Papa?" the girl asked, bright spots in her cheeks spoiling the haughty tilt of her chin. "I—"

Saltash didn't move.

Jasper glanced at Laura, then focused again on Saltash through narrowed eyes. "How unforgivably clumsy of me. I'd always assumed—your daughter—I mean—"

Laura took her cue and laid a hand on Jasper's arm. "Darling. Don't say anymore." She bestowed a twinkling smile on her poleaxed uncle. "The next act is about to begin and I think we should take ourselves off before causing more mischief. Of course, you are welcome to the wedding, aunt. And you too, cousin." She started for the door. "So sorry! The most regrettable accident! Au revoir!"

She made it to the corridor before seizing Jasper's arm. "How did you know?" she asked, pulling him aside, close to the wall. She'd never suspected. Her mother had never even hinted at such a thing, but she must have known. Why else all those worries for her sister?

"That she's not his daughter? I didn't. Just trying to be as offensive as possible. Never dreamed I might be hitting the truth. Though once I said it, I remembered certain facts—"

"Their faces," Laura whispered. "He couldn't have known."

"Foolish of him to ignore the evidence. He must be truly awful at cards."

He grinned so provokingly she had to hide her mouth behind her fingers. Even so, a half-squashed laugh escaped. "Yes, but what have you done?"

"Given him plenty to think about," Jasper countered. "It's the least he deserves."

"But my poor aunt!"

"I know." Jasper squeezed her hand. "She must have had some spirit once. Trust her to find it again. It's not your trouble. He's behind you now and that's bound to be a good thing."

————

"You took your time returning," Henrietta said when they retook their seats.

"We were recovering in the corridor," Jasper said. "I shared a joke with Saltash."

Henrietta glanced at the duke, then eyed them suspiciously. "He doesn't look like he enjoyed it. I trust you are all right now?"

Laura nodded. She would be.

————

CRAMMING the whole family together was more diverting than Jasper expected, but surprisingly fatiguing. Sophy and Tom were here, staying in Rushford house instead of Tom's London home. They claimed it was so Sophy could have more time with Lord and Lady Fairchild, but Jasper suspected his mother still wasn't entirely reconciled to Tom's unfashionable address. She kept urging him to sell.

Anna and Alistair came by most days with their son Henry,

who along with Henrietta's boys wreaked the sort of havoc that, for now, Ollie could only dream of. Jasper watched Sophy's startled eyes following those three terrors whipping through the library, then coming to rest on the daughter bundled in her arms. "Give her another year," Jasper said, unable to resist.

"Nonsense. She's perfect," Tom said, lifting Ollie from Sophy's hands. He kissed her waving fist and passed her to Jasper just in time for her to spit up on his coat.

"What did I tell you?" Tom said, smirking at Jasper as Sophy searched for a handkerchief.

"Ours will be drier," Jasper called to Laura. "Make a note of it, please!"

"I didn't think you cared overmuch for children," Laura said.

Jasper shrugged. "Seems an unavoidable fate." Walking to the long windows, he freed one hand to close them and fasten the latch. "You're not so bad," he said, looking down at Ollie, "but your cousins, now..." He glanced at Laura again. "Ours will be quieter."

"If you say so," she said.

He hoped so, but didn't plan on finding out straight off. Children and family were well and good, but they undoubtably kept him from seeing Laura alone. After sharing her all week with his parents and nephews and cousins and sisters, he thought it would be nice to keep her to himself for at least a little while.

"I'll return her now," Jasper said, tipping Ollie back into her father's arms. "It appears I need to change." At the door he caught Laura's eye and she followed him from the room.

"Ready to escape this madhouse?" he asked.

"Don't pretend you don't enjoy it." She smiled at him. "You'd better hurry up and kiss me while there's still time."

Jasper inclined his head. "I am, as ever, your obedient servant."

———

OF COURSE they didn't have long before she was summoned away for a final dress fitting. At dinner he could only watch her down the length of the table making conversation with his father and Alistair while he tried to keep up things at his end with Sophy and Henrietta and Laura's brother Jack. Superstition, and his mother, kept Laura hidden from him the next morning until Tom and Alistair commandeered him and brought him to church. They were early—in order to have plenty of time to roast him, Jasper suspected. He didn't mind. But he did keep an eye on his watch.

———

"THINK THEY'LL EVER LEAVE?" Jack asked, peering from the window of Laura's room as Jasper's family trickled out the door and into the waiting carriages. "We'll be late."

"Lady Fairchild doesn't believe in punctuality. That's for lesser mortals," Laura said. "We'd better wait a quarter of an hour or we'll get to the church before them."

"They're not a bad lot I suppose," Jack said.

"Even Jasper?"

"I could grow to like him," he said.

"Do," Laura told him.

Jack smiled and crossed the room, picking up her hands and turning her around. "Very pretty," he said. "But Maman would have stitched it better. She'd be happy, though. And proud."

"Are you?" Laura asked.

"Yes. And sorry. I shouldn't have stayed angry with you."

"I forgive you," Laura said, with an airy wave of her hand.

Jack laughed. "Good. Maybe you'll forgive me too, for going round and thrashing that doctor friend of Saltash's. Condemning him in a letter to the Royal Society was not quite enough."

"You didn't!" Laura gasped at him.

"I'm afraid I did. Wanted to do the same to Saltash, but Jasper said no, you'd both taken care of him. I think—" Jack hesitated. "He's right about—well, he's both right about you and right for you, it seems."

"I was too headstrong," Laura said. "I'm sorry, Jack. But it turns out well, doesn't it? We'll both be in Suffolk. You'll have to get yourself a housekeeper, though. The state of your cuffs—you look as if no one cares for you and it isn't the case."

"I was almost enjoying letting myself think so," he said. "But self-pity gets old after a while. Can we go? Has it been fifteen minutes yet?"

"I don't know but I'm tired of waiting." She beckoned him and together they went downstairs. "Thank you for coming to give me away."

"I'm glad to do it. Easier than trying to keep you." But he smiled as he said it and pressed her hand.

———

THE CHURCH WAS full of society gogglers, as Lady Fairchild declared it should be. Waiting to walk down the aisle, Laura felt a similar excitement to the kind she used to feel before the rise of a curtain. With Lady Fairchild as an example, it was easy to see she'd still have opportunities to perform, if not the same range of parts she used to enjoy. A small sacrifice but worth it, to marry Jasper.

He was at the front of the church, looking too handsome to

be allowed. Laura whisked her face out of sight. "Am I presentable?" she asked Jack, more worried than she cared to admit. She'd played to larger audiences countless times, but this —this was real. Jack's reassurances didn't make it to her ears. Her legs felt shaky and her stomach dived as the music cued her forward. Taking Jack's arm, Laura miraculously made it to the altar without stumbling—it would have ruined the solemnity and infuriated Lady Fairchild. The unfamiliar fidgets left her once she took Jasper's hands. Abandoning habit, she forgot the watching eyes. They might have vanished, every one. Even when Jasper raised her veil and turned her round for all to see, Laura saw only a blur of faces as they hurried from the chapel.

He helped her into the coach. Laura sighed. "The breakfast now, I suppose." Lady Fairchild had made all kinds of plans. Breakfast and chatting and congratulatory toasts seemed terribly prosaic things just now. She felt new and the feeling wouldn't last once they were brought out for general inspection.

"Would it break your heart if I told you no?" Jasper asked.

Laura looked at him and felt a glimmer of hope. "Mine will survive, but I don't know what it will do to your mother's."

"She has my father to console her."

A smile was creeping out despite her efforts. She ought to stop him, but she wouldn't.

"See, my darling wife, it's a little backwards, but I realized when we were in the church that we were both cheated in the matter of marriage proposals. So I propose we do it over again. I'll ask you the right way and you can accept me without the intermediary of Mrs. Stoke."

"We're already married."

"I just—I just want everything to be right."

"It won't be, you know," Laura cautioned. "We'll probably fight over our children. Maybe I'll turn extravagant. I was too tired to notice before, but perhaps you snore."

"I don't mind a good argument as long as it's civil," Jasper said. "I like to win and though I've not had much practice at it, I can turn out a decent apology when required."

"I know," Laura said.

"You also like to argue, to have your own way, are not extravagant, but I can indulge some of that should you choose to be. I don't want to think about children yet, though I intend to practice making them, and I assure you I would never be so coarse as to snore."

"Then I suppose that's right enough for me," Laura said.

"Me too. Now. My proposal." He cleared his throat. "Miss Edwards, in the course of our acquaintance I have become most sincerely attached to you. Will you do me the great honor of becoming my wife?"

Laura snuggled into his shoulder. She could reply in languid syllables, 'I suppose so,' or laugh and call him a nod, reminding him she'd already done so. If she were an utter fool. He was right. They both deserved the best from each other. She would speak only the truth. No acting.

"I'm not sure I deserve you," Laura said, stopping his protest with her fingers. "Let me finish. You have my heart. And if, impossibly, I've earned your regard, I accept it because you are the truest man I know. And because I love you." She kissed him.

"Well, that's good," Jasper said, sliding his arm around her. "It would be mortifying to be as in love as I am and not have the feeling returned. No, really," he said, over her laughing protests, "I made myself ill trying to hide it from you."

"Simpleton," Laura said. "I've loved you for ages. Before you brought me to London even. Probably ever since that breakfast at your sister's house when you kept flinging lines of Sheridan, trying to catch me out. Couldn't you tell?"

"No, but I like that story," he said, crossing his ankles. "Tell me more."

Where to begin? "There once was a girl who needed thirty pounds." Laura paused, struck by how different life had become. She'd been so wrong-headed. Happiness wasn't a finite something you wrested for yourself. It stuck to your fingers as you gave it to others. Just look at Jasper. He gave her happiness in abundance and still had smiles to spare. With a smile of her own, Laura settled back in her seat to tell her husband exactly how she fell in love with him.

AFTERWORD

I started writing Fairchild because I ran out of books to read by Georgette Heyer and Eva Ibbotson. Often imitated, never duplicated they say, and I suppose the end result is something like that.

Sophy's story began as a retelling of Hans Christian Andersen's Princess and the Pea. The second book in the series, Incognita, shaped itself around another Andersen fairy-tale, The Steadfast Tin Soldier. Jasper's story is different. He speaks to me easily—more than any other character, which may be why he is such a general favorite. True to form, his story didn't want to behave. I stacked my bedside table with collections of fairy tales, but couldn't pull myself away from eighteenth century comic playwrights like Farquhar, Goldsmith and Sheridan. Layered deceptions, villainous schemes, headstrong ladies and dashing blades exiting and entering scenes at a flying clip: this world was irresistible.

The Fairchild stories, to me, are about family. Sometimes you have to listen. So I did.

ALSO BY JAIMA FIXSEN

Fairchild

Incognita

The Reformer

A Holiday in Bath

ABOUT THE AUTHOR

Jaima Fixsen is a USA Today and International best-selling author living and writing in Alberta, Canada. Her novel, The Girl In His Shadow (co-authored under the pen name Audrey Blake), was selected as Libby's 2022 Big Library Read, and has been translated into six languages.

Jaima studied Occupational Therapy at the University of Alberta, and her experiences learning anatomy and dissecting cadavers began her fascination with the history of medical science, which often figures in her stories. Her debut crime novel, The Specimen, released this year. Jaima still works in health care, supporting children with disabilities and their families. She loves history, snow, reading, snow, and spending as much time as possible in the Canadian Rockies